Early Praise for *Virtual Sabotage*

"Strap in and go for a ride with *Virtual Sabotage*, a thrilling change of pace for Julie Hyzy. She takes us on a mind-bending trip into a world where villains set the rules, and heroes can't believe what they know to be true. Fascinating, fun, and deeply satisfying."
—Joseph Finder, *New York Times* bestselling author of *Judgment*

✦

"*Virtual Sabotage* blurs the borders between man and machine, sounding a warning about the safety of social media. Think Michael Crichton with a cyberpunk twist. Breakneck pacing, seamless prose, and authentic research—Julie Hyzy is definitely the voice to heed in high-tech thrillers."
—K.J. Howe, bestselling author of *Skyjack*

Also by Julie Hyzy

Playing with Matches
Artistic License
Made for Murder (short stories)

THE ALEX ST. JAMES MYSTERY SERIES
Deadly Blessings
Deadly Interest
Dead Ringer (with Michael A. Black)

THE WHITE HOUSE CHEF SERIES
State of the Onion
Hail to the Chef
Eggsecutive Orders
Buffalo West Wing
Affairs of Steak
Fonduing Fathers
Home of the Braised
All the President's Menus
Foreign Éclairs

THE MANOR HOUSE SERIES
Grace Under Pressure
Grace Interrupted
Grace Among Thieves
Grace Takes Off
Grace Against the Clock
Grace Cries Uncle
Grace Sees Red
Grace to the Finish

VIRTUAL SABOTAGE

Julie Hyzy

CALEXIA PRESS

Calexia Press LLC
525 W. Monroe St., Suite 2360
Chicago, IL 60661
www.calexiapress.com

ISBN: 978-0-9835067-3-7

Library of Congress Control Number: 2018937723

Book design by Prideaux Press
Cover design by Bookfly Design

Publisher's Cataloging-In-Publication Data
(Prepared by The Donohue Group, Inc.)

Names: Hyzy, Julie A.
Title: Virtual sabotage / Julie Hyzy.
Description: Chicago, IL : Calexia Press, [2018]
Identifiers: ISBN 9780983506737 | ISBN 9780983506744 (ebook)
Subjects: LCSH: Virtual reality--Fiction. | Brainwashing--Fiction. | Conspiracies--Fiction. | LCGFT: Thrillers (Fiction)
Classification: LCC PS3608.Y98 V57 2018 (print) | LCC PS3608.Y98 (ebook) | DDC 813/.6--dc23

*In memory of Ray Bradbury,
whose short story "The Veldt" planted the seed
for this tale in my brain.*

ONE

FOR IMMEDIATE RELEASE

Much like the rapid evolution of cell phones, from the handheld mobile "bricks" that few could afford in the 1980s to the slim, pocket-size computer smartphones most consumers carry today, the past several years have seen the rise of virtual reality (VR) as it morphed from simple cardboard headgear displaying 3-D visuals to sleek, discreet implanted devices providing fully immersive, near-tangible adventures.

Behemoth company Virtu-Tech, with proprietary technology that taps directly into a participant's brain, has infinitely expanded users' VR experience. Always offering free upgrades—like their much-anticipated 6.0 model—Virtu-Tech provides the widest, most fulfilling opportunities to consumers at a price nearly everyone can afford.

Although all virtual encounters are perfectly safe, the human mind can be fooled into believing that the simulated experience is real. Because there may be danger to the participant if the delicate balance between reality and perception is breached, Virtu-Tech has taken the extraordinary step of employing envoys to rescue users who have been pulled in too deep. Celia Newell, president and CEO of Virtu-Tech, calls them "lifeguards for the brain."

In this twenty-first-century world of cheap mass-produced trinkets, experiences have become more highly prized than material goods. Virtu-Tech adventures offer options for exploration, learning, living, and testing one's limits while adrenaline pumps, rushing participants to new highs. All while remaining perfectly safe.

It's no wonder with its groundbreaking technology, Virtu-Tech has surpassed all others to become the number one choice of entertainment in the world.

TWO

Kenna Ward yanked her ponytail tight. She hated when hair stuck to her sweaty face during rescues, and this one promised to be her most difficult yet. Pacing the floor here at AdventureSome, outside the door to capsule number five, she waited for Stewart to give her the all clear.

She drew a long breath and pushed it out slowly: a vain attempt to steady the rolling gyrations in her stomach.

"What the hell is Charlie doing in there, anyway?" she asked.

Studying the capsule's control panel, Stewart didn't look up. "I don't know, Kenna. I was as surprised as you."

She rubbed her eyes, still filmy from the deep sleep she'd been in when she'd gotten the call. "Stewart?" she asked. "Who's in there with him?"

"No idea, but it doesn't matter right now, does it?" he replied. "Just get in there and get them out." He expelled a breath. "Okay, we're ready."

She took her position inside the safety capsule as Stewart stepped forward to place a chain around her neck. "Can't forget this," he said.

Her signal medallion. She hoped to God that Charlie had remembered to wear one, too.

Kenna flexed her jaw as Stewart inserted sound dimmers into her ears, then adjusted a dark shield over her eyes. He snaked the shield's command microphone around the curve of her ear, allowing its delicate receiver to follow the line of her cheek.

She hated going in without complete information. Charlie knew better than to enter a scenario without leaving a trail—but he'd left no plan, no lead. An unauthorized incursion. "He's going to have a lot of explaining to do," she said.

As she spoke, Stewart probed the hard bone area behind her right ear. A half second later, his fingers found her implant. She felt the tiny, familiar pressure as he inserted the component that would connect her mind to Charlie's reality.

There was a faint *click*, then the link's accompanying tingle as VR accessed her brain. She winced.

"Let this be the worst of it," she whispered.

She settled her mind, breathed in, and felt the familiar wave rush up to meet her.

"Sight," she said.

As always, the moment hovered. A breathless instant of absolute nothingness.

Blackness shot from deep to pale gray, then froze. Kenna muttered impatiently as the operating system's logo, an infinity symbol with the words "Virtu" and "Tech" on each side, shimmered into view. The warning came next: the soothing female VR voice relaying the ominous reminder that Kenna was about to enter a scenario at her own risk. The voice faded with an admonishment to play responsibly. As the logo dissolved, visions behind it moved with rippling grace, gently solidifying into three-dimensional silhouettes.

"Come on," Kenna said.

With tentative virtual steps, she urged the program to

move faster. "Sound," she said. "Smell. Taste." She raised her right hand. "Touch."

Flat images acquired depth; noises grew more distinct. Familiar dizziness engulfed as her synapses struggled to transform these sparkling clouds into recognizable shapes.

Charlie was here. And she would find him. But even that knowledge wasn't enough to quell the trepidation in her heart.

Stepping into another person's virtual reality uninvited was always risky. But that's what envoys did when things went wrong.

Like smoke in a vacuum, the fog disappeared. Sudden brightness sharpened Charlie's world into crystal clarity.

She blinked. She was in.

THREE

The moment Kenna was settled, Stewart stepped away from her capsule and returned to the instrument panel against the wall. He tugged on his headset and patched into the adjacent room. "Tech support?" He waited half a beat. "Vanessa?"

Static distorted Vanessa's voice—she was probably fitting her own headset on as she spoke. "I'm here."

"Status?"

"Hold on. The medics just arrived." Noise filtered through to Stewart—delayed, discordant scuffles coming from both the corridor and through his earphones. "They're interfacing now." Her voice cracked. "My god, Stewart, what was Charlie thinking, going in cold with no one running tech?"

"He should have known better." Stewart ran his fingers along his brow. His gaze flicked over to the capsule where Kenna moved slowly, exploring the world around her. He'd left the access door open to keep an eye on her. Like a mime, she moved silently in the opaque tube. The setup allowed freedom of movement while the smooth-walled boundary provided security. Stewart drew in a breath.

"Who's the client in there with Charlie?" Vanessa asked.

"Don't know. But Kenna will get them out," he said. "She has to."

Over the interoffice connection, Stewart heard the medics in Vanessa's room issue crisp commands. He hoped that was a good sign. Knowing Vanessa had control of the other chamber, the one housing Charlie's and the client's physical forms, gave him a measure of peace. Yet, this situation was so out of the ordinary and so fraught with peril, he wished he could be in two places at once. As much as he wanted to see for himself, there was no way he'd leave Kenna alone. Not after so much had gone wrong tonight.

"Charlie preset the program," Vanessa said in a tight voice. "Why didn't the backup safety protocols kick in?"

"I'm checking." Stewart worked the console, issuing a voice command: "Fail-safe status, report."

The computer answered his inquiry with an audible, "One moment please," and on-screen appeared a tiny infinity symbol with a blue streak racing along its never-ending path.

Stewart used that moment to chance another look at Kenna. She was petite but powerful, from the determined thrust of her chin to the tension in her shoulders. When she went into VR, she was the master. He'd never encountered an envoy with better intuition or improvisational skills.

Stewart rubbed his hand against his late-night beard stubble. He would have said the same thing about Charlie. Until today.

Still watching Kenna while he waited for the system report, Stewart spoke again into his headset. "What's the status on the client?"

"Unknown at the moment. Medics are too busy to talk." Vanessa's voice rose. "What were they doing here, anyway? If the auto alarm hadn't tripped, we wouldn't have found them for hours."

Before Stewart could answer, a harsh alert pulled his attention back to his fail-safe inquiry. "This can't be," he said. "Someone turned off the damn safety program." Fingers flying, he input the code sequence to reengage the system.

"Charlie wouldn't have done that." Vanessa's voice wavered. "Would he?"

The wall console buzzed: an error message.

Stewart frowned. Must have fat-fingered. "He had the capability. But he knows better." Taking a breath, he inputted the code a second time—carefully—then hit "enter."

Again, the computer buzzed its refusal to comply.

His fingers raced over the keyboard. "This can't be happening."

"What's wrong?" Vanessa asked.

Stewart stepped back, scanning the set of controls as though looking for a physical way in. Sweat trickled from his hairline into his eyes. He blinked it away. "Nessa," he said, pulling his microphone close. "Quick. Reestablish the fail-safe from your station. Use your override code."

"But what's—"

"Just do it!"

Through the headset, Stewart heard the familiar melodic beeps as she worked at her control panel. During the long pause waiting for acknowledgment, Vanessa's breaths came short and fast.

The error message sounded as loud as if it had buzzed inside Stewart's brain.

"That's it," he said. "Let's get Kenna out before we try this again."

"She'll be furious if we initiate an extraction," Vanessa said. "You know how long those take." A second later, she shouted, "Oh, God!"

"What?"

Vanessa swore again.

"What's wrong?" he asked.

"Stand by."

Stewart stretched his lips back and forth, pulling at his neck muscles, trying to work out the tension. He listened. The medics' calm directives, at first mumbled in the background, had gotten progressively louder, more urgent.

"What the hell's going on?" Stewart asked.

Vanessa didn't answer. Instead, she cried out, "What can I do? What do you need?"

A male voice answered, "Backup. Get us backup."

Stewart turned at a loud *whump* to his right. Kenna's body arched against the capsule's wall; head up, she let out a long guttural cry.

"Vanessa!" he shouted. "What's happening?"

FOUR

Kenna shoved the hanging leaves out of her way as she crept forward. Heat and humidity made it impossible for her to take five steps without having to wipe sweat from her face.

"Charlie?" Storming through overgrowth heavy with the smell of damp moss, Kenna called out her partner's name. Leaves the size of panthers blocked her view of everything but the lichen-covered ground. Warm sunlight glowed through the greenery to her left. She moved toward it, slamming more foliage out of her way.

"Charlie?"

She swiped again at her face. Although Kenna knew that the imminent perils of the situation were all products of virtual reality, she also knew the danger to Charlie and his client was real. There was only so much perceived stress a human mind could assimilate without lapsing into mortal absorption. Her job was to prevent that, at all costs.

Kenna clenched her teeth. In the old days, renegades moonlighted in these kind of clandestine gigs, but Charlie faced huge fines—even termination—if he got caught on an unauthorized jaunt. There was no reason he should have been here tonight. She hadn't even known he was gone until Stewart called. She'd been sound asleep, oblivious to the fact that Charlie had even left their bed.

Whatever the reason, it had better be good.

A second later, she blinked. Last night, Charlie had made an offhand comment about finally getting answers. They'd been discussing his concerns about Virtu-Tech's corporate management—a topic he'd brought up several times in recent weeks. Whenever Kenna had pressed him for details, he'd hedged. Last night, however, when he'd brought up the subject again, he told her he'd soon have solid facts to share. He'd seemed enthusiastic, upbeat.

Could this unexplained incursion be related? That would make sense. Stewart's reputation for dealing swiftly and forcefully with potential problems was well-known. If Charlie suspected negligence or misconduct among the corporate higher-ups, he wouldn't risk alerting Stewart until he had solid proof.

Above the quivering calls of birds and clicking insects came a low blast from her far left—the sound was out of sync with the environment. She changed direction and called for Charlie again.

The deep bellow split the jungle's calm a second time. The flat blare of a car horn blasted, then faded to an intermittent bleat.

Kenna picked up her pace, using her right arm like a windshield wiper to thrust away the plant barriers a split second before she broke through.

Other than the basic olive T-shirt, green khakis, and hiking boots envoys usually started out wearing when entering VR, she'd come in with nothing. She hadn't known enough about the scenario to properly outfit herself. Now as she ran, she whispered commands to the program, arming herself with as much firepower as she could, given this reality's parameters. Concentrating on her needs slowed her down, but one never went into a potentially hostile scenario unarmed.

The system responded briskly to her orders. A leather belt appeared at her waist. Seconds later, she felt the added weight as a whip, hefty switchblade, rope, and other armaments latched on. In the next moment, a bow in a shoulder harness along with a quiver of arrows bounced against her back. Her left hand searched the new belt to locate the machete she'd called up. She stopped dodging branches long enough to slide the weapon from its sheath. Properly armed, she raced forward again, slicing at the heavy vegetation.

As she ran, her silver heart pendant bounced just below her neckline. It lay tucked beneath her shirt, clicking brightly against the signal medallion Stewart had slipped over her head.

Insects dive-bombed her face, biting and pinching. She blinked stinging sweat from her eyes. The source of the horn blasts couldn't be much farther. The pounding pulse of her feet on soft soil matched the beat of her heart.

"Charlie?" she yelled, straining to hear him answer.

She nearly tripped on a deep groove in the muck. Tire treads.

At a small clearing, Kenna sheathed the machete. The land rose sharply before her, and she blew out power breaths as she sprinted up the steep embankment, grasping for handholds, fighting the bursting heat in her lungs.

At the top she stopped, breaths coming in shallow gasps. The tire tracks ended just ahead, at the edge of a grassy precipice. She raised an arm to shield the sun's glare. Before her, spanning a canyon-like gorge, a primitive suspension bridge swayed as though someone heavy had just bounded across.

On a wide outcropping ten feet below, a camouflage-green Land Rover lay upside down like a helpless turtle, its wheels twisted at odd angles. Kenna blew out a breath of relief. This had been easier than she expected. Finding lost adventurers was often the hardest part of an envoy's job.

The Land Rover had obviously gone off the precipice. Charlie and his client would likely be hurt—tactile experience was part of VR's allure, after all—but safety protocols kept participants from suffering mortal wounds. The two were probably unconscious, unable to activate their signal medallions.

All this worry for nothing. She should have known Charlie better than that.

She dug her heels into the crumbling ground and grasped sturdy weeds to slide sideways down the shallowest path toward the vehicle.

Warbling screams rent the silence, echoing in the chasm below her. So raw, so primordial were the cries that chills trickled up Kenna's sweaty neck. She scanned her surroundings but couldn't pinpoint the sound's source.

A heavy silence settled in. What sort of fantasy was this place? The sooner she got the two of them out of here, the better.

She'd just made it to the rear of the upended Land Rover when a man crawled out on his forearms, panting. Bloody spittle dangled from his lips. Long-limbed and thin, he had sun-crusted skin and scrub brush–short pale hair.

Kenna took a step closer. "Where's Charlie?"

The man's eyes widened and his mouth went slack. He scrambled to his feet.

No doubt about it, the man was a sentient. This must be Charlie's client.

He started toward her. "Who the hell are you?"

From high above, more trilling screams.

The man stopped. His eyes went wide.

"Shit." Turning, he ran.

Kenna started to follow, but the cries were much closer now. When she looked up, five warriors lined the ridge of the embankment. With armor worn across their shoulders and chests, they glistened in the sun. Pointy helmets topped their strangely elongated heads. They carried bows, arrows, ropes, and pickaxes. These were Huns, or someone's interpretation of them, at least. All men, they wore skirts made of patterned metal scales that clacked and snapped as they lumbered closer to the precipice's edge.

One of them bared his teeth and aimed his pickax at the pale-haired man. The projectile whistled past Kenna, chunking into the sentient's right arm. The impact sent him rolling sideways in a shower of blood. He screamed. Kenna started for him, intent on helping, but the man managed to get to his feet on his own. He took off toward the suspension bridge. From the way he cradled his right arm, she knew he'd been hurt—or at least, he believed he had. Out here, pain wasn't the enemy. Panic was.

Kenna spoke quietly into the program again to provide the command necessary to take charge of the scenario—to make these warriors disappear. Overriding existing parameters required a standard four-digit confirmation code. As she recited the proper sequence, she looked up in anticipation of watching the men vanish.

Nothing.

She tried again. Still nothing. Whoever had designed this scenario had password-protected elements of the scene. Frustrated, she smashed her hand against the Land Rover. It hurt more than it should have. Had she actually smacked the wall of her capsule in real life? That would be a first.

An arrow chucked into the ground next to her. The five Huns warbled rallying cries.

As one of the attackers raised a rope as though to lasso her into submission, Kenna yanked the bow from her back, nocked an arrow into place, and drew back the projectile with ease. She pulled a deep breath, held it, and let the bowstring roll off her fingers. The arrow whistled through the air.

The point plunged straight into the neck of the closest warrior with a cleaving sound that made her smile. Killing virtual bad guys was always fun. And with VR's safety protocols in place, she knew she couldn't be seriously hurt. Not physically, at least.

The warrior fell over, hands clutching at his throat, heels banging the rocky ground. The other men raced down the precipice. Kenna nocked another arrow into place and sent it screaming into the left eye of the next closest warrior. He sprawled backward onto one of his comrades. Those behind them rushed forward, heaving axes at Kenna.

She cut to her far left and had just pulled up another arrow when she spied an arm flopped outside the Land Rover's open window. Distracted, she aimed at the lead Hun, only to have her shot deflected by a well-timed sword swing.

Kenna slung the bow back over her shoulder and raced around the far side of the Land Rover, using it for cover. She threw herself to the ground and peered in.

"Charlie?"

He didn't answer.

Ducking her head, she crawled on elbows and knees along the inside roof of the vehicle to reach him. Suspended from his seat belt, his neck was twisted sideways and backward, wedged between the vehicle's roof and the steering wheel. Kenna's breath caught in her throat. Inching closer, her knees scraping against the edges of the open window, she reached across the cramped area and dug her fingers into his neck to twist his face in her direction. Half of it had crushed in on itself.

Kenna recoiled, then blew out a quick breath of relief. Not Charlie. It had to be a virtual.

The man's arms drooped like twin vines, swaying side to side as the vehicle shifted under Kenna's weight. She scooched closer to inspect a metallic glint at his waist. This virtual had been equipped with a Beretta? How odd. She hauled the firearm free, taking two precious seconds to engage the arming overrides.

As she drew back, her fingers grazed a chain around the man's neck. She tugged, disbelieving, until a bright silver medallion came loose from beneath his shirt. She stared at the two-inch oblong in her hand. There was no mistaking the emergency signal button. This man was very real. Belatedly, she noticed he was also very dead. But he couldn't be.

"My god," she said, dropping the medallion as she inched away. She hadn't expected to find two unknown sentients here. What the hell was going on?

Screaming wails brought her back to the present. She scrambled back out of the Land Rover and dispatched the remaining Huns with swift nine-millimeter spits to their foreheads.

A second later she heard crazed yells in the distance. It wouldn't be long before replacements arrived.

FIVE

Charlie snapped awake to find his wrists and ankles bound together tightly behind him. His quads and shoulders screamed with hot pain. His chin pressed hard against cold dirt so packed and scuffed that it had taken on the luster of black linoleum. He gritted his teeth to keep from crying out.

Three steps away a man was turned from Charlie, hands clasped behind his back. His boot heels made quiet creaks as he rocked back and forth.

To keep his mind alert, Charlie fixated on a spot just to the right of his captor's foot where a prickly weed had managed to break through the tight soil floor.

Where was this place? Where was Larry? Who had done this to him?

The standing man twisted to his right, pacing the length of what appeared to be a small hut. Charlie breathed through his nose, keeping his gaze on the tough little weed, watching it flex back and forth in the air caused by the man's footsteps. Focusing on the sharp-edged leaves helped Charlie keep his mind off the pain. He needed all his strength to figure out what was happening.

The man's heels made soft chuffing sounds against the dirt floor as Charlie worked his aching jaw, tasting a metallic gush of blood when his swollen tongue disturbed a flap of sliced cheek.

Something was very wrong.

VR technology allowed for sophisticated tactile interaction, but limits in the program and safety protocols prevented participants from experiencing this level of pain. At least, they were supposed to. Charlie blinked, trying to clear his muddled mind. Then it started to come back to him. How Larry had promised to demonstrate what he'd uncovered about Virtu-Tech's experimental remote technology and about the company's alarming future plans.

Larry had been driving the Land Rover when an explosion threw them over the nearby ledge. Charlie remembered the bone-crushing pain upon landing, as well as unlatching his seat belt to reach for his and Larry's emergency-signal necklaces. That's when he had been yanked out of the Land Rover, rolled onto the ground, and smashed in the face with what felt like ten pounds of pipe.

Now, with his nose pressed into the dung-smelling dirt, his face crusted with dried blood, he lifted his head.

"Finally awake, I see," the man said. "Good. This was not how I'd envisioned our meeting, you understand. My apologies for that."

Charlie raised his head to get a look at his captor. He blinked to clear his vision. "Who are you?" His voice sounded as broken as he felt.

The man wore a sharply tailored dark suit over a ramrod body that spoke of pride and middle-aged paunch. The jacket was double-breasted with shiny buttons, and polished black boots poked out from beneath crisply seamed dark pants. The boots took two steps back, and the man folded himself into a crouch, resting his elbows on his knees, as though ready to address a recalcitrant toddler. "Exactly who do we think is interrogating whom?"

His vaguely familiar face was unremarkable and bland with gray hair cropped so short to be nearly invisible. He had hard green eyes, their whites oversize and bloodshot, brows wiry and furrowed.

Charlie remembered the signal medallion on the chain around his neck. If he could access it—press the emergency-rescue button—he'd be pulled from this scenario before anything else could go wrong.

Charlie coughed. "What do you want?" he asked. His gaze swept the floor. If he could buy time—if he could find a rock or other outcropping—and position himself against it just right.

The man extended two fingers, touching the underside of Charlie's chin, which he raised until their eyes met. "Answer my questions and the worst you'll face is loss of your envoy status. Fight me and I'll see you locked up," he said.

Reaching into his coat, the man pulled out a folded leather wallet and flipped it open. The top half of the identification bore his unsmiling face and his name—Werner Trutenko. Recognition clicked even as Charlie's eyes glossed downward to the insignia below. Virtu-Tech's infinity logo.

Fighting the nausea of knowledge and pain, Charlie stared up into Trutenko's icy gaze. "So we were right?"

"Yes, Mr. Russell." He smacked Charlie's bloody cheek to punctuate his words. "But the time has come for you to open your eyes."

Charlie tried to blink away the pain.

Werner Trutenko stood, clapping his hands together in a thoughtful motion. "The world is in chaos, young man. You see it every day. And without intervention, there will only be more of the same. Can't you understand that?"

Charlie turned his head.

"Why do you fight us?" Trutenko asked. "Join us. You're

an envoy; that alone elevates your status. You can be part of the solution instead of one of our problems."

Charlie stared again at the scrappy weed. He ordered himself to focus on it as he blew out a long breath, releasing as much pain as he could. He rocked himself backward, trying to urge the medallion on the chain around his neck to swing a little so that he could locate its position under his shirt.

The silver oblong didn't sway when Charlie moved. Rather, it stuck to his sweat-covered chest. He grimaced so hard he felt the blood rush inside his sliced cheeks. Fighting waves of nausea, he stretched his bound limbs, inching toward his captor. Trutenko's boots were pointed. Pointed just enough.

"You clearly don't appreciate the trouble I had setting up our meeting here today." The man took a step backward. "You thought you were going to trap *us*. You thought you could slow us down. Oh, Mr. Russell. That level of hubris astounds me."

Noise outside the hut pulled Trutenko's attention. Charlie twisted his head to see what was going on. The hut's walls shook. The door opened, and a light-haired man with sun-roughened skin broke through. Charlie took a sharp breath as recognition hit. The guy who'd pulled him from the Land Rover. The guy who'd smashed his face.

"Tate?" Trutenko said. "What are you doing back here?"

Blood soaked the man's beige flak jacket and he held his right arm tight against his body, eyes wild with panic. "We gotta get out," he said. "Now. Hurry."

"What about Wendell?" Trutenko asked. "Where's he?"

"Dead. When I went back there, I tried pulling him out of the car wreck, but his death must have triggered some alert because they sent an envoy in. Totally screwed up the program, and then the damn warriors attacked *me*." Proffering his bleeding arm, the man raised his yellow-blond brows in anticipation. "What do we do?"

Trutenko's face reddened. "No one was supposed to die." He paced twice. "Damn it."

"Yeah, well, at least this one's still here," Tate said as he delivered a sharp kick to Charlie's midsection.

Charlie's battered body jerked in an effort to double over, but his bound arms and legs restricted his defense.

"Stop!" Trutenko shouted. "I told you I wanted him persuaded to cooperate, not beaten into oblivion."

Tate grunted.

Charlie closed his eyes, longing for that pain-free existence unconsciousness could provide. But with whatever strength remained in his heart, he forced himself to keep alert, straining to listen in on their conversation.

"Can't you sidetrack this other envoy? Cut off access to the program?" Trutenko asked.

The pale-haired man shrugged. "I don't know. She saw me. I'll bet she's on her way here now." He kept one twitchy hand on the door as he bounced his gaze between Charlie on the floor and the quiet jungle outside.

"She?" Trutenko asked. "A female?"

"Little thing." Tate gripped his bleeding arm again, then shook his head as though unwilling to believe what he'd seen. "But tough. I watched her take out two of those armored goons in the space of three seconds."

My god. Charlie sucked back a gasp. *Kenna's here.*

Trutenko spun. He lifted Charlie's face with the toe of his boot. "Tell me who she is."

Vomit and blood dribbled from Charlie's mouth onto Trutenko's foot. The big man swore, stamping the ground to shake off the filth. His heel came down hard on the little weed in the floor, destroying it. Charlie winced.

Trutenko crouched one more time. "Who is she?" he asked again. "Does she know about Sub Rosa?"

Charlie worked his tongue around the inside of his mouth. "No," he said, in a rasp so soft that Trutenko had to lean close to hear.

Charlie worked his lips as though trying to say more.

Trutenko pressed closer.

"But she's going to find out," Charlie said, and spat in Trutenko's face.

The big man reared back with a yell. He jumped to his feet, face contorted as he muttered furiously, wiping his face with the back of his hand.

"She's almost to the bridge," Tate shouted. "We've got to get out of here."

"Kick her out of the program; it should be simple enough," Trutenko said, grimacing as he wiped his face again. "Didn't you establish control before we started? I need time. I have more questions for Mr. Russell."

"I didn't expect an envoy. I'm not prepared," Tate said. He pulled a small device from a back pocket and flexed the fingers of his injured arm. He hesitated, working the controls with start-stop jerkiness. "This contraption is new to me, too, remember. The best I can do is slow her down. Maybe."

Trutenko glared. "Hurry."

Tate shot him a furious glance. "You're the one who wanted the safeties off, but I'm the guy who got sliced in the arm, okay? I'm moving as fast as I can." He sent a quick pointed look that encompassed both Trutenko and Charlie. "No matter what I do to intercept the girl, the longer we stay, the more chance whoever is monitoring her will discover our link. Then all bets are off. Meaning, we have to get out. Now."

Trutenko's nostrils flared. He took a deep breath before answering. "This has been a colossal waste of effort. Can you reboot his implant? Erase this episode? Get him to forget why he's here? We can't risk him talking to others."

"I know what I got to do, boss," Tate said.

Trutenko nodded, pressed his medallion, and disappeared.

Tate made an incoherent noise. He finished inputting something into his handheld control, then sprinted across the room. "You're a damn fool, you know that?" he said, yanking away Charlie's signal medallion and placing it around his own neck, making it clink against the one already hanging there. He pulled a gun from the back of his waistband and aimed its deadly barrel at Charlie's forehead.

Charlie clenched his eyes and thought about Kenna.

"I'll erase your brain, all right," Tate said. He squeezed the trigger.

It clicked.

Charlie's eyes popped open. He managed a grin through his ravaging pain. The idiot didn't know enough to engage the arming overrides. Kenna could take this guy. She was the toughest envoy of them all, and she was on her way.

"Damn," Tate said. He patted his pockets.

Charlie stared at the door, willing it to open, willing Kenna to burst into the room and take this guy out.

Tate yanked a ten-inch serrated blade from a sheath at his side. Using his uninjured arm, he raised the knife high and dropped to his knees next to Charlie. "God, I hate getting my hands dirty."

SIX

Stewart pressed the earpiece tight, as though doing so would help him hear better, as though it would compel Vanessa to answer.

"What's happening?" Blood rushed up, pounding behind his eyes. "Vanessa," he said, his voice an order, "come in. What's happening with Charlie?"

Listening as the medics' staccato imperatives grew terse, Stewart waited for what seemed the longest five seconds of his life. He kept an eye on Kenna. Her body tensed, her sweat stains grew, but she seemed in no danger at the moment. Still, given the situation, he'd do well to have a set of paramedics in here, too. Just in case.

"Vanessa?"

Her voice cracked when she answered. "We're losing him, Stewart."

"But..." Stewart said, not knowing what to say next. They'd never lost an envoy. "Kenna's there," he finally said. "She'll get him out."

Vanessa said, "They want me to do a cold shutdown."

"No!" Stewart said. "That risks brain damage."

"Don't you understand?" Vanessa's voice hissed over the phone. "Charlie. Is. Dying," she said, punctuating each word. "It's the only chance we have left to get him out at all."

"Try to hold them off, Nessa. Kenna's there. She'll do it. I know she will." With another glance in Kenna's direction, he added, "I'm going to call for backup medics." Shaken over the recent events, he rubbed his face. "Kenna's fine now, but with the safeties off—"

"I'll send two of them over," she said.

"But the client—"

"The client is dead, Stewart. He doesn't need them anymore."

SEVEN

Kenna scrambled away from the Land Rover, taking cover behind a shrub. She peered over it, gauging activity on the ledge. No one watching. Keeping to a low crouch, she bolted, intent on following the blond man's path. Just beyond, the suspension bridge spanned a rocky gorge. She didn't know who the guy was, but there was no doubt he knew where to find Charlie.

She'd taken two steps when warbling screams from the ledge warned her that more Huns had arrived. New warriors stamped their feet and raised their weapons. One of them launched an arrow.

The projectile, benefiting from both the downward trajectory and the warrior's uncanny aim, shot straight for her. Anticipating the hit, she threw herself backward, rolling into a ball to protect her face and vital organs. Although VR safeties were always engaged so that injuries participants sustained would be equivalent to getting dinged with a paintball, she'd seen the guy in the Land Rover. She wasn't about to take chances.

The moment the arrow *thunk*ed into the soft ground next to her, Kenna unfolded herself and pushed to her feet, going for the thirty-yard dash to the suspension bridge. She forced herself not to look back, knowing that with each long stride she pulled farther out of harm's way. Grasping at her ear, she sought her command microphone. She'd do well to create some sort of shield for herself.

Her fingers came up empty.

Damn. She must have lost it when she'd rolled to the ground.

Focus, she told herself. The first tenet taught at envoy school. Focus is what gets your targets out safely. And you out safely with them.

A wood-hewn threshold signaled the entrance to the bridge just ahead. She kept her eyes on the goal, ignoring the battle cries from above.

She heard the whistle of another arrow slicing the air toward her. Risking a glance to her left, she redoubled her speed.

Too late.

It caught her mid-stride.

Doubling over, grasping at her leg, she howled and rolled to the ground. The warriors' triumphant shouts from above nearly drowned out her scream. *That was no imaginary impact.* Fabric, torn away by the projectile's graze, gaped around a bloody wound the size of her fist. As a pickax sailed her direction, Kenna clambered to her feet. The shot missed her by a breath.

This isn't real.

But it sure felt real.

Time to get rid of these creeps. She took out the Beretta that she'd recovered from the dead guy in the Land Rover. Aiming at the closest Hun, she squeezed the trigger. He fell in a burst of red, but the gun's slide racked back.

Out of ammunition. And no way to order more.

She tossed the gun away.

Sucking back the pain, she limped toward the bridge. She still had her signal medallion around her neck; she knew she could get out now. But, other than Stewart, there were no other envoys at AdventureSome right now. Charlie couldn't wait.

This VR was very wrong. Charlie's only chance of survival rested with her.

Arrows hit the ground, their points chuffing into the soil behind her, their hollow shafts vibrating on impact. Kenna concentrated on the threshold, focusing her energy on reaching the bridge's opening. She repeated the envoy mantra. "'Nothing is real. Everything is perfectly safe.'"

Mind over matter, she told herself, biting down hard on her upper lip. Every step shot hot pain up her body as though a torch pressed against the inside of her skin. Fear-sweat ran down her legs and soaked into the open wound, causing her to flinch as she ran.

Agitation kept her moving. Mantra or not, it wasn't supposed to hurt like this. As she cleared the threshold, she glanced over her shoulder to see the Huns climbing down the ledge.

At her first steps, the bridge's floor swayed hard to the right, then corrected itself by swinging left. Kenna's hands shot out to both sides and she gripped the rope handrails, instinctively looking downward, an eye on her footing. Over the side, the gorge was deep with greenery as far down as she could see. Concentrating even as she eased her way across the tenuous bridge, she caught the sparkle of a river, so small that it appeared no bigger than a vein in her wrist.

Kenna shuddered as her foot slipped on the wooden slats. Catching her balance, she stepped down too hard on her injured leg. She cried out. Behind her, amid wails and yells, the warriors closed in.

A sudden fog rolled onto the bridge from its far side. Kenna couldn't begin to guess what that meant. She needed to force the pain out of her mind long enough to get across. Going back was not an option.

Holding tight to both sides of the rope bridge, she widened her legs in a spread-eagle stance and shook the structure, hard. The bridge swayed, but it didn't list so far to either side that Kenna thought it would throw her. Safe then. For now.

She closed her eyes for a precious second, then tightened her body in anticipation of the agony ahead.

She ran.

The bridge wobbled but held as her feet clattered across the bouncing floor. Her hands skimmed along the rough rope sides and she counted her steps to keep her mind off the hot throbbing in her leg.

"Charlie!" she yelled, not caring who heard her. She wanted him to know she was there. The growing gray fog now obscured the bridge's far side completely. Sounds of movement, however, arose from its depths.

"Charlie?"

She had gotten about halfway across when the floor jerked, then jerked again as the Huns plodded onto the bridge behind her. Turning, Kenna whipped the bow from her back and nocked another arrow into place. Just as she released, the lead warrior stomped hard. The bounce caused her aim to falter. She watched the arrow fly helplessly over the side.

Backing into the fog, she decided to try again. She set her stance on the shaky bridge, hoping that the leading edge of the gray cloud would render her invisible to the advancing warriors. Closing one eye to aim at the lead man, she released the arrow, sending it straight into his neck. Arms flailing, he staggered backward, tumbling into two comrades. The bridge bounced and swung as they all toppled. Kenna, gauging the sway as she aimed, took the opportunity to fire again.

"That's for you," she said as the arrow landed solidly into one man's uncovered thigh. It made her own wound feel better. She nocked another arrow into her bow and allowed herself a triumphant grin when it pierced the other man's eyeball.

Still watchful, Kenna took another step back.

Her form was probably obscured from the warriors' vision by the fog now, although she could still see the remaining two making another attempt to rally. The guy with the arrow in his leg grimaced in an expression of pure pain as he reached down and tore the arrow from deep within his thigh, releasing, as he did, a cry so fierce that Kenna shivered, despite herself.

Another heavy tremor on the bridge.

From behind her, this time.

She eased herself far left, pressing her body against the rope side, giving whatever loomed behind her wide berth. Tilting her head, she kept one eye on the Huns. Below her ponytail, the tiny hairs on her neck stood up on end. A prickly feeling of closeness forced her mouth tight. Remaining as still as she could, she held her breath.

Far to her right, the bridge shuddered again. Harder this time.

Kenna released her breath, her attention seized by the action of the Huns. They'd also felt the movement. The two still alive looked up toward the fogged area with twin expressions of wariness. Bearing axes at shoulder height, they took decisive steps forward.

Kenna inched sideways to avoid causing movement of her own, but when the Huns broke into a run, their brutish progress covered Kenna's advancement.

Completely swallowed by the fog now, Kenna could no longer see the warriors as they charged. She dropped to her knees, both to be less of a target and to crawl-feel her way across the rest of the bridge. Maneuvering blindly, she knew that any miscalculation or lost floorboard could mean the end of her. And Charlie. She kept low and moved quickly, her senses on high alert.

A low rumble just ahead. Rhythmic and menacing, it sounded exactly like a dog's warning before it attacks. The throaty growling paused long enough for her to hear and feel an exhalation of warm air. Something very large panted. It sniffed the air near her ear.

Thinking fast, she snugged her arms around the bridge's rope handrail, took a steadying breath, and hauled herself over the side. Holding tight, she dangled in the sweep of empty space below.

At that moment, the fog lifted. With a strangled cry, the Huns stopped running. An enormous, doglike form bellowed, then lunged across the bridge, headed directly for the two warriors. Kenna had never seen anything like this creature in any scenario ever before. And she'd seen a lot.

The men screamed, heaving axes at their attacker. However, the jerky swing-sway of the bridge disrupted their aim and they missed. Kenna's heart pummeled a beat in her throat. Hold on, hold on, she told herself. Having turned to flee, the warriors took no more than three steps before the creature was upon them, raising up onto its hind legs to seize the men, one at a time.

Kenna froze for a breathless moment, mouth agape. How did a monster like this get into a jungle VR scenario? This level of inconsistency made no sense.

Putting the anomaly aside, she swung her uninjured leg up, hooking it between support ropes. With effort, she dragged herself back onto the bridge.

God, that hurt, she thought as she rolled to a crouch. Behind the beast now, she crept backward—gingerly—so as not to attract attention.

It stood at least eight feet tall, its spine a sinuous ripple beneath a brush of short golden fur. Torn remnants of a tan shirt and pants clung to the monster's back and legs, as though it had been wearing clothing that had suddenly become too small.

When it had sprung past her, it had moved like a giant wolf—hind legs powerful, forelegs stretching. Now it moved more like a man, standing tall. Its profile revealed alert, intelligent eyes. Blue eyes. But the face, with its forward-thrusting jaw and wide mouth—exposing yellow teeth that dripped saliva—was like nothing she'd ever seen before. Like a golden werewolf, but more human, with hands as large as basketballs.

The werewolf grasped one of the men's arms in its teeth and wrenched it off amid tearing flesh and screams.

Kenna didn't wait to see more. She scrambled to her feet. That short respite had caused the wounded muscle in her leg to stiffen, and she bit back a cry as she forced herself to hobble across the rest of the bridge.

As she cleared the far side's threshold, the creature roared again. Kenna chanced a look back. Its long snout turned. Its ears pricked up. Straightening, it dropped what remained of the Huns and stomped across the bridge in her direction. Those long legs would close the distance between them in seconds.

Kenna knew her arrows would be ineffective against such a coarse hide. She yanked her machete from the belt at her waist and stood at the edge of the bridge, hacking at the left side railing with overhand chops. The rope was sturdy, but it was rope, thank goodness. Not wire, not synthetic. Two hacks. Three. Four. With encouraging squeaks and the *whup-whup-whup* of unraveling rigging, it began to split.

The left side of the bridge lurched downward, and the werewolf dropped to all fours, growling as it maintained precarious balance, too unsteady to spring.

With new desperation, Kenna hacked at the right side handrail; it gave way with a grinding wrench that registered in the creature's pale blue eyes. Sensing immediate danger, the werewolf lunged—its claws almost gaining purchase on the ledge at Kenna's feet.

It missed. Triumphant, Kenna watched the monster fall—but just as its final yelp echoed through the canyon, the beast vanished into thin air.

The werewolf's disappearance froze her in place. Had the creature triggered a signal medallion? Could it have been an avatar for *another* sentient being? How many were in this scene?

She shook herself out of it. Charlie. She had to get to Charlie.

Kenna spied an isolated hut not thirty feet away. She sprint-hopped toward it, ignoring the knifelike stabs from her wounded leg.

Twenty more steps.

She grimaced, fighting the screams of pains from her nerve endings.

Not real.

Ten more steps.

Through gritted teeth she repeated, "Not real."

Five steps.

As she reached the door, she withdrew her knife. She paused to listen. Low moaning. Charlie's voice.

Opening the door, she cried out when she spotted Charlie, bound and bleeding, on the dirt floor. Survival instinct kicked in, and she stopped herself from running to him until her eyes swept the small area.

Four flimsy walls—but no one else there. Safe.

In a heartbeat she was at his side. "Charlie," she whispered.

He didn't react. Didn't move. A deep gash in his abdomen flowered open, blood gushing from his severed belly skin. As horrific a sight it was, Kenna felt a peculiar sense of relief. Charlie was still alive.

His face had gone slack, his dark hair lay plastered against his head with sweat, and beneath Kenna's hand he trembled.

"Charlie," she whispered. "It's okay. I'm here. It's going to be—"

When he opened his eyes, she sucked back her next words.

Red rims had begun to form around his irises.

"No!" she shouted. Charlie could never succumb to mortal absorption. Not possible. He knew better.

She used her knife to slice his bonds. "It's all in your mind." Cut free, he grimaced in pain. Kenna adjusted his limbs with care to get him to lie flat on his back. "Charlie," she said sharply. "Listen to me. It's not real. You're coming back with me."

Her fingers explored his chest for Charlie's signal medallion. If she could activate it…

But it wasn't there. She searched again. It had to be. Charlie would never have taken it off. He knew better.

"Where's your medallion?"

Charlie's blue eyes arced slowly until they met hers. She watched tears form and fall to track through the dirt on his face. Keeping eye contact, he blinked. The red rims around his irises thickened.

Oh, God, no.

"This isn't real." She fought rising panic, striving to achieve the soothing, strong, calming tone they'd learned when they trained to be envoys, so long ago. "None of this is real. *You* are in control. Nothing bad can happen."

Charlie's cracked lips moved again. "Virtu—"

"Right. Virtual reality. That's where you are. This isn't real. This is all in your mind."

He shook his head, the movement obviously causing him great pain.

"Your body's far away. Safe." Kenna started to dig her signal medallion out from beneath her T-shirt. "I'm going to get you out of here now," she said. "They'll send someone back in for me, so I'll be right behind you. You are fine," she added, putting emphasis on the word "fine," but the aching wound on her leg gave her doubts. "You aren't here, Charlie. Remember? You're safe. Your real body is back at AdventureSome."

Kenna lifted the medallion's necklace over her head. "I'm going to put this in your hand, okay? It'll take you—"

"No!" Charlie coughed the word out, his red-rimmed eyes clenching shut as his body tightened in on itself. More blood poured from the gaping wound. She suppressed a startled cry. He opened his eyes again. "No time."

"Listen," Kenna said, refusing to accept that Charlie was near complete mortal absorption. If he believed all this was real, his body back in his capsule would react as if it were true. Unless she could convince him otherwise, he'd die from his own sympathetic response to perceived injuries. "This is *not* real."

Charlie's left hand flew up. He grabbed hers, harder than she expected. "Sub…Rosa," he said.

She tucked the medallion into Charlie's other hand. It slid through his slack fingers and fell to the floor. More blood leaked through the gash in his abdomen.

"Please," she said, her voice betraying her rising dread. "Please, Charlie. You're whole; you're safe. We just have to get you back. That's all."

"No time. No chance," he said. "Kenna." His bright eyes clouded—the red had completely surrounded the blue, and he had trouble maintaining focus. "Sub Rosa. You have to... stop it."

She shook her head. "We'll stop anything you want," she said. "We'll do it together. But you have to come back first." Snatching the medallion from the floor, she pressed it into his hand again. "You have to go. Now."

His right hand fell open again, limp, even as his left maintained an uneasy grip on hers. His eyes, watery and wide, pleaded for understanding. "Too late. Just stay with me now."

"I'm here," she said, cradling Charlie's head in an awkward embrace. "I'll always be here."

EIGHT

A lthough she'd visited Virtu-Tech's headquarters countless times for product training, Vanessa had never been called before the Board of Inquiry's Tribunal. Of course, she'd never experienced the loss of an envoy before. She sat next to Stewart in the fourth-floor corridor near the elevators, not quite knowing what to do with herself until they were summoned. She scratched her upper arms.

Her attention settled on the monitor affixed to the wall across from them. Soothing music set the tone for the new Virtu-Tech advertisements. Seeking escape from the recent terrors she and Stewart—and Kenna, poor Kenna—had lived through, she let herself be mesmerized by the score, marveling at the effort that she knew must go into creating new ads every month or so. Not that they needed updating. People flocked into VR facilities so regularly she wondered why the Virtu-Tech big shots felt the need to advertise Implant 6.0 at all.

Like all prior implants, this new one would be provided free to clients. Claims that 6.0 would further improve the customer's VR experience had generated considerable buzz. Yet, nearly everyone was addicted to VR already. How much more money did the company expect this upgrade to generate?

She let her fingers wander to the small area behind her right ear until she found her own implant, the 5.0. Although there was nothing wrong with it, she—like a good little lemming—intended to upgrade once the new version was available, too.

When Stewart shifted again, she glanced his way. The man hadn't stopped fidgeting since they sat down.

He wiped at his hairline and blew out a breath. "I'm going to hit the men's room."

"Again?"

"Got to." He was down the corridor before she could remind him that they might be called in at any second. The last thing she needed was to face the Tribunal alone.

Returning her attention to the screens, she watched the busy ads, studying the quick scene changes as smiling people rappelled down the sides of cliffs, explored the underwater mysteries of the sunken *Titanic*, and walked on Mars. All within the safe confines of VR. She curled her fingers inward and looked down at her ragged cuticles, wondering how she'd answer the Tribunal's inevitable question: What went wrong?

Vanessa gave an involuntary shrug, then scratched her leg again. She was so itchy lately.

A voice rang out over the monitor's murmuring hum. "Nervous?"

Her head jerked up.

A man grinned down at her. "I guess you are," he said. "Didn't mean to scare you."

"It's okay," she answered automatically, wondering if he was part of the Tribunal. She'd pictured three police detectives, interrogating from behind bright lights.

This man was in late thirties, slim, tall, and blond. "Hi," he said, extending his hand. "I'm Adrian. Adrian Tate."

"Nice to meet you, Adrian." She half rose from her chair and pointed to his bandaged arm as they shook. "What happened?"

He gave a short, scratchy laugh. "Ah…me and power tools don't get along."

"Are you one of the board members?"

"Board member? Ha! No, I had to drop something off at one of the offices down the hall." He yanked a thumb backward as he lowered himself into the chair next to hers. "But then I saw you sitting here all by yourself, and I said to myself, I gotta find out who that beautiful creature is."

Vanessa blushed. "I'm waiting to be called into the Tribunal."

Adrian's face contorted in an exaggerated comical grimace. "That sounds intimidating." He raised his free hand up near the side of his head, wiggling his fingers as he lowered his voice. "The Tribunal."

Despite herself, Vanessa laughed.

Adrian tilted his head as if studying her. "You've got a gorgeous smile."

Vanessa flushed, pleased. "Thank you."

Adrian glanced down at the floor, then back up at her, shaking his head. "I'm sorry. That was pretty forward of me, wasn't it?"

Vanessa smiled. "No worries."

"I mean," he said, "I don't usually come on so strong. I'm usually much better behaved."

Vanessa thought he was behaving quite nicely, thank you very much. Her face grew warmer still. "Even if it was forward, it was a very nice thing to say." Over Adrian's shoulder she caught sight of Stewart headed back from the men's room.

Adrian must have noticed the distraction. He twisted around to look before continuing. "Boyfriend?" he asked.

"No, that's my boss," she said before lowering her voice. "And he's almost old enough to be my father."

Adrian nodded, his eyes straying momentarily toward the crooning monitor. "This Tribunal thing you've got going," he said. "When do you think you'll be wrapped up?"

Vanessa tucked a lock of hair behind her ear. "I don't really know," she said. "I've never been here before."

Adrian pulled out his phone. "Would you give me your number? Or at least, take mine. When you're done, if it's not too late, maybe we could go out somewhere? Get a bite to eat?"

Stewart strode up, and the look of concern on his face momentarily stalled Vanessa's answer. "I'd like that a lot," she finally said.

After they exchanged information, Adrian eased to his feet. "I'll catch you later then," he said, with a wink. He pocketed his phone, headed to the elevators, and hit the down button. As though it had been waiting for him, the gold doors of the left car slid open and he disappeared inside.

"Who was that?" Stewart asked.

Vanessa shrugged, dragging her fingers along her forearm. "A guy who stopped to talk."

Stewart looked gray in the face again. "Nobody called for us while I was gone?"

"Nobody," she said in a voice she hoped conveyed confidence. "I meant to ask—did you talk with Kenna today?"

"Yeah," he said. "She refuses to take any time off. She's convinced she needs to be at the office to hunt down what went wrong. I've allowed her access to all our records, and she understands that our VR is offline until further notice. I hope I made the right decision to let her dig."

"You did," she said, and patted his hand.

"She's as tough as they come, but dealing with the aftermath of Charlie's death is taking more out of her than she realizes." Stewart stared up at the ceiling. "That's another reason I didn't want her here today. The people at this inquiry"—he gestured toward the ads playing on the screen—"want answers. That girl can be stubborn," he said with what sounded like pride. "If she lost her temper, it could hurt us all."

"There's something I don't understand," Vanessa said. "Why have Virtu-Tech directors come all the way out here to question us? Wouldn't it have made more sense to fly the two of us out to DC?" She started to scratch at her thigh again. When Stewart noticed and shot her a questioning look, she stopped.

His nostrils widened as he pulled in a breath. "I asked them the same thing." His gray brows came together in concentration. "They're coming from three different locations. To rule out bias, or so they say."

"Do they have the authority to shut down AdventureSome?"

"If they think we're a risk, yeah," he said. "Definitely." He wiped at his face again. "But that isn't all I'm worried about."

"Then what?"

"Criminal liability." Stewart took a deep breath again, then stood. Vanessa thought he was fighting off a faint. He paced the small area, gesturing with undisguised agitation. "We're a good facility. Our record is pristine, and we fly so straight and narrow that they don't even remember that our franchise exists. I like that. And we're a clean operation financially, too. I don't go for any of this 'taking money for product placement' or similar shenanigans." He nodded at the screen; it had shifted to a doctor who talked about the safety of VR. "Aboveboard," he said. "And safe."

Vanessa knew all that, but Stewart obviously needed to reassure himself, so she said nothing. She scratched at her upper arm again.

"Are you okay?" he asked.

She nodded.

Stewart stared away. "I have to convince them that our recent accident is just a fluke. That we're not to blame. Otherwise, they can put me away. They can put Kenna away." He fixed a look at Vanessa and she felt herself blanch.

"Me too?"

"If they find evidence of negligence, they can prosecute us all." He continued to pace. "It's not something they do often, nor easy for them to prove, but with Charlie being there after hours, unsanctioned…"

"They can't blame you for that."

"Can't they?"

"Who was that client anyway?" she asked, desperately searching for someone else to blame.

He shrugged. "He wasn't in our database. I'm sure we'll discover his identity once the authorities complete their investigation."

"Listen, Stewart," she said, feeling a tingle of panic running along her arms and up her back. "We'll face the Tribunal, and we'll tell them the truth."

"But what is the truth?" he asked sharply. "I don't know what the hell Charlie was doing in there." He shook his head, twitching. "A tribunal is assembled only in the gravest of circumstances. Virtu-Tech takes security issues very seriously. Losing a client is unfortunate, but accidents do happen. Losing an envoy to mortal absorption…" He crumpled into his seat, dropping his head into his hands. "I don't know how we're going to get through this."

NINE

Patrick Henry Danaher heard Werner Trutenko coming. Outside the closed office door, his half brother dropped orders like fiery bombs on the employees who sat in his path.

Patrick could have turned to watch Werner's approach through the office's inner windows. Instead, he chose to use these last few seconds to marshal himself. He sat up straighter, his bulk protesting the restriction of the molded chair's arms. The past twenty-four hours had been among the worst he'd experienced in his adult life. Impatient as he waited for further updates, he'd paced, grimaced, and wished life had taken him elsewhere. Now, he ran a hand over his sparse red hair, and twisted his chin to loosen the snug of his collar.

Werner's office door slammed open. "Patrick!"

"I'm here," he said, getting to his feet. "What do you need?"

Werner wrenched off his suit jacket and threw it against the open chair. "I'm going in," he said.

They stood for a moment, staring at each other, Patrick trying to read his half brother's expression.

"I don't understand," Patrick finally said.

The two men were similar in height and build, both carrying more heft than their large frames required. Though separated by nearly fifteen years, the two men seemed much closer in age. Elder brother Werner still sported a full head of close-cropped gray hair, whereas Patrick felt as though his bald spot expanded by the day.

"The Tribunal," Werner answered. "I can't leave this to chance. I'm taking over."

He shuffled through the papers on his desk. "Where the hell did I put my phone?" he asked.

Patrick reached across to where it sat next to the monitor.

His brother took it from him with mumbled thanks. "About that envoy, the one from the botched operation—"

"Charles Russell?" Patrick asked.

Werner grimaced. "After everything we've just gone through, do you actually believe I'd forget his name? No, I meant the woman. The one who came in after him."

"Kenna Ward? What about her?"

"I've gotten word that she won't be in attendance." Werner pointed upstairs. "The owner of the franchise and the tech who was on duty that night are here, but Kenna is not."

Patrick didn't know how to respond to that.

"I'd intended to find out how much Charles Russell had shared with her." Werner gave Patrick a pointed look. "If she was his fiancée, I have to assume she's working with the dissidents, too."

"My sources believe he kept her in the dark," Patrick said.

"How confident are you with these sources?"

"Pretty solid." Patrick shrugged. "They're the same sources who warned us about Tate."

"I should have listened to you." Werner worked his jaw.

Patrick held up both hands. "He's trouble, Werner. I think we ought to cut him loose now before he causes more problems."

His brother shook his head. "We can't. Not after all this. He could ruin everything."

"He's too unpredictable. Give him to me. I'll find a job for him in the organization that keeps him busy but limits his influence."

"Thought of that. Won't work," Werner said as he sat. "Tate may be easily manipulated but he's not stupid. Any position not reporting directly to me will come across as a demotion." Grimacing again, he added, "He's proud of himself for what he did. Can you believe that? Proud."

Patrick sat, too. "He's sick."

"Maybe, but we're stuck with him for now." Werner turned his attention to his laptop screen and studied the display. "How well did you know Charles Russell?"

"Not well enough to anticipate something like this." Patrick ran a hand over his head. "Why?"

"Who recruited him?"

Patrick rubbed his lip. "I don't recall." Shifting his weight, he added, "I could find out."

"Do it. Investigate the recruiter thoroughly. Russell may have accessed sensitive data. If so, he most likely passed it to that damned underground organization." He shot Patrick a look of fury. "If whoever brought him on was part of the underground, too, I want that man's balls on a silver platter."

Patrick gave a crisp nod. "I'll see to it immediately."

"No," he said. "I want you to search Charles Russell's apartment first."

"Excuse me?"

"Get in there any way you can and bring me everything that looks even remotely suspicious. Assemble a team to help you." Werner placed his big fingers on the keyboard, tapping slowly, squinting as he worked. "Use people who know how to keep their mouths shut. Tell them what to look for, but don't tell them why. And watch them. Make sure nothing gets past you. If this Russell was able to infiltrate our ranks, there's no telling how many other spies we have in our midst."

"Got it," Patrick said.

Werner stopped typing and turned to his brother. "But perhaps we can fight fire with fire."

"How?"

"You." He pointed his finger like a gun. "Get inside the rebel underground."

Patrick struggled to conceal his surprise. "How do I do that?"

"How the hell should I know? That's your job," he said.

Patrick shook his head. "This could take some time—"

Werner cut him off. "You knew Charles Russell. Exploit that friendship."

"I wouldn't call our relationship a friendship."

"You're the only person I completely trust." Werner threw Patrick a baleful look. "Get in there. Do whatever it takes."

TEN

A brick outhouse of a woman appeared from around the corner. "Stewart Mathers?" she asked. When he and Vanessa stood, the woman ordered them to follow her, navigating the narrow hall with such verve that Stewart feared she might bounce against the walls. He didn't like her expression. He didn't like anything about this place. He'd never been called before the regulatory board before, and he wished to God he had some idea of what he was going to say. There was no explanation for what had happened. None. Sledgehammers pounded his heart. Sharp pincers gripped his stomach. He needed to heave.

The squat woman pushed one of the tall doors open with an authoritative flat hand. "In here," she said.

The room was empty, though large enough to seat a hundred. Far across the dark-carpeted expanse, behind a skirted table and silhouetted by tall, bare windows, sat three individuals on a raised platform. Flanking the wide wall of windows were two portraits of the men who'd started Virtu-Tech, Vefa Noonan and Simon Huntington.

"Come in," an amplified voice beckoned.

The words echoed as if they had been shouted in a cave. Stewart and Vanessa walked in behind the woman, who quickly outpaced them. She made it to the front and settled herself at a small desk. Within seconds, she'd triggered a small camera and waited, fingers poised, to begin recording the proceedings into a laptop computer.

Taking a breath, Stewart shot Vanessa a look of encouragement. He strode in purposefully. No sense in looking weak even if that's how he felt.

He took a seat at the table facing the three judges, Vanessa to his right. Live microphones arced into their personal space. Spotlighting bathed them in personal pools of glow. Could this get more intimidating?

Stewart couldn't make out the faces of the Tribunal members. The bright windows behind them kept him from being able to discern much more than that they were all male. His eyes scanned down to the court reporter facing him, ready to start the proceedings. She spread her lips in a smile that did nothing to ease his discomfort.

"Welcome," came a voice from above. From the slight shift in the center figure's shoulders, Stewart deduced it was he who'd spoken. "We are very sorry to meet you under these circumstances," he continued in a nasal tone, spreading his arms as if to encompass the situation, "but I am certain that with your cooperation, we'll have matters settled soon and be able to move forward with confidence."

Stewart spoke into the microphone. "Um. Yes. Thank you. I agree," he said. Out of the corner of his eye, he noticed Vanessa nodding. The woman at the computer began to type.

The voice continued in the slightly higher pitch of introduction. "As you know, we represent Virtu-Tech's governing body for mind-directed entertainment. I am Dr. Brennan, and to my right is Dr. Sachs. Dr. Larson is unable to be here today, but we are fortunate to have another associate here in his place to conduct the questioning." He took a slip of a breath, then turned to his left. "Dr. Trutenko, you may begin."

The large man leaned forward, bringing his body enough into the overhead light to allow Stewart a good look at him. He didn't like what he saw. Buzz-cut hair, middle-aged scowling face.

"We summoned three individuals to this inquiry. Why are there only two of you here?"

The man's tone churned up Stewart's uneven stomach yet again. He cleared his throat. "I ordered the envoy—the one who attempted to save the lives of Charles Russell and his client in the fatal VR scenario—to remain back at our facility."

"Why would you do that?" Trutenko asked.

"A judgment call on my part," Stewart said, with every bit of confidence he could muster. "She and Charlie...Charles Russell...were close." He kept his gaze steady. "She needs time to deal with her grief. I believe that putting her through this inquiry would have been damaging to her."

Trutenko appeared to be ready to ask another question, but Stewart interrupted. "Because both the client and Charles Russell were dead or nearly dead by the time she reached them, I don't believe any analysis of her actions is relevant to these proceedings."

Trutenko's jaw worked out some inner tension. He consulted notes. "This envoy," he said finally, "her name is Kenna Ward?"

"That's correct."

"You say that she and Charles Russell were close. In fact, they planned to be married, didn't they?"

Stewart clasped his hands together. "That's correct."

Trutenko scratched a few notes. "Isn't it rather unusual for romantically involved envoys to work together?"

Vanessa interjected, "They were a team first. An excellent one. They always worked together." She shot a glance toward Stewart, then amended, "Well, until recently."

"Then how do you explain Mr. Russell going in without tech support?" Brennan interrupted from his center chair. "Why no backup?"

Stewart bit his lip. Here it was. "Charlie accessed our system without authority. He and the client apparently came in after hours to participate in the client's adventure."

"Without authority, you say? Why was that?" Brennan pressed. "What prevented this client from coming to the facility during normal hours? And how did he manage to hire one of your envoys to accompany him?"

Vanessa glanced over at Stewart as though she read his mind. He had no choice but to tell the truth.

"We don't know. We couldn't identify the client. We couldn't find anyone who fit his description in our records. We couldn't find him anywhere, as a matter of fact." Stewart dropped his gaze. It sounded ridiculous. *Everyone* could be found nowadays. The fact that they couldn't identify this user was inexcusable. Stewart looked up again. "The authorities are investigating. I'm sure they'll come up with answers. We assume that the name the client provided was an alias."

"Why would he fake his identity?"

Stewart had given this a great deal of thought. "My guess is that, whoever the man was, he'd been on a list of prohibited VR users. By using a fake ID and coming in after hours, he circumvented the system so that no one would know he'd participated."

"But because you don't know who this individual really is, you don't know for certain that he was prohibited. Correct?" Brennan pressed.

"Yes. We can only speculate that he'd demonstrated a high risk of immersion in the past." Stewart stared down at the table. He scratched at the linen with his fingernail. "Apparently he was very susceptible."

The room was silent save for the tiny tapping noises as the court reporter recorded Stewart's last few words. Long slivers of sweat trickled down his back. He shivered in the chill. His fingertips had gone numb.

Outside, the afternoon sun clouded, darkening the windows and bringing the three men's faces into better focus.

Trutenko leaned forward again. "Back to the viability of your franchise. How many envoys do you have on staff?"

"After the loss of Charlie, we're down to three."

"Including Kenna Ward?"

"Yes. That includes Kenna."

"What are her plans? Brennan asked. "Will she return to the job? Or has the experience at AdventureSome traumatized her? Is it possible you'll be left with fewer envoys than you're required to have on staff?"

"I offered to bring on a couple of registry-level envoys," Stewart said, "but Kenna refuses to take time off."

Trutenko pursed his lips. "You do understand that, for a facility your size, four full-time envoys are required."

"I can step in as needed."

"You're certified as an envoy?"

Relieved to be able to answer at least one question with confidence, Stewart nodded. "I am."

"When was the last time you tested?" Brennan asked.

"Less than a year," Stewart said.

Brennan made a sound that could have indicated disbelief. "We will feel more comfortable allowing AdventureSome to reopen once you're fully staffed."

"I've taken steps to hire a replacement"—Stewart nearly choked on the word—"for Charlie."

"Good," Brennan said.

Trutenko held his pen poised above the desk before him. "You say that Kenna Ward and Charles Russell were lovers," he said. "They lived together?"

Stewart lowered his head toward the microphone. "Yes."

"If I understand the sequence of events correctly, Ms. Vanessa Rickert was on call the evening of the recent deaths." He nodded toward her. "She was summoned in by the automated alarm system when the unknown client's life signs began to fail. On her way into the facility she notified you, yes?"

"That's correct."

"You assessed the situation and made the decision to summon Ms. Ward to attempt a rescue."

A long moment of silence. Finally Stewart said, "Yes, that's true."

"Why did you choose to summon Ms. Ward? Why not someone else?"

"Kenna's my best envoy. There's no one—"

"Is it because Ms. Ward *already knew* Mr. Russell was there without permission?"

"No." Stewart frowned. "Kenna didn't—"

"Come now, Mr. Mathers. Charles Russell was operating in stealth. You've already admitted as much. Wouldn't it make sense to summon an envoy who was aware of his covert activities?"

"Absolutely not," Stewart said with resentment, the flush of anger rushing to his face. "Kenna didn't even know that Charlie was there that night."

"How can you be certain?"

Stewart stared Trutenko straight in the eye. He knew that the man was here to do a job, but he couldn't help hating him. Maybe because this hearing represented how Charlie died, or Stewart's own inability to prevent this tragedy from happening in the first place. No matter. Stewart refused to allow Kenna's reputation to be questioned.

"Listen," he said, when he composed himself. "If Kenna had found out about an unauthorized trip in, she would have kicked his ass, if you'll pardon the expression. Kenna has seen firsthand what can happen when rules aren't followed. I'm sure Charlie was keeping her in the dark."

"Why is that?"

Stewart took a deep breath, then answered. "I can only guess that he may have been trying to earn extra money before they got married."

Placing one hand over his microphone, Trutenko motioned for his colleagues to lean in. They spoke in low tones before returning their attention to Stewart and Vanessa.

Brennan leaned forward. "Because your facility has a solid record, we have decided to allow AdventureSome to reopen. That's assuming, of course, our techs find nothing out of order during their investigation."

Stewart's shoulders relaxed. "Thank you," he said.

"Not so fast." Trutenko held up a finger. "We have also opened an investigation into Kenna Ward's liability for this recent tragedy. We expect your complete cooperation."

"Kenna had nothing to do with it."

"So you claim," Trutenko said. "Let us hope the facts support that assertion. In the meantime, you are both hereby admonished to say nothing of this aspect of the investigation to Ms. Ward."

"Please, listen to reason," Stewart began.

"No, Mr. Mathers. You need to listen," Trutenko said, cutting him off. "While your facility is in no danger at the moment, the loss of an envoy is a singularly alarming occurrence. If those who are trained to protect are in jeopardy themselves, then our entire industry is threatened. We need to minimize that risk. There may be other forces at work. From your testimony here today, I believe it is possible that Mr. Russell was keeping more secrets than even you were aware of. One of these secrets may enlighten us as to why he was unable to survive a relatively mild VR adventure."

"I don't understand."

Trutenko's glare bore down on him. "And that is precisely why we need to step in and analyze the situation. We don't know much about this Charles Russell. We don't know the sort of person he was, or who this Kenna Ward is. We don't know their friends or acquaintances. We must investigate the possibility that they may have set out to sabotage Virtu-Tech's systems."

"Sabotage?" Stewart choked an indignant huff. "You've got to be kidding."

"I assure you, I am not. There are enough questions here to raise suspicion. I don't want to falter in my investigation. I choose, rather, to cover every possible alternative."

"Charlie wouldn't be involved in anything underhanded. I'd have trusted him with my life."

"Be very glad you never acted upon that trust, Mr. Mathers. His client apparently did and died for his naïveté. You will provide whatever assistance is required to facilitate our covert investigation." He blinked twice, then smiled.

"You can't do that."

"Indeed, I can. AdventureSome is a franchise of Virtu-Tech, is it not?"

"Yes, of course."

"Then you may wish to review the contracts all franchise

owners are required to sign before being granted permission to operate."

"I protest." Stewart stood, barely aware of Vanessa's restraining hand on his arm.

"Then let me submit this observation to you, Mr. Mathers. With your cooperation, our Tribunal will be willing to overlook your recent misfortunes. If you choose to thwart our investigation, then I will have no choice but to close down AdventureSome immediately and indefinitely."

ELEVEN

S itting together on a train station bench, Kenna and Stewart didn't speak. Instead, they stared straight ahead.

Kenna appreciated the silence. Guilt and grief combined to make the past several days among the most difficult she'd ever endured. Robbed of the words to explain to Charlie's family, she'd nonetheless assisted his mother in arranging for his cremation. At the memorial service, his mom had silently squeezed Kenna's hand. Forgiveness? Understanding? Kenna would never know.

Through it all, Stewart had been steadfast and supportive. He'd listened as she recounted her experiences in Charlie's fatal VR scenario, as baffled as she was regarding the program's anomalies and Charlie's involvement in a clandestine adventure. They, together with Vanessa and the other techs at AdventureSome, had tried to make sense of the situation, but no matter how deeply they dug, they found no answers. At this point, Kenna was simply talked out. She craved anonymity and oblivion. When Stewart announced his errand, she'd volunteered to go along. Where better to blend in than at a busy train terminal? Commuters, travelers, shoppers, and families scurried past against the backdrop of an unceasing procession of long- and short-distance shuttles. Sleek and glistening white, the snakelike monsters slid in and out of Chicago's Union Station with graceful precision like a reptilian ballet. The trains made slow U-turns behind curved Plexiglas. They stopped long enough to disgorge arrivals and absorb new passengers before shushing off again through dark feeder tunnels. Above the Plexiglas barriers, ever-changing readouts silently displayed gate assignments and departure times.

And on every vertical surface in the station, billboard screens advertised the latest in VR entertainment.

Kenna let her gaze fly from one wall-size display to the next. In concert, dozens of screens presented their ever-repeating ads filled with laughing people of all colors, shapes, sizes, and ages. Every one of them spoke earnestly into the camera.

"Experience the adventure of a lifetime," they urged in a sea of sincere eyes and bright teeth.

An elderly man with cherry-red cheeks winked. "As often as you want!"

A clean-cut woman in a lab coat and a name tag reading "Doctor" stepped into the frame. Carrying a clipboard and wearing look of satisfaction, she gave her notes a theatrical glance, then smiled at the swell of cheerful people before turning to address the camera herself. "The new 6.0 implant will be available soon. Sign up today to be first in line for the free upgrade when it's released," she said. Brightening her smile, she added, "It's perfectly safe."

Perfectly safe. Yeah, right. Kenna fingered her silver locket. An engagement gift from Charlie. Her most treasured possession. Her only tangible link to him now.

The last thing Kenna wanted to think about was the pervasiveness of VR, but there was no escaping the animated billboards chanting happy claims from every direction. She couldn't summon the will to even look away. Instead, she studied the ads, dispassionately estimating that they cycled about every seven minutes. Jason's train had been delayed, and they'd been here for four rounds already.

Next ad: Simon Huntington: wizened face, youthful energy, sharing the story of his friendship with Vefa Noonan and the tale of their wondrous invention. Everyone, even little kids in school, knew VR's origin story. Kenna had learned it herself years ago, and mentally recited along with old Simon.

There had been any number of virtual reality gadgets on the market before Simon Huntington and Vefa Noonan came along. They'd expanded on the concept, taking it deeper. First into the realm of education and health care, saving countless lives in the process. That the technology had now morphed into entertainment—becoming Virtu-Tech's crown jewel—was simply bonus. For both eager consumers and its owners' bank accounts.

The full advertising cycle wouldn't be complete without a word from Celia Newell. Vefa Noonan's only child—and now the powerful president of Virtu-Tech—she smiled into the camera, coolly reminding everyone to come in for free implant upgrades.

"Virtu-Tech and I care about you," Newell said for the fourth time since Kenna had sat down. She sincerely hoped the trains wouldn't be further delayed. She didn't think she could sit through four more iterations.

"You're sure you don't want at least a few days off?" Stewart asked, breaking into her reverie. He sat forward, elbows on his knees, hands clasped, thumbs rubbing together.

They'd argued this point several times already. She turned to face him. "Until the diagnostics are complete on AdventureSome's system, I can't get into the program to retrace my steps. Keeping busy, even if that means sitting in a train station, waiting to meet this new envoy, is about the only way I'm able to hold myself together."

"I'm sorry," Stewart said for at least the hundredth time.

"Not your fault." Kenna turned her attention back to the ever-rearranging trains. Gliding along on single rails, their movements were shushed in the din of the cavernous station.

"Are you sure there isn't anyone you can call?" Stewart asked. "To come stay with you?"

"Stay with me for how long, Stewart? Is there a proscribed timeline for grief?"

His cheeks colored.

"Sorry." Kenna looked away. "No," she said. "No one to call."

"Adventure of a lifetime." The old man with the cherry cheeks winked again. "As often as you want!"

Stewart stared at the floor, nodding. He took a deep breath. "Have you made your appointment with Dr. Baxter?"

Kenna gave a brief nod. "Tomorrow morning." Yet another hurdle in her path to finding Charlie's killers: safety protocols required a psych evaluation before Kenna would be allowed to return to envoy duties.

"Before Jason gets here…" Stewart began then stopped.

Kenna waited, tightening her mouth when Stewart faltered. He was the closest thing to family she had. She wanted to curl up and cry into his chest. She wanted him to rock her with strong arms and promise her that things would be okay.

But things would never be okay now that Charlie was dead.

Bright-backlit signs above the third set of tracks announced Jason's train was due to pull in in two minutes. She moved to stand.

Stewart stopped her with a touch. "Wait," he said.

The warm feelings she had for her mentor snapped the moment she saw the look on his face. "What?" she asked.

His blue eyes held the same concern they'd had right before she'd gone in to try to save Charlie. Kenna blinked the memory away.

"It's about the Tribunal, isn't it? What haven't you told me?"

He scratched his head, looked away, then finally returned his gaze to meet her stare. "If this new envoy, Jason, doesn't work out, I may be forced to shutter AdventureSome. At least temporarily."

"Whoa," she said, not even attempting to tamp down her anger. "You never said anything about the Tribunal ordering you to close your doors."

"They didn't order it. Not in so many words, at least. But the threat is real because, well, Jason was the only applicant for the job." He winced. "And regulations state that we can't be open unless we're fully staffed."

"What about registry-level temps?" she asked.

"You know what a hassle that can be," he said. "And with the release of the new 6.0s in the coming months, the shortage of full-time envoys is going to get worse, not better." He tried to work up a smile. "The good news for you is that—once you're cleared to get back to work—your skills will be in high demand. Even if we shut down, there will be opportunities for you elsewhere." Stewart's eyes sought something in Kenna's but apparently didn't find it.

Kenna said nothing.

Stewart's face tensed and his words came out jerky and flat. "I thought you ought to know," he said. "I thought it was only fair to tell you."

"Thanks," she said, looking up at the train signs again. Jason's train was due in forty-two seconds. Forty-one. "What's causing this shortage anyway? Do you know?"

"Fewer people willing to give up VR as entertainment these days," he said. "And of those who do enter the training program to become envoys, only a small percentage succeed."

"I guess that's true," Kenna said. Charlie had complained about how inescapable VR had become and how envoys were among the last remaining participants who managed to remember that life existed outside the capsule.

She glanced up at the VR ad's doctor who said, "Perfectly safe."

A gleaming set of cars slid into its bay. The Plexiglas safety curtain slid up, and the doors opened. Among the disgorging passengers was a fellow with a duffel bag slung over one shoulder. About Kenna's age, he glanced around, his shaved head reflecting the overhead lights. It looked like he was eating something.

"There he is," Stewart said, waving.

The bald guy cocked a dark eyebrow, then made his way over. He finished chewing, then swallowed. "Hey," he said. "You must be Stewart. I'm Jason." Stuffing his half-eaten Flaxibar into the pocket of his duffel bag, he reached out to shake hands. Turning to Kenna, he said, "And you must be my new partner. Nice to meet you."

"Mm-hmm." This was so wrong she struggled with pleasantries.

Jason studied her for a moment too long. "You okay?"

She nodded. "Tough times," she said.

"Yeah, I heard." His expression sobered. "I'm sorry about your friend Charlie. I know how it is with partners. I won't try to replace him or anything..."

"Like you could." Kenna's tone was bitter.

Stewart laid a hand on her arm. "Charlie wasn't just Kenna's friend. He was her fiancé."

"Geez, Stewart." Kenna fought for control. "Why not share my whole life story?"

Stewart apologized as Jason's eyes widened.

"I didn't know," Jason said. "I really am sorry."

"Not your fault." Kenna gave a brief nod. "Let's just get going, okay?"

As they made their way to the car, Jason asked about apartments in the area and if Stewart or Kenna had any recommendations. Stewart gave some advice as he drove.

"You're not taking me to AdventureSome first?" Jason asked when they pulled up to his hotel.

"They're not letting anybody in," Kenna said as she turned to face him. "System is completely down."

Stewart forced a smile. "Only until I get the all clear. My techs assure me they'll be out of our hair soon. I'll text you as soon as I know more. Could be as early as tomorrow afternoon."

"Should have been today," Kenna said. "I have work to do."

Jason alighted from the back seat. "Looking forward to getting in there," he said. "Whenever we can."

✦

When it was just the two of them in the car again, Stewart turned to her. "Go easy on yourself, Kenna. Please."

She nodded. "Yeah."

TWELVE

Later that night, when Adrian Tate rolled off of her to fall almost immediately asleep, Vanessa let out a sigh of confusion. The man had kept up an incessant chatter during sex that could have been erotic if he'd only kept his attention focused on her. When she'd asked about his injured arm—no longer bandaged—he'd claimed he was completely healed. "Mind over matter," he'd assured her. Whatever that meant.

He'd started out well enough. When she'd taken off her clothes and he told her how beautiful she was, Vanessa had almost been convinced that she'd landed one of the good guys this time.

As his hands roamed, however, so had his attention.

It still wouldn't have been so bad, except all he wanted to talk about was Vanessa's experience before the Tribunal. After she'd told him the circumstances that had landed her there, he'd become fixated on all the details regarding Charlie's death.

If, after these past few grueling days, Vanessa hadn't been looking forward to an evening of vigorous, casual sex, she might have pushed back. Instead, in an effort to maintain his interest, she indulged him. She shared more about the tragedy at AdventureSome than she normally would have with a new acquaintance, but she was careful to avoid mentioning any of her colleagues by name.

He seemed fascinated by her job. What harm could there be?

By the time his eyelids fluttered an hour later, Vanessa's mood had begun to improve. Adrian wasn't a bad-looking man. And when his face broke out into a lazy, just-awake smile of pleasure as he gathered her in his hairy blond arms, she talked herself into giving him another chance.

He turned her so that her back was to him. Pulling her close, he nuzzled her neck. "Have a nice nap, gorgeous?"

Definitely worth another chance. "I stayed awake watching you."

"Oh?" He gave a rumble of pleasure. "What time is it?"

She propped herself up on one arm to see the alarm clock over his shoulder. She squinted to read the digital numbers in the dark. "Eleven."

Closing his eyes, he made an indistinguishable noise as he pressed his face into the pillow. "Morning or night?"

Vanessa laughed and was heartened to see the corners of his mouth pull up. "Nighttime, silly."

"Thank God."

"Why?"

Reaching over, he grabbed one of her nipples and tweaked it. Extricating himself from her as he sat up, he rubbed his face. "I have to get going."

Vanessa looked at the clock again, as though it might have lied to her the first time. "Now?" she asked, her voice taking on a tone of petulance she didn't try to disguise. "So late?"

Adrian swung his long, wooly legs over the side of the bed. Though there was little ambient light, Vanessa noticed that his feet were hairy, too. Long and lean, like the rest of him. "This isn't the middle of the night, sweetheart," he said. "It's still early."

"Where are you going?"

"Duty calls."

"Duty," she repeated with heavy skepticism. "I thought you said you were in sales." She couldn't remember what industry he'd said he was in. "You can't possibly be seeing customers at this hour." Maybe he was married and not one of the good guys after all. Drawing the sateen sheets up to cover her exposed breasts, Vanessa tried again. "What's so important?"

By now Adrian had pulled on his khaki pants and dark polo shirt. He slid his sockless feet into brown loafers and brushed a hand over his short hair. "Couple of things I have to take care of."

In the dark she couldn't see his expression. Was he teasing her? "That's pretty vague."

He leaned across the bed to kiss her.

Vanessa touched her lips to his. "Will I see you tomorrow?"

"Hope so," he said. "But I may be out of town on business for a few days."

"Where are you going?"

Still almost nose to nose with her, he waggled his blond brows. "Big project I'm working on." Standing straight again, he worked at his fly, making sure the zipper was shut. "Real big. Can't put this one off. But I'll call you just as soon as I get back. Okay, babe?"

Long after Adrian clicked her front door shut, Vanessa stared after him, realizing that he'd never once called her by name.

THIRTEEN

D r. Sadie Baxter tilted her head. "Would you like something to drink, Kenna? Tea, perhaps?" She gestured across her office, toward a small countertop along the wall. Outfitted like a miniature kitchen, the space held all the comforts of home. There was even a plate of cookies, no doubt standing ready to soothe anxious patients.

From the engraved brass nameplate centered on her desk, to framed letters of commendation, to a dozen different diplomas both earned and honorary, the psychiatrist's name was everywhere in this walnut-paneled room. The ostentatious display of intelligence and postgraduate education did nothing to improve Kenna's mood.

"No," Kenna said, "I'm fine," hoping the good doctor would pick up the hint.

The wide wall of windows behind Dr. Baxter's desk overlooked Lake Michigan, sparkling blue green in the morning sun. Kenna squinted. She couldn't wait to get this over with. The sooner her psych evaluation was behind her, the quicker she'd be able to dive back into VR and find out what went wrong.

"Oh, let me get that." The doctor stood up, closed the draperies, and flicked on a small lamp. Slim, midfifties, with dark skin and shoulder-length graying hair, Dr. Baxter looked exactly as Kenna had expected. Her eyes were bright, alert, and framed by wrinkles probably worn in from years of narrowing her gaze at patients. She wore blue jeans and a long-sleeve top. The deep V of her neckline showcased the sagging skin of her neck and décolletage.

Returning to her seat, she leaned both elbows on the desk. "There," she said, a self-satisfied smile on her face. "That better?"

"Thank you, Doctor," Kenna said.

"Call me Sadie," she said. "I like to keep things informal."

"Informal," Kenna repeated. She resisted a crack that if the woman wanted informal, she ought to have mentioned that to her decorator. This room epitomized stiff-brow snobbery. Now, with the light suppressed, it was unbearably dull as well. Kenna shifted in her seat, desperate to be away.

"Yes," Dr. Baxter said smoothly. "And while we're on the subject, is there any way I can make you more comfortable? Would you prefer to sit together on the couch?"

Kenna rolled her eyes. This woman could play a psychiatrist in a movie; she was such a stereotype. "Uh, no," she said. She enunciated again: "I'm fine."

Dr. Baxter stared downward at the neat-as-a-pin blotter on her desk. Her slim fingers framed its edge as she adjusted it slightly. Her lips twitched before she raised her eyes to meet Kenna's. "Not quite." Cool smile. "You're not fine until I say you are."

Kenna stared back, breaking away only when the clock in the corner clicked a new minute.

"Now that we have that settled," Dr. Baxter said with a tone free from gloat, "let's get started, shall we?"

Keeping her narrative sterile and precise, Kenna recounted every step of the tragic VR scenario. Instead of making eye contact with Dr. Baxter, she stared at one of the wooden panels across the room. She appreciated its subtle grain marking.

From the psychiatrist's probing questions, Kenna realized that the woman must have scrutinized her dossier before this interview and that someone—probably Stewart—had divulged that she and Charlie had been engaged. And, of course, that became exactly the raw spot the shrink wanted to pick at most.

Kenna faced Dr. Baxter. Let her chew on this: "What somebody needs to explain to me," she said, "is who that other guy was. The one who ran away from me. Where did he come from? Why was he in there?"

"Aren't there usually others in these scenarios?" Dr. Baxter asked.

"You don't understand. This guy was different. Sentient. I could tell. There was something about him…" Kenna's hands tightened in her lap. She stared at the wall again; these were the questions that kept her up at night. "It doesn't make sense. And what about that werewolf thing? A creature like that doesn't belong in a jungle."

Dr. Baxter said, "Why do you *think* it was there?"

"I don't know." Kenna's face warmed. "That's my point."

Dr. Baxter said nothing.

"Look, I don't know how much you know about VR scenarios, but they have a natural progression." Kenna gestured as she spoke. "They follow—for lack of a better term—a storyline. That's why ninety-nine percent of the time, participants get out safely. The story ends. The VR is over. People gradually resume consciousness and walk away. But there were inconsistencies in this one. Like the Land Rover and the gun. In a scenario with Huns, neither should have existed."

"I thought the gun didn't work."

"It did work." Kenna tried to keep the exasperation out of her voice. "But only because I remembered to change the arming override. There's a specific fail-safe built into any scenario that involves firearms."

Dr. Baxter didn't seem to be bothered by that.

Kenna continued. "And the werewolf. There shouldn't be werewolves—even in a fictional Hun attack. It doesn't fit the scenario's parameters."

"Can't those parameters be overridden?"

"Of course," Kenna said, "but the system wouldn't allow me to program anything anachronistic. That means that certain parameters were in place. My ability to change the scene was limited. But not, apparently, for whoever set this one up."

"Charlie?"

"Not a chance." Kenna fingered her silver locket. "This one didn't have Charlie's style."

"So you're telling me this was different?"

Didn't I just say that? Frustrated, Kenna tried to keep her voice even. "It was personal." As she gave voice to the notion, she realized its truth. "The werewolf came out to stop me."

Dr. Baxter nodded. "Have you ever experienced mortal absorption?"

Kenna slammed her hand on the desk. The doctor flinched. "No, dammit. Listen. The werewolf didn't belong. It appeared because I was getting close to Charlie. It came to get *me*." Kenna bolted from her chair. She paced away from the desk, running her hands through her hair. She hadn't intended to get into this, but now that she'd started, she couldn't make herself stop. "I know how paranoid it sounds, but the werewolf looked at me. He had sentience. I saw it in his eyes. He was out to get me."

"Okay," Dr. Baxter said slowly, clearly unconvinced. "But why—"

"And I'll tell you another thing." Kenna pointed her finger at the doctor. "That guy I saw running..." She stopped herself from saying that the blond man had the same eyes as the werewolf creature. "He didn't belong there, either." She sat.

Dr. Baxter lifted one eyebrow. "You suffered an injury in the scenario, didn't you?"

Kenna's hand reached involuntarily to the back of her leg. "The safeties were off," she said. "Sometimes your body can sustain a shock effect that mimics an actual injury, but my brain wasn't immersed, if that's what you're thinking."

Dr. Baxter's patient silence was starting to drive her crazy. Exactly what she didn't need right now.

Kenna sighed. "VR scenarios aren't real. I haven't forgotten that. Unfortunately, Charlie"—she hated that her voice cracked—"suffered mortal absorption. I know that now. What I'm trying to convey is that this scenario was wrong in a way I can't fully pinpoint yet. Charlie was the best." She looked away to stare at the walnut paneling again. "Something had been changed. Technically, I mean. Why were the safety protocols shut down?" She shrugged and looked down at her lap, measuring her words. "VR is safe. It isn't real. Unless someone is immersed, there's no chance of danger. Nothing goes wrong in ninety-nine percent of the adventures. For that other one percent, they have us, the envoys. We rescue those who've become mortally absorbed."

"Like Charlie?"

Kenna bit her lip. "Like Charlie." She watched her thumbs rub against each other. "I could have saved him, too, if I'd gotten to him sooner. He should never have gone in unsanctioned."

"Or without the safeties."

Kenna nodded.

"Do you think that Charlie was responsible for turning off the safeties?"

Kenna knew that Charlie would never do anything like that. She knew it deep in her core. But to sit here and insist that the blond man, the werewolf, and the system were all in some sort of conspiracy to kill Charlie sounded ridiculous. "No one else there had the codes," she said. "Not that I know of, at least."

"So, you're saying now that it was Charlie's fault?"

Damn it all to hell. Kenna steeled herself, took a deep breath, and decided to give the good doctor what she wanted. "He wasn't authorized to be there, he hadn't taken the necessary precautions, and he let himself become mortally absorbed. Yes. It was his fault."

"What about the rest of it? What about it being 'personal'?"

"That was just my emotion talking a minute ago," Kenna said, injecting a little hitch into her words. "I always knew I was safe. I could have pulled myself out at any time. Nothing went wrong other than human error."

Dr. Baxter waited a beat. "Nice speech."

Kenna's head shot up. "Excuse me?"

"Now that you've gotten the party line out so convincingly, why don't we start from the beginning, and this time, instead of werewolves and attacking Huns, let's talk about how angry you are with Charlie."

FOURTEEN

I don't like this one bit," one of Patrick Danaher's men said during their brisk and efficient examination of Charlie Russell's apartment. "Doesn't seem right to be nosing through other people's business when they aren't home. You sure this is legal?"

It wasn't, of course. "Take a look." Patrick pulled an official-looking document out of his pocket and unfolded it. "Our subject's signature, right here." He pointed. "She gave us authority to poke through her apartment if we think it could help. Said she didn't want to be here while it was going on."

"I wouldn't let strangers into my place without me being there."

Patrick refolded the paper and tucked it away. "She wants to get to the bottom of this as much as Trutenko does," he lied. "And she's okay with our being here as long as I oversee the process."

"Still feels like a violation."

Because it is.

As soon as the two-man team completed their search, Patrick Danaher dismissed them, telling them he'd take it from there.

"We didn't find anything incriminating," one of the men said. "Not that I could tell, at least. You sure you got the right apartment?"

"Give me what you have, and I'll figure it out," Patrick said.

The man complied and said, "Good luck with that."

When the door shut behind them, Patrick scratched at the scant hairs spanning his freckled pate and breathed a long sigh of relief to finally have time alone.

Seated on the couple's worn leather sofa, he began the Herculean task of sorting through the amassed detritus. All the journals, notes, and other personal items the team had collected during the seizure sat before him. Patrick closed his eyes to concentrate on his next moves.

Werner wanted everything of interest in his hands as soon as possible. "Don't bother me until you have proof," he'd said. "I want to know everything Charles Russell suspected. I want to know everything the girlfriend knows, too."

Now, as Patrick stared down at the two overflowing bins and the sprawl of paperwork that blanketed the small coffee table—all that was left of Charlie's bold, brave, and inquisitive nature—he heaved a resigned sigh. This was a job for one set of eyes, and his were the only ones he trusted.

He ambled into the kitchen and opened the right-hand cabinet next to the stove to grab a tall pilsner drinking glass. Turning back, he opened the refrigerator and swung his hand to the shelves inside the door for one of the bottles of beer he knew would be there. Twisting it open, he poured the amber brew into his glass, shook the bottle empty, and then bent to toss it away in the recycle bin next to the sink.

Grimacing, Patrick lifted the glass upward, in salute. After a quick sip, he headed back to the living room. With his knees bumping the low sofa table, he scratched at his head again, then reached for the notes.

FIFTEEN

Jason looked up when she walked in. "Hey, Kenna. How's it going?"

Having come in to work at AdventureSome directly from her appointment with Dr. Baxter, Kenna sucked in a breath at the sight of Jason sitting in the cubicle next to hers. Charlie's station. Of course he'd be there, she reminded herself. Where else would Stewart have placed him?

"All good." She fought the prickles of pain his presence triggered as she busied herself settling in. "Have we gotten the all clear on our system yet?"

"Not yet. I figured I'd get a jump on things, though. You know, kind of check the place out." Gesturing toward the monitor, he nodded. "You've got some sweet equipment here."

"Where did you work before?" she asked.

"A franchise in Muskogee. Small shop."

"Oklahoma?"

"You know of any other Muskogees?"

"Touché," she said. "What brought you here?"

Reaching upward, he leaned back, making Charlie's chair squeak. "Bigger city, more opportunities. A life. Back there, VR is all there is. That, and gambling. When I wasn't working, I was bored out of my mind." He smirked. "Pun intended."

"Chicago has plenty of options, that's for sure," she said. "But VR is a giant presence here, too."

"Yeah, I'm getting that impression. All the shops we passed yesterday. Big ones, small ones. Hundreds, it seems." He dropped his elbows onto Charlie's desk and pointed with his chin. "And Virtu-Tech headquarters practically right next door. How do you guys compete?"

"We don't," she said as she sat. "The location down the block is an office building for Virtu-Tech regulators, marketing people, research and development teams—stuff like that. Couple of bigwigs, too. Virtu-Tech itself doesn't open its doors to the public. VR services are provided by franchisees. Of which we're the closest one."

"Must give this place an edge over other spots."

"What gives us our edge is all this sweet equipment you mentioned." *Thanks to Charlie's connections.* She pulled in a tight breath. Charlie's friend Lib, a hotshot at Virtu-Tech, kept AdventureSome supplied with state-of-the-art upgrades. She hadn't talked with Lib since Charlie's death. She'd have to reach out to him soon.

Stewart walked in from one of the adjacent rooms. "Kenna," he said with what sounded like relief. "How did it go?"

"Fine, just fine," she said, hoping to quash the conversation before he could press further. She didn't want to share any details in front of Jason. "How soon before we get back in?"

"That's what I was coming to tell you: we're back online. Our techs have given me the go-ahead but I won't open for business until you two are ready. Feel free to start your team exercises whenever you like."

Finally, something going her way. Kenna fisted both hands. "Yes."

"I'm ready right now," Jason said. He turned to her. "How soon do you want to jump in?"

"Give me a few," she answered. "I need a word with the boss. Stewart, you have a minute?"

He held out his hand toward his office. "Always. Come on in."

Kenna shut the door behind them.

"What's up?" Stewart asked. "Any problems with Dr. Baxter?"

"No, everything's fine." She didn't want to get into particulars of their discussion. How Dr. Baxter had managed to coax information from Kenna about her parents, her early losses, her pride in learning to fend for herself. Stewart already knew Kenna's history; she saw no need to revisit any of it with him now.

"Will there be follow-up?"

"Not sure," she lied. Sadie Baxter had already scheduled the next two sessions. "That's not what I want to talk about, though. It's about me borrowing a capsule later tonight."

"After hours, you mean?" He took a seat behind his desk.

"Yeah," she sat across from him. "I haven't had a chance to revisit the program—Charlie's program—since he...since we lost him. I need to get back in there and find out what went wrong."

"Are you sure that's a good idea?" he asked. "It hasn't even been a week yet. Don't push yourself."

"It's something I need to do."

"Does Dr. Baxter support this?"

Kenna knew with absolute certainty that Dr. Baxter would not approve. "She's urging me to face the truth about Charlie's death." That much was true. "Facing reality involves understanding what drew him into that jungle in the first place and then caused him to be immersed."

"He'd been logged in more than six hours before you got there," Stewart said gently. "That's way over the limit. Even for an envoy."

She pulled in a breath. "I know. But I also know that I won't be able to find closure without revisiting the scene."

He nodded. "It's important to find closure."

"It is." *And that means finding his killer.*

"Keep in mind that we're going offline late tonight for a software update," Stewart said.

"We couldn't have gotten it done during all our diagnostics?"

"This is a scheduled update." He shrugged. "You know how those go. They're always scheduled for off-hours. We don't get to choose what time, though."

"Got it." Kenna nodded. "But you're okay with my staying late?"

Stewart frowned. "I'm out this evening, but maybe one of the other techs can hang back and run the system for you." He adopted a stern look. "You promise not to go in cold?"

"I won't," she said. "I'll talk with Vanessa. See if she can do it."

"If she's willing, it's all right with me."

✦

"Fifteen," Kenna said.

Hands on hips, Jason stared at the climbing wall before them, his gaze traveling up and down the fake rock with the multicolored footholds. "No way." He frowned as he ran a hand over his shiny scalp. "Twenty," he said, "minimum."

"You've got to be kidding," she said. "Fifteen. Easy."

"What are you trying to say? That you Chicago envoys are tougher than little Muskogee brats like me?"

Kenna grinned in spite of herself. Side wagers often brought out the best in envoys, and she relished a challenge. "Aww, is little Okie afraid to be shown up when I complete it in fifteen?"

He gave the fake rock another long look. "Eighteen, at least."

"You want to bet?"

"Bet?" His mouth twitched. "Yeah," he said, "sure."

Kenna nodded and began double-checking all the clips and connectors of her climbing harness. This was the third VR station she and Jason had encountered so far, and although training was taking place entirely at AdventureSome, she enjoyed no home-field advantage. Sophisticated algorithms kept challenges fair and even. Stewart had insisted that they run through the complete set of team-building exercises before assigning them to a case. That would take a few days. Kenna had argued for an abbreviated version, but Stewart had been adamant, insisting that she and Jason find their comfort zones with each other before working together in scenarios with real consequences.

Jason's eyes, the color of shiny mud, reflected the ceiling's hanging light fixtures in tiny white circles. The sight reminded her of Charlie's eyes turning red. She looked away.

"What are the stakes?"

Kenna affected a careless once-over of the rock. "Name it."

He strolled past the structure, his hands clasped behind his back, his lips pursed.

The climbing wall sat like a stark monolith in the center of this otherwise empty, white-walled room. With each "pass," in this training scenario, the VR controls would conjure up a new and slightly more difficult test of teamwork. They were required to achieve a minimum 70 percent score over the ten exercises. But Kenna wasn't interested in achieving minimums.

Jason got to the far end of the edifice and affected a military spin. "I got it," he said. "Loser buys dinner."

She glared at him. "Not a chance."

"Okay, then," he said, as though he'd expected her response,

"Loser buys the Flaxibars."

"Flaxibars?"

"Yeah. A case of them."

"Ick," she said. "Flaxibars are disgusting."

He shrugged. "I think they're pretty tasty." Keeping his hands behind his back, he maintained a neutral expression. "Buying me a case shouldn't be too much of a burden for a well-paid envoy like you."

"I don't plan on losing," she said.

"Then the loser buys dinner."

"I don't want to have dinner with you."

"Geez, I'm not talking dinner-dinner," he said. "I mean we grab something to eat. You know, kind of get to know each other because we'll be working together. But, I hear you." He pursed his lips again, looking deep in thought. "Okay, how's this? You win, I pay for dinner. You go eat all by your lonesome if that's what you want. But if I win, you pay, and we go together." He raised a dark eyebrow and added, "And I pick the place."

She wanted to slap the smirk off his face right then, but realized it'd be so much better to enjoy his reaction when she made it to the top with time to spare. "You're on."

Jason donned the ground harness. He maintained control of the belay ropes as Kenna got herself situated. They argued for a while as to whether the timer would start with Kenna flat-footed on the ground, or with her hands and feet snugged into the first holds. Kenna now stood, ready to leap into action, her back to Jason, waiting for his signal to go.

"Fifteen seconds, right?" he asked.

"Fifteen," she said, without turning.

"And you think you're going to make it?" He made a clucking sound. "No cheating, now."

"Start the damn clock," she said.

"*Tsk*. You're a talented envoy, but such a potty mouth," he said. "You ready?"

Kenna nodded.

"Okay," he said. "On my go." The room fell silent for three long beats. "Ready...Go!"

Kenna sprang into action, finding the first foothold, boosting upward. She counted to herself: one.

Her right hand grasped at another hold—two. Bearing most of her weight as her left foot sought purchase, her arm muscles shuddered.

She moved like lightning, scrambling up the mottled wall like a spider advancing on prey. Three. As she stretched up her left arm to grab a handful of blue plastic, hot slices of pain shot from her shoulder, radiating across her back. Heaving herself upward, she bent the left knee, jamming her foot against a cup-shaped toehold of brown. Four.

She reached upward with her right arm, aiming for a red plastic grip a good six inches out of her range. Sweat broke out at her hairline, but she refused to take the time to wipe her face on her sleeve. Five.

With a determined look upward, she spied the bell at the top. She could feel it waiting for her, just as she could feel Jason's mocking grin at her back. Six.

Down to nine seconds now.

Damn.

Kenna made the split-second decision not to dry her sweaty left hand on the side of her leggings before lunging for a handful of bright orange. Not much farther now. She could do it in three seconds if she pushed.

She managed to hook two fingers over the rounded edge of the hold, but as she started to clamber upward, they slipped.

Bracing herself with her right arm and both legs, Kenna didn't fall away from the wall, but it took a beat and a half for her to grab the orange hold again, and to regain her momentum.

She lost count.

Just as she started to reach upward again, she was overcome with a sudden weightlessness.

"What the hell?"

The bell's ringer cord was in reach.

"Ring it," Jason yelled from the ground.

He'd boosted her up with the belay cords—pulling her to the top.

"Ring it," he shouted again.

The stopwatch buzzer went off.

"Damn you!" She stared down at him. "Why the hell did you do that?"

Jason grinned. "Looked like you needed help."

Furious, Kenna faced the wall, bracing her legs and grasping the rope to begin her rappel downward. "Get me down," she said.

"What? I can't hear you."

"I said get me the hell down."

"Guess we have to call it a draw," he said with a laugh when she landed.

"Do not *ever* do that again." Glaring, she called out to suspend the program, activated her signal medallion, and disengaged.

SIXTEEN

There was very little talk among them at first. Murmurs mostly. Three men and two women formed a haphazard circle in this low-rent motel room. One member of the group slouched in a hard chair, another sat tightly cross-legged on one of the twin beds, leaning against the headboard. One sprawled face up on the other mattress. One paced. They all pored over documents, making faces as they read.

Back end perched on the edge of a low dresser, Patrick rubbed a weary hand over his head. He'd been at this for hours, sorting through files, taking pictures, and printing copies. Letting his gaze wander over the group of young people, he cleared his throat. "Everyone just about finished?"

He waited until all their eyes met his. They were the unlikeliest group of rebels he could imagine.

"I don't get it, Pat," Maya said, leaning forward from the headboard. She pushed a strand of her dark hair behind one ear as she glanced up. "Why was Charlie sitting on all this?"

Edgar rolled from his back onto his stomach, tucking his packet of information under his chest. "Charlie called me last week," he said with a lilt of regret. "I asked him what was up, but he said he wasn't sure. That I should come take a look. Sabra and I were getting ready to fly in when all… this"—Edgar gestured around the room—"happened."

Sabra spoke up from the chair. "The important thing is

that we have more information now. But, what I want to know is...hang on." Flipping back several pages, she squinted while the group waited for her to continue. "Here it is. This guy, Larry Collins, was supposed to be sharing details about the new interface device with Charlie." She frowned. "But you're telling us he was actually a Virtu-Tech operative."

"That's right," Patrick said, knowing what was coming next. "He was."

The last member of the group, Aaron, stopped pacing to face Patrick. "And you didn't warn Charlie? It would have saved his life."

"Larry Collins is an assumed name. His real name was Wendell Long. I didn't even know Charlie had connected with him," Patrick said. He pushed off from the dresser to meet Aaron face-to-face. Half his age and six inches taller, Aaron packed double the muscle under tight, black skin.

Patrick continued, "You know as well as I do that Charlie did all this on his own. He didn't talk to anybody." Lasering his gaze at Edgar, he added, "The fact that he called you last week is something. He may have begun to have doubts. He may have been looking for guidance."

"But you believed Virtu-Tech wasn't targeting the Chicago market yet," Edgar said.

Aaron lifted one dark eyebrow. Held his ground. "Obviously, you were wrong on that," he said. "*Dead* wrong."

Edgar eased himself off the bed to join the two men. "Listen, we all thought they'd wait until New York and DC were up and running before moving out here." He placed gentle fingertips on both men's chests, moving them slightly apart.

Aaron gave an insolent head shake and stared at Patrick. "I thought you said you knew everything Trutenko knows," he said. "Maybe it's the other way around?"

"Come again?" Patrick said, inching forward, hands flexing. "What are you trying to say?"

"What do you think?" Aaron asked, mocking. "You're Trutenko's little runaround boy, sucking up to your big brother, practically spit-shining his shoes. Maybe we're not getting classified information on Virtu-Tech like you keep assuring us we are. Maybe Virtu-Tech is getting classified information on *us*."

"Back it up, both of you," Edgar said, exerting considerable pressure against Patrick's chest. Edgar pushed between them, keeping his back to Aaron as he faced Patrick in a subtle but effective message: two against one. "We've gone over all of Charlie's notes. And I have to admit," he said, "it looks like he was set up. Question is: Why didn't Trutenko let you in on this operation?"

"I don't know." Patrick's hands came up; he took a conciliatory step back. He hated the suspicion that stared at him from four sets of eyes, but he couldn't blame them for doubting him. Charlie wasn't just another operative. He'd been their friend. "Charlie *was* set up. But Trutenko never meant for things to go this far"—Patrick lifted his chin to forestall their collective outcry—"I didn't find out about it until after." Patrick's voice faltered. "After Charlie had been killed."

"Convenient," Aaron said.

"Look," Patrick said, "would I have pulled this group together if I was in on it?" He didn't wait for them to answer. "Of course not," he said. "My brother confides in me, but he doesn't tell me everything, okay?" He met each of their gazes in turn. "You've read the notes. Charlie thought he could do it all himself. He thought that once he got hold of the interface device, he could use it to infiltrate Virtu-Tech's systems and boost the chances of our plan's success."

Maya swung her legs over the side of the bed and looked up. She finished his thought. "But then Trutenko noticed him."

Patrick nodded. "My brother decided to interrogate Charlie. Apparently, he wasn't convinced Charlie was any kind of real threat at first. That's why he never mentioned him to me. Trutenko couldn't conceive of anyone so far away from DC headquarters being able to mess with the plan."

"The guy's never heard of hackers?" Sabra asked.

"Celia Newell believes that Virtu-Tech's systems are impenetrable," Patrick said.

Maya wiggled her fingers. "No system is impenetrable."

"Exactly." Patrick smiled. "But the longer they believe that, the better it is for us."

"Trutenko didn't say squat to you," Aaron said. "About Charlie."

It wasn't a question, but Patrick answered anyway. "No, he didn't. Trutenko pulled in Collins and a guy named Tate. Tate's the one who—" Patrick cleared his suddenly hot throat. "He's the one who killed Charlie. It wasn't meant to go that way."

"You're not defending Trutenko, are you?" Maya asked.

"No, of course not. Just trying to share the facts as I know them. Collins was supposed to trick Charlie into divulging information on the dissident movement. They expected names, locations, and plans, but Collins lost control of the scene. My best guess is that when Charlie realized what was going down, he tried to escape with the new technology. Unfortunately, we'll never know for sure."

Patrick revisited the moment Werner had told him the news of Charlie's death. Like a swift, deep punch to his soul, Patrick had lost ability to draw air into his lungs, and—barely able to remain standing—strove for phony outrage over Charlie's incursion as he struggled to fake nonchalance.

"They sacrificed Collins," he added.

"Trutenko killed one of his own?" Sabra asked.

"More like they sent him in without understanding the consequences," he answered. "Collins wasn't an envoy. Neither is Tate. They programmed limitations to their power and didn't know how to work around them. They lost control of the scenario. Trutenko, incidentally, is furious. He was determined to get Charlie to talk. You'll all be relieved to know that Charlie didn't breathe a word about what we've uncovered on Sub Rosa."

"Of course he didn't. None of us would." Aaron relaxed his stance enough to let Patrick know he'd gotten through. "What about Charlie's girlfriend?" he asked.

"Fiancée," Patrick corrected.

"How much does she know?"

"Not a lot. Kenna can be bullheaded." *That was an understatement.* "He knew that if she caught a whiff of wrongdoing, she'd take it up the chain until she got answers."

"That ain't gonna work," Maya said. "Not in this situation. Way too dangerous."

"Exactly," Patrick said. "She gets laser focused on righting perceived wrongs. Makes her an excellent envoy."

Sabra nodded. "But tough to corral."

"If Charlie never told her about us," Aaron said, "maybe he didn't trust her."

"Charlie trusted Kenna," Patrick said. "Completely."

"Yeah?" Aaron worked his jaw. "Well, let me say what we're all thinking here. This is serious shit we're dealing with, and sometimes it's hard to know who you can trust and who you can't." He looked around the room. "If Charlie didn't talk to his own fiancée, then what's that say about her? Maybe it isn't that she'd go running to 'right the wrongs.' Maybe she's in on Sub Rosa. Maybe she's one of them."

"Charlie trusted her," Edgar said. "When I talked with him last, he said he intended to bring her in on all this as soon as he had something solid." He waved his hands to encompass the group. "Maybe he was just trying to protect her. That's what I'd do in the same situation."

Sabra and Maya sent him twin looks of disdain. "Big man protecting his little woman?" Sabra said.

Edgar frowned. "You know what I mean. It's not a gender thing. You try to protect those you love."

"Lotta good it's doing her now," Maya said. "Nobody's watching her back."

"Kenna is a kick-ass envoy. Better than Charlie was, even," Patrick said. "And I'm watching her back. What I need to do now is to convince Trutenko that Kenna's not worth his effort, so that he calls off the dogs."

"How?" Edgar asked.

"I sorted through Charlie's notes to identify the ones that make it clear Kenna isn't involved. I'll be sure he understands that."

"You're going to hand over Charlie's notes to Trutenko?" Aaron asked.

"I've got to give him *something*." Patrick's tone was clipped. He was tired of trying to hide his irritation. Tired of having to behave like a good Virtu-Tech soldier, only to turn around and have to justify his actions to the dissident team. "He knows I went through Kenna's apartment. He knows Charlie was onto him. If I come up empty, it'll only raise more questions." He rubbed his hand over his head again, tension and exhaustion seeping through his weary words. "I'm not going to give him anything that could bite us."

"You'd better not," Aaron said.

Patrick ignored him. "He flew to DC to meet with Newell. He's returning here the day after tomorrow. With any luck, he'll bring me up-to-date with her plans." He nodded to them all, as though soliciting cooperation. "You guys got copies of everything Charlie found before he went to that final meeting."

"He uncovered a hell of a lot in a short amount of time." Maya said.

"Yeah," Patrick said. "Now we just have to figure out how best to use it. Decide on our next steps."

"Charlie's notes make perfectly clear what our next step should be," Maya said, holding the documents aloft. "We recruit Kenna."

SEVENTEEN

Kenna locked AdventureSome's front door and returned to the VR control area. "I really appreciate your help with this, Vanessa," she said.

Vanessa sat at a monitor, tapping at her keyboard. "What exactly are you hoping to find by re-creating the scene?" she asked. "I can't imagine any way revisiting it will help you understand what happened to Charlie."

Picking up her VR headgear, Kenna turned to face her friend. "No one believes me," she said. "And I get it. What I described doesn't seem possible. But I swear that creature on the bridge was an avatar of a sentient being."

"There wasn't anyone else here, though," Vanessa gently reminded her. "Someone can't enter another person's scenario. Not remotely. They have to be together in the same facility if they plan to share an adventure."

"I know that," Kenna said. "But I also know what I experienced. That thing knew exactly what it was doing when it activated a signal medallion."

"The werewolf."

"I know how it sounds." Kenna returned to confirming her capsule's readiness. "And to answer your question, I don't know what I hope to find. But I have to start somewhere, and this is the only option I've got."

"Let's do it then," Vanessa said. "I've set you up with full permissions and command for self-direction. Ready when you are."

"Thanks," Kenna said. "This means a lot to me."

Once in, it didn't take long for Kenna to get her bearings. She ordered herself to see, hear, and smell the surroundings as they assumed shape. Sunlight emerged, filtering gently through umbrella-size leaves, warming her bare arms and casting shadows through long fronds onto the soft soil underfoot.

She took a deep breath of the mossy air, fighting the quiver of anxiety that jolted her heart. This is how it all began before. But this time, she told herself, she wasn't looking for Charlie; she was seeking clues to his killer. And unless all aspects of the program had been permanently purged, she'd find him.

Kenna sorted through all the possible ways to go about searching. The blond man wouldn't be here, of course, but because he'd appeared in Charlie's final VR scenario, his matrix was on file in the global database.

Somewhere.

Kenna made her way to the clearing in the jungle. She had no warriors to worry about this time, no overturned Land Rover beyond the edge of the cliff. All she had to help her concentrate was the sun beating down from the clear sky above, and a view of the rope bridge that had finally led her to Charlie's side.

She stood at the cliff's edge, trickles of perspiration beading and dripping down her sides and back. Turning her face to the sun, she found herself relishing the feel of toxins pouring from her body.

Charlie had been murdered. Despite what Stewart, Vanessa, and Dr. Baxter all argued, Kenna knew Charlie hadn't simply become mortally absorbed. He was too good for that.

The blond man from the VR jungle scenario was key to discovering what was really going on. Somehow he'd manipulated the program's parameters, and her best plan of attack was to locate his matrix. Then, it would just be a matter of tracing that matrix back to its source.

Kenna remembered his height, his build, his coloring. By self-directing—controlling the parameters of her VR while inside it—she would be able to search the global database for matches. She sat on the sun-warmed ground and stared down over the outcropping. Concentrating, she began her quest.

This scenario wasn't precisely the same as the one in which Charlie had been killed. It was close, but she'd had to settle for an amalgam of different images and different scenes because there was nothing unique enough about a jungle with a rope bridge to trace back to its source. She needed to narrow her search.

Kenna made her way down to the outcropping and started across the wobbling bridge. She held on to the rope sides, gazing down at the gorge, so far below. The bridge's far side offered no hut, but VR huts were ubiquitous. Hun warriors less so, but because they were a popular option among warfare-loving VR participants, there was no way to isolate the very ones she'd encountered. To attempt to re-create them here would be foolish, and a waste of time.

But.

Kenna stopped at the center of the bridge and looked down at the water and thought about the werewolf. It had vanished before hitting the bottom. That meant it was either programmed to do so or, as Kenna suspected, it was a sentient being's avatar.

That hadn't been typical. Not by a long shot. While certain types of VR adventurers often included mythical creatures in their scenarios, the light-eyed monster with oversize hands might just be unusual enough to be tracked.

Kenna hurried across to the bridge's far side, her steps making hollow sounds as she clattered along the plank floor. At the far end, she turned. Focusing on the middle of the bridge—where she'd seen him last—she triggered the global database as she set up her search parameters. Best guesses. She specified the color of the creature's fur, and, most important, those pale blue eyes.

"Come on," she said.

When the werewolf appeared, Kenna laughed in spite of herself. It was Wary Wolf, a familiar cartoon character Kenna used to watch as a child. He glittered to life, grinning. Wary Wolf, bright-eyed and scrawny, spent his days chasing a chicken he never could catch. Worse, he was terrified of the little thing.

Three more tries, three more werewolves. Kenna gritted her teeth in frustration. How many damn blue-eyed werewolves were there? Details, she thought. I need details. She closed her eyes and tried to conjure up every minute feature she could recall. She changed the parameters to exclude those she'd already found, and tried again.

After what seemed forever, Kenna saw a faint shimmer at the bridge's center. She stared at the spot, holding her breath as the shimmer grew larger, and larger still. Silvery and striated, like a streaked mirror, it molded itself—body first, then appendages. The wood floor of the rickety structure began to sag from added weight. Before the form came into sharp focus, she heard a low growl.

A familiar growl.

The werewolf came to life with its back to her. The sight of it sent apprehension buzzing down her neck. It stood upright, exactly the way it had when it snatched and killed the warriors. Everything, from its yellow fur to the size of its hands, was exactly right. And when it slowly turned its massive head to fix its light blue stare on Kenna, she knew she'd struck gold.

"Yes!" she said aloud.

With a fix on the creature's matrix, Kenna was confident she'd be able to find its creator. She wanted nothing more than to tear the ugly monster apart with her bare hands. But that would solve nothing. Instead, she focused on getting the thing recorded. Saving its file. All she had to do was interface with the system long enough to record the creature's specifications. Then, it would be just a matter of time before she tracked its originator down.

"We meet again," she said to the growling monster. "But this time—"

All went gray. Then black.

Kenna blinked. But everything stayed black.

She whipped the VR headgear off her face, screaming in frustration. Outside the capsule, Vanessa met her with an expression of apologetic pain.

"What the hell happened?" Even as the question escaped her lips, Kenna knew the answer.

"I'm sorry," Vanessa said. "The software update is about to kick in. I had to ease you out before it shut you down."

Hands fisted, Kenna paced the small area to work off her anger. Vanessa had been right to ease her out. A system shut down in the middle of an excursion was not good for the brain. "I was so close," Kenna said. "So close. Five more minutes, tops."

"I'm so sorry," Vanessa said.

"Not your fault." Kenna found herself saying that a lot lately. "I should have worked faster."

"We'll get you back in tomorrow," Vanessa said. "Count on it."

EIGHTEEN

Her fiancé was dead and now her apartment destroyed. Cool moonlight bathed her living room with a silver-blue sheen that could have been beautiful if every single paper she owned hadn't been trashed.

After a long moment staring at the mess, Kenna dropped her duffel bag inside the front door. Her shoulders sagged, weighed down by too much reality.

"What's wrong?" Vanessa asked. "I waited for your lights to come on, but—" She sidestepped Kenna and moved into the room. "Yow. What happened here?"

"I don't know." Kenna strode across to the nearest lamp, reached up, and twisted the switch. "Who did this?"

"Thieves, most likely," Vanessa said. "You should call the police."

Kenna's legs gave out, and she collapsed onto her sofa. Whoever had been here had made a mess of the house but had inexplicably cleared off the coffee table, except for one piece of paper folded in half.

She opened the note.

> Kenna—
> Come see me as soon as you get in. Don't call.
> Don't tell a soul you found this. We need to
> talk.
> Lib

Charlie always called him Liberty, Lib for short, because of his full name: Patrick Henry Danaher.

"What's that?" Vanessa asked.

Don't tell a soul you found this.

What was going on?

"Nothing." Kenna stuffed it into her pocket. "An old grocery list."

NINETEEN

Vanessa stared down at the information she'd printed out, trying to find something—anything—that didn't belong. She held an open but untouched candy bar in both hands, forearms steepled, head resting against them.

"I don't get it," she said aloud. A moment later, she looked up to see Stewart and Jason walking in. "Good morning, guys."

"You don't get what?" Jason asked.

"I'll tell you what you're *going* to get," Stewart said. "A mess of chocolate dripping down your arm if you hold on to that thing much longer."

Vanessa glanced up at her forgotten candy bar. "You're right," she said. It was starting to get soft already. "Ick." Grabbing a tissue from a box on the corner of her desk, she set the candy down where it wouldn't smear the reports.

"How can you eat that stuff?" Stewart asked.

"Good question." Vanessa eyed her boss's slim frame and, not for the first time, envied his apparently active metabolism. The man could pack it away with the aplomb of guys twice his size but never gained an ounce. She glanced over at the messy blob. "I don't even like these very much," she said.

"I love Flaxibars," Jason said. "One of my all-time favorites."

"I haven't bitten into it yet. You want it?" she asked.

"Sure, thanks," Jason said as he reached for the proffered

snack and took a bite. "You're here early. I thought AdventureSome didn't open for another couple of hours."

"Yeah, well. I have lots of questions and not enough answers."

Jason chewed, looking thoughtful. "I was hoping to get some capsule time alone before Kenna gets in. Is that going to be a problem?"

"Shouldn't be," Stewart said. "Kenna has an appointment this morning. She'll be in by early afternoon."

"I won't stop you," Vanessa said, indicating the paperwork on the desk before her. "This is where I intend to spend my morning."

"How late were you here with Kenna last night?" Stewart asked.

"Late," Vanessa said. "She stayed in until the software update started."

"Ha!" Jason said. "I had a feeling she'd sneak in to practice when I wasn't around."

"That's not why she was in there," Vanessa said.

"Did she find what she was looking for?" Stewart asked.

Vanessa made a so-so motion. "She swears that if it weren't for the update, she would have extracted the werewolf matrix."

"Werewolf?" Jason half laughed. "What the heck are you talking about?"

Realizing how crazy that sounded, Vanessa hurried to explain. "The werewolf is one of many unexplained inconsistencies Kenna experienced last time she went in."

"The scenario where her fiancé died."

"Yeah," Vanessa said. "You have to understand. Charlie was too good of an envoy to suffer mortal absorption."

"Yet, he did."

"Kenna's convinced otherwise. She found a number of

anomalies in the program," Vanessa said. "Like a werewolf in a jungle with attacking Huns."

Jason shrugged. "So someone with a wild imagination put those elements together. I've seen worse."

"Except," Stewart said, "the program was locked against anachronistic details."

"Then how—?"

"We can't explain it," Stewart said.

"And all the safeties were turned off," Vanessa said.

"Okay, wait." Jason said. "Messing with safety protocols is no simple task. You'd have to have high-level permissions to make a change like that."

"Exactly," Stewart said. "And we've checked and double-checked. We can't find any evidence of our system being compromised. We have multiple redundant fail-safes in place for every possible consequence. In fact, one of our fail-safe mechanisms is how we were alerted to Charlie's imminent mortal absorption."

"Which Kenna can't accept," Vanessa said. "She's convinced that someone set out to deliberately hurt Charlie, or his client, and tapped into the system remotely."

"That's not possible," Jason said.

"Doesn't matter," Stewart said. "What does matter is that we allow Kenna time to grieve in her own way. If revisiting the scenario to seek out a giant werewolf helps her accept the truth, I'm willing to give her the latitude she needs."

"Sounds pretty messed up," Jason said.

Stewart took a seat at a desk across from Vanessa's. "Can you imagine how it *feels*? We all trusted Charlie. This has been a blow to business, sure. But it's an even harder blow to those of us who knew him. Kenna most of all."

"Sorry," Jason said.

Vanessa couldn't tell if Jason was expressing sympathy or remorse for having accepted the AdventureSome job. "Hey, you came in early to get a head start," she said. "Don't let us keep you."

Jason took the hint. "Thanks. Talk later."

The moment he was gone, Stewart leaned back in his chair. He pinched the bridge of his nose and focused his gaze upward. Pulling his attention back to Vanessa, he gave a feeble smile. "He seems like a decent kid," he said. "Maybe it was a mistake to bring him in so soon. Maybe we should have shut the place down for a month."

"Right," Vanessa said. "You think Kenna would sit still for that long?"

"Good point." A second later, he blinked. "Seems as though you're not scratching anymore," he said.

"Yeah," she said with a touch of wonder in her voice. She'd forgotten that itching spell. "Must have been nerves. I'm a lot better now."

"But you still haven't found anything that would explain Charlie's actions that last day?"

"Not a thing. I do have a few more avenues to investigate," she said. "Out-of-the-loop ideas, though. I'm not holding my breath."

Stewart leaned forward again, rubbing his eye sockets with more pressure than Vanessa thought his poor eyeballs could handle. "I just don't know," he said. "We've checked everything we can. There's nothing to indicate that Charlie and his client had anything beyond an ordinary VR adventure planned."

"Unless"—Vanessa gave a deep sigh—"something really was wrong with the whole setup."

Stewart opened his eyes. "What do you mean?"

"We're trying to trace what went wrong—why Charlie was mortally absorbed in a scenario he'd programmed."

"Right. And we checked the system's internal diagnostics. Everything was functioning normally, within acceptable parameters. And when Charlie set up the VR chamber with his codes, everything was working perfectly. Exactly the way it was designed to."

"Except a client and an envoy are dead."

Stewart seemed to age ten years at Vanessa's words. "Yeah, except for that."

"Which means the safeties got turned off after they were in."

"No kidding," Stewart said. He compressed his lips and added, "Sorry. Didn't mean to snap at you. But who could have monkeyed with the safeties? There was no one else here when they went in."

"What if Kenna is right?" Vanessa asked. "What about someone from the outside? With a remote VR interface?"

Stewart frowned. "That's still in developmental stages. Nobody has that technology yet. Not even the military."

She stared down at the printouts again, silent for a long while. "What happens if Kenna can't let this go?"

"If she clears her psych evaluation, then we'll put her back in. If not—" He let the thought hang.

"If not, we'll need to hire another envoy," she said. "Kenna won't like that very much."

Stewart blew out a breath. "Let's hope it doesn't come to that."

TWENTY

When Trutenko was shown into her office, Celia Newell got to her feet. "Why didn't you tell me things had gotten out of hand?"

Startled by her full-throated growl, Trutenko hesitated. Coughing up a smile, he resumed his approach and feigned nonchalance.

Thin and shapely as a lamp pole, Celia clearly reveled in the way her oversize desk and massive, windowless office dwarfed her. She liked being perceived as small. Trutenko had learned the hard way that her power lay in being underestimated.

High on the curtained wall behind Celia's desk, portraits of Virtu-Tech's eccentric founders, Vefa Noonan and Simon Huntington, stared down. Impossible, but both appeared terrified of her, too.

Trutenko rubbed his hands together. "Everything is under control."

"Under control?"

Marionette lines bracketed Celia's thin lips. Deep grooves spanned her forehead, speaking of a lifetime of fierce concentration and scorn.

She leaned forward, fingertips pressed hard against her desktop, poised as though ready to lunge and bite. Her dark hair fell to her shoulders in waves—an incongruous display of softness in an otherwise severe package. She was lean, hard, and as bitter as Lake Michigan in winter. As unforgiving, too.

To admit he'd made a tactical error would be suicide.

"Yes, of course," he said, draping a hand over the back of a chair. "May I?" Without waiting for her assent, he sat, brimming with manufactured confidence. "And how are operations progressing in the other divisions? Are they on schedule?"

Newell levered herself into her seat. She sucked in her cheeks, making her look like an even angrier puppet than she had before. Without breaking her gaze, she picked up a remote from her desk and hit the power button.

Machinery above him clicked, then hummed. The room's lights dimmed.

Drapery on the wall behind Celia lurched, the heavy fabric sliding away to reveal six large monitors. Three positioned to the right of the founders' portraits, three to the left. Each screen displayed a different VR advertisement.

Spinning her chair to face the big screens, Celia pointed her remote and tapped a couple of buttons. All six screens went black.

"The new ads?" Trutenko squirmed. "How are they working?"

She ignored him. The six screens remained dark for another few seconds before five of them pinged alive, each with a different man's face and each so huge Trutenko could practically see the men's pores. These were the other five Virtu-Tech directors. Headquarters remained here, in DC, and these other men managed New York, Houston, Miami, Los Angeles, and Seattle. The silent sixth screen, the Chicago market—Trutenko's market—remained blank.

Celia studied the remote before tapping its controls again. A moment later, Patrick Danaher's face flickered into view on the final screen. He acknowledged the two-way communication with a nod.

"Patrick," Trutenko said. "Report."

"Not so fast." Celia angled herself to be able to eye both Danaher and Trutenko at the same time. "Tell me, Werner," she said, "why is Patrick in charge? Why not Tate?"

Trutenko glanced over to his brother, whose face remained damnably passive. "Patrick is handling the underground resistance," he said with exaggerated authority. "He needs to maintain control."

Apparently unimpressed, Celia lowered her chin so that her eyes bore into his. "I was under—the impression," she said, taking a pause where none was required, "the underground had been—handled—already."

Trutenko waved her comment away. "Yes, of course. I'm talking about a small loose end we discovered."

She turned to face him, completely leaning forward, alert, as though he were the most important person in the world. If it weren't for the piercing fury in her eyes, he may have been flattered. "Expand," she said.

The six faces watched him, waiting. "In accordance with your directive," Trutenko began, looking to the five other directors for agreement, "our operatives sought out those involved in the rebel movement. Once we established that Charles Russell was secretly involved with my Chicago operation, we devised a plan to trap him." Trutenko's mouth was dry, but he persevered. "We didn't get as much as we needed from the infiltrator. He…expired before we could interrogate him fully."

Celia sat eerily still, immobile as the rapt audience behind her.

"But Patrick," Trutenko indicated the screen with his chin, "completed a search of the infiltrator's apartment. And I, myself, questioned the owner of the VR facility where Charles Russell's death occurred."

"Why?" Celia's eyes bore into him.

"Why...what?"

"It was my—understanding—Werner," Celia said in that oddly cadenced way of hers, "that this 'accident' came as a direct result of your involvement. You caused the very incident you were purporting to investigate." She paused, raising a dark eyebrow and sucking in her cheeks again. "What was the purpose of personally interviewing the franchise owner? What could you have possibly hoped to uncover?"

What a ridiculous question. "It would have looked more suspicious if I hadn't." He was about to add that he'd made a good show of it, but she interrupted.

"Dr. Larson was scheduled to head the Tribunal inquest. And yet you usurped his position. Why?"

"We needed to find out how much Charles Russell had uncovered," Trutenko answered, defensiveness creeping in. "I needed to know," he said. "This matter needed to be handled expeditiously. Who better to handle it than I?"

Her eyes lasered in on him. "You acted without authority."

His chin came up. "I'm in charge of the Chicago operation. Despite the fact that we know there were no malfunctions, I had to make the investigation look good."

"And now, individuals outside our organization know your face," she said through scarcely moving lips, "thereby compromising the project's overall stealth."

Trutenko searched the giant eyes of the five on-screen directors who still watched and blinked, their expressions identically unreadable. He stared up at Patrick. *Say something, dammit. Tell her why I'm right. Tell her that we've got it all under control.*

Celia watched him for a long moment. Sweat from Trutenko's brow seeped along the sides of his face.

"I'm certain Danaher would be willing to step into your position, Werner, as you are apparently no longer capable of carrying out my orders." She turned toward the monitors. "Patrick," Celia said, addressing the monitor again, "what do you say?"

Bursting from his seat, Trutenko interrupted. "I compromised nothing!" His gaze shot back and forth between Patrick's obvious surprise and Celia's derisive stare. "Charles Russell's files are in our hands, thanks to me. We now know everything he knew." Trutenko banged his fist on her desk. "Because of me."

Five large sets of eyes blinked. Their nervous gazes began to rove as they made eye contact with one another via monitors and satellites. Only Patrick's attention never wavered.

Trutenko wiped his free hand across his brow and sat back.

"Tell us exactly"—Celia dropped her voice—"what it is you have on Mr. Russell that we didn't know already."

Damn it to hell. Patrick held that information. Trutenko hadn't had a chance to thoroughly debrief his brother since the raid on the apartment. He needed something, anything, to convince Celia he was in still in control. "Russell may have had an accomplice."

"Oh?" Celia arched a brow.

Emboldened, he flicked a glance up toward the attentive audience. Patrick's face, in particular, seemed to register apprehension. "Shouldn't we talk privately?" Trutenko asked.

Celia considered it, and with a decisive click of her remote control, all six monitors went black. "I'm listening."

Trutenko squared his shoulders. "Her name," he said, "is Kenna Ward."

TWENTY-ONE

D r. Baxter didn't say a word about Kenna's tardiness, nor did she give her watch the exaggerated scrutiny Kenna expected she might.

Instead, she welcomed Kenna into her office with a smile. "You're very lucky," she said, gesturing toward the same chair Kenna occupied before. "The appointment immediately after yours has canceled. That gives us extra time today to talk."

Kenna dropped into the seat. "Great."

Dr. Baxter maintained her tolerant expression but didn't wait a beat before jumping right in.

"Did you find what you were looking for in Charlie's VR scene?"

Kenna sat up. "You've got to be kidding. Who told you I went back in?"

Dr. Baxter folded her hands atop the neat blotter. She wore a small but triumphant smile. "You just did."

When Kenna opened her mouth to retort, Dr. Baxter cut her off.

"Call it an educated guess," she said. "After our first meeting, I had little doubt that you'd return there as soon as you possibly could. What I'd like to talk about is why you felt the need to engage programs that simulated the scenario where Charlie died. Let's start there."

Kenna's mouth opened again. She wanted to tell this woman it was none of her damned business why she'd re-created the jungle scenario and sought out the werewolf. Before a single vituperative syllable flew from her lips, however, she caught herself and bit it all back.

Starting slowly, she searched for the words that would satiate the doctor's curiosity and provide what she wanted to hear. "Yes, I went there," Kenna said, reminding herself to stick with the truth as much as possible. "I was looking for something."

Dr. Baxter's head tilted slightly to her right. "Looking for something," she repeated. "What were you looking for?"

Staring down at her hands in her lap, Kenna let her thumbs play together for a couple of beats. "Closure," she said.

"And did you find it?"

"I believe I did," she said. "Going back in there helped me face the truth. I'm starting to see my way out."

Dr. Baxter was quiet for a very long time. So long that Kenna risked a curious glance her direction. From the woman's amused expression, it seemed she'd been waiting for Kenna to look up. "Good. That's *very* good," Dr. Baxter said, as though there'd been no lapse in the conversation at all. "But do you think it's helped you enough?"

Kenna didn't understand. "Enough?"

"Would you be prepared to delete the scenario today if I determine it's in your best interests to do so?"

"What? No," Kenna said, shocked by the suggestion. "Not yet."

"Oh? Why not?"

"Because," Kenna began. She thought fast, desperate to come up with a reason Baxter would accept.

"Tell me if I'm wrong here," Dr. Baxter said. "But the idea of losing access to certain elements of the program terrifies you, doesn't it?"

Kenna opened her mouth to protest—Dr. Baxter lifted a finger.

"It terrifies you because of all the loss you've endured in your short life, already." She narrowed her eyes again. "Right?"

"If you mean my parents," Kenna said, regretting that she'd even mentioned them at their last meeting, "I've come to terms with that."

"Have you?"

Damn her. Kenna wanted to shove at the desk, to knock the woman's prim arms off their restful perch and to watch her run from the room, sorry that she'd ever brought the subject up. "Yes," she answered, her jaw tight. "I have."

"I found this, Kenna." Dr. Baxter drew out a print copy of an internet news article from all those many years ago. She pointed to its final paragraph. "You were placed in a psychiatric ward."

"For two days. For observation." Kenna practically spit her next words. "Of course I was taken in. I was fourteen when they died. A kid. They were killed in a fire at home when I was at a friend's sleepover. I skipped away from my completely ordinary life one day and woke up to a nightmare the next. Does that article tell you how every little tiny precious bit of our lives—all our photographs, my mom's journals, all their books—every single thing was destroyed? Gone. I had nothing of them anymore. Nothing."

Kenna words had come out fast, sharp, hot. The tragedy had happened such a long time ago, she'd convinced herself she'd made peace with it all. Apparently she hadn't.

She took a deep breath, let it out. "If I can survive that," she said finally, "I can certainly survive this."

"But at what cost?"

She sat forward, punctuating her words with her index finger on Dr. Baxter's desk. "I'm here. I'm active. I have a job and a purpose in life. I'm good at what I do. What more do you want?"

Dr. Baxter glanced down at Kenna's insistent finger for a long moment. She placidly raised her gaze.

"I want you to be happy."

"Then I'm happy. Can I go now?" Kenna worked her jaw.

"No." Dr. Baxter smiled. "Indulge me for just a minute, Kenna, and consider this: When you lost the two most important people in the world, you not only missed having them in your life to help shape yours, but you were robbed of every memento, every reminder of them, too."

Kenna patience waned. Hadn't she just said all that?

Dr. Baxter tilted her head, squinted those sad eyes again. "Now that Charlie's gone, it's natural for you to fight to keep hold of his memory. You're convinced that's all you have left, and so you're re-creating Charlie's death scenario as a link to him. But you don't realize how much harm you're doing to yourself. Rather than keep Charlie's memory alive with reminders of the joy you shared together, you're choosing to keep—at the forefront—a 'souvenir' of his death. I can't begin to tell you how damaging that can be to you."

Kenna wondered what the psychiatrist would think if she knew the real reason she'd revisited the jungle was to begin a quest for vengeance. She didn't expect Dr. Baxter would approve.

Adopting an earnest expression, Kenna softened her voice. "Just a little more time, and then I'll purge it. I just need to keep it for a while. That's all."

Dr. Baxter seemed to study her for a long moment. She shook her head, speaking slowly. "No, Kenna. I can't allow it."

"What do you mean, you can't allow it?"

Dr. Baxter turned to her computer monitor and tapped at the keys. "I'm prohibiting you from engaging in any VR activities until further notice."

"You can't forbid me from VR," Kenna said. "This is supposed to be an evaluation, not a sentencing."

Dr. Baxter resumed typing, still studying the display.

Kenna persisted. "I'll fight."

Without missing a beat at the keys, Dr. Baxter tilted her head again. "Do what you must," she said. "You can go off and spend your life chasing ghosts in VR scenarios to your heart's content." Then she turned to fix Kenna with a no-nonsense stare. "But until I give authorization, you'll never work as an envoy again."

TWENTY-TWO

Standing dead center in front of a blank screen, Glen clapped his hands together, commanding the small group's attention. "Virtu-Tech is poised to strike," he said. "And we"—he took a long moment to make eye contact with each audience member—"are poised for greatness."

Werner snaked a sideways glance at Celia, wondering why she'd chosen to sit next to him. The small conference room featured three tables and a dozen empty seats. Nick, Celia's right-hand man, sat front and center, taking notes. Tall, trim, handsome, and handpicked by Celia to help her lead, Nick sat sideways in his chair, one arm draped across its back. Early thirties, dark hair, dark eyes, he wore casual, expensive clothing and an air of supercilious disdain.

Werner had chosen a chair at the back of the room far from the door, certain that Celia would opt for a position at the head of the class, near golden boy Nick. Why hadn't she?

The five other Virtu-Tech directors from the earlier meeting were back—attending again via live-feed and the wonders of instant transmittable information. Werner wanted nothing more than to escape this stuffy meeting and get back to Chicago. Patrick was back via monitor, too, looking uncomfortable in the role of ersatz director.

Celia leaned closer. "Pay attention," she whispered, loud enough for everyone to hear.

Werner faced Glen. A big guy in his early fifties, he wore a shiny suit and a dull grin. His teeth, a bit too big to be real, accentuated the sibilants in his speech. Projecting an air of commiseration, he paced in front of the blank screen.

"As you all know, our first three initiatives met with only limited success."

Celia raised her hand but didn't wait to be called upon. "Glen, please"—her tone carried a reprimand—"let's not be coy."

Glen's frown softened. "Our first three initiatives," he said with a sigh, "were undisputed failures. But I truly believe we are now on a path to victory. What we failed to take into account is that—as enthusiastic as people are to participate in VR scenarios—they aren't always able to make time to visit a facility."

Celia nodded.

Glen continued. "It goes without saying that if people aren't regularly accessing their implants, they're not able to respond to our messages. We needed to find a way to either encourage more VR participation or"—he paused long enough to flash his big teeth—"design an implant that accesses our subjects' brains around the clock."

"Which is where we are now, yes?" Celia asked.

"Very much yes," he said. "The 5.0s were our first foray into the continuous-contact model. Two weeks ago, we initiated a trial directed toward those 5.0 users, and"—he paused, smiled again—"we hit our target. Then, last week, when we ran a second, more comprehensive test"—he paused again, beaming triumphantly—"results *exceeded* our expectations."

He pressed a button on a handheld control. The screen at the front of the room zinged alive. Glen directed their attention to a brown-and-white bar of soap atop a silver tray. "Two weeks ago," Glen said, eyebrows arching, "people around the country began buying Clifft soap. A *lot* of Clifft soap. Why?"

Everything about this man was manufactured. Werner knew it; they all knew it, but they were too deep into the initiative to resist hearing what he had to say.

"Clifft is actually inferior to the top brands, and five percent *more* expensive," Glen said. "It irritates the skin. And look at it. What marketing genius decided that soap should be brown? No one in their right mind would buy this soap. And yet, consumers did, in droves. Why?" Like a magician mesmerizing his audience, all eyes in the room and on-screen followed him. "Why did they buy so much Clifft soap?" he asked rhetorically.

He waited a couple of beats. "Because we *told* them to."

Murmurs of admiration bubbled up.

Glen clapped his hands. "People!" He paced again, his tone heralding the resumption of his power persona. "Clifft soap was just the beginning." With a few deft clicks of his remote, the screen behind him sizzled then changed. "Last week, everyone in the country decided to stock their pockets with Flaxibars." He pointed to the beige wrapper with the bright green letters. "They look like chocolate and smell like chocolate but they're made with flaxseed." Glen scrunched his face. "They taste terrible." Grinning, he added, "But stores can't keep them on the shelves."

Nick waved his pen to catch Glen's attention.

Glen clapped his hands again. "Question, Nick?"

"This is all fascinating," Nick said. "I can certainly sleep better at night knowing that people in the country are keeping themselves clean with itchy brown soap." He caught Celia's eye and sat up a little straighter. "But let's face facts here, Glen. This is all child's play. When are we going to see the real results? When are we going to get to the real payoff?"

"Glad you asked," Glen said, though Werner thought he looked rather annoyed. Arms outstretched, he encompassed the group. "We all know how price is determined, right?" He pointed at Werner. "Remind us. How is price determined?"

Startled, Werner's mouth opened.

Nick rolled his eyes. "Supply and demand," he said in a tone that suggested impatience. Heat pounded Werner's face.

"Exactly!" Unfazed, Glen turned back toward the rest of the group. "But Virtu-Tech's new implants are skewing that principle. Our implants are responsible for sales that have nothing to do with supply or demand. We are changing the rules of economics. Do you have any idea the power we hold?"

Directing his commentary to Nick now, Glen spoke animatedly, all big teeth and hissing spittle. "Clifft soap sold better during our one-week trial than it had in the past *year*—despite its high price, nasty color, and tendency to cause skin irritation. Flaxibars sold out almost everywhere—despite the fact that they're awful. That's precisely why we picked those products for our tests. We chose them *because* they're substandard. And"—he waggled his eyebrows—"in a shrewd bit of optimism, we chose to invest in their parent companies the weeks before we ran our little experiments."

One corner of Glen's mouth curled up as he faced the group. "What that means, folks, is that in addition to our unqualified successes, Virtu-Tech made a considerable profit. Even better, we're making inroads on Canadian and European markets that give every indication of proving equally successful."

Nick interrupted, again waving the pen. "We're not here to congratulate ourselves on some piddling investments. We're here to talk about—"

"Nick." Celia's voice was sharp.

He leaned forward. "But—"

"Later," she said.

Clearly confused, Glen leaned forward as though expecting an explanation. When none was forthcoming, he widened his smile and waited.

Nick sat back, tapping his pen against his lips.

Directing her comments to Glen now, Celia kept a cool, expressionless look on her face. "Have you followed all the protocols we set up at the start of this venture?"

"Of course," he said.

"You haven't shared any of your findings with individuals outside Virtu-Tech?"

"Why would I? What we've created here," Glen said, "is light-years beyond what other marketing departments are even dreaming about. We've broken new ground with VR—we're determining a new order in consumer control. This technology is beyond valuable." He held out his hands in a helpless gesture, then grinned. "It's also illegal."

"Yes," Celia said. "We're aware of that."

"Still," Glen said, "I haven't gotten where I am in the world by turning my back on opportunity. Virtu-Tech has the power to control consumer choices over everything from soap to candy bars to vacation spots. Armed with that capability, your company can direct worldwide trends while profiting from prognostication." He shrugged. "I'm happy to be one small part of this plan, and I'm looking forward to sharing in the company's future earnings."

"Yes, well," Celia said, "we'll have to discuss that."

Glen's cheerful look of anticipation fell. "It was my understanding—"

Celia raised her hands. "Don't get me wrong, we plan to take care of you, but I can't act until we're certain that we've covered everything."

"But isn't that why we're here today?" he asked. "The 5.0s have proved themselves—and without around-the-clock brain stimulation. Once we launch the 6.0s and consumers can't escape Virtu-Tech's influence, we'll be unstoppable."

Nick sat forward, actively watching the interchange between Celia and Glen. "Only once we reach market saturation, right?" he asked. "When will that be?"

Glen addressed the younger man. "Ask your directors," he said. "They're in control of distributing the upgrades." He glanced up at the six screen attendees. "Our initial goal was to produce enough implants to outfit forty-five percent of the population. We've exceeded that, too. Which means," Glen said, with an arrogant lilt to his voice, "that we can go live with the next program as early as today. Right now. The rest of the public will go crazy catching up when they see how popular the new 6.0s are." He smiled up at his audience. "What are we waiting for? Are all your divisions ready?"

Patrick cleared his throat. "If I may…" He shot an uneasy glance at his brother before continuing. "In theory, everything in Chicago is ready to go. Our experiences with 5.0 were exactly the same as in all the other locations across the country." He nodded to the other directors. "And Chicago *could* have been ready to go live on time, except for one problem…"

Werner broke into a cold sweat. Before he could open his mouth, Celia turned and spoke to him through clenched teeth. "What problem is this, Werner?"

His mind raced. His mouth opened.

She didn't waver. "Werner?"

"I..." Bile rose up at the back of his throat, hot and sour. "I don't know," he managed, hating the words he forced himself to say. He made eye contact with Patrick in a silent plea for help. "There were no problems when I left."

"I'm sorry." Patrick blew out a breath. "Chicago has no upgrades."

"But they arrived more than a week ago," Werner said.

"I'd hoped to break the news to you in a less public setting, but—" Patrick gave an apologetic shrug. "I'm sorry to report that the dissident group apparently intercepted the shipment. We have no 6.0 upgrades to disperse."

"That's impossible," Werner said to Celia. "I saw them myself." He spun in his chair, practically shouting at his brother. "We examined the shipment together. You saw them. We both did."

Patrick's homely face took up the entire glittering screen. "They weren't 6.0s."

Werner sputtered, "But—"

"Fakes?" Celia said. She turned to face him again. "What kind of idiot are you?"

He didn't have the chance to answer that because Nick broke into the conversation. "If Chicago's not ready to go, we shouldn't move forward in the other areas. Not yet. Moving forward piecemeal could jeopardize the initiative."

"Jeopardize?" Glen asked. "How? The beauty of all this is that there is no time frame."

Nick straightened. "Glen, you don't understand what's at stake here." A pointed look from Celia made Nick hesitate before continuing. "What I mean," he began again, "we don't do things haphazardly in this company. From the very start, we agreed that we roll out all divisions together."

"It would hardly be haphazard," Glen said.

Celia held up a hand to stop him from arguing further. She turned to Werner. "We deserve an explanation."

Werner turned to his brother again, his anger growing. "Patrick?"

"They're not fakes, they're..." Patrick took a breath, then started again. "This all just came to light. We've been scrambling to trace how it happened. I wanted to have better news for you by this time. At least we have an idea of who's responsible."

"Who?" Werner asked.

The entire room leaned closer as though to better hear Patrick's answer.

"Tate. Instead of destroying the 2.0 supply that's been sitting in the warehouse for the past year—the way you ordered him to—it appears he sold them for scrap and pocketed the profits. We imagine he called some recycling company to pick them up. Someone switched labels before the hauler showed up."

"Tate couldn't have done that. He's busy elsewhere," Werner said.

Patrick blinked. "I guess I would have beaten a path out of here too if I'd pulled a move like that."

"No, he's...," Werner started to explain, then stopped. "He's on special assignment."

"I hope he handles this one better than the last one. He told me to my face that you were having him look into an important matter. Next thing I know, the warehouse is cleaned out and his signature is on the paperwork. I know he's going to deny any involvement, but I have to tell you..."

Like hungry dogs with treats dangled in front of them, the group again leaned forward to hear what Patrick had to say. "We've got a couple million 2.0s here and not a single Six."

TWENTY-THREE

Kenna left Dr. Baxter's office intending to take a walk along the lakefront to excise her high aggravation. When she stepped outside the building's doors into heavy cloud cover and the tang of impending rain, however, she groaned in frustration. Annoyed, she took in her surroundings, gauging options. She wasn't ready to return to AdventureSome for another day of exercises with Jason. Not yet.

Across Michigan Avenue, Millennium Park's Cloud Gate—affectionately known as "The Bean"—reflected the sky's gray dreariness as well as the day reflected Kenna's mood.

Spying a cheerful café on the next block, Kenna hurried across Washington Street with four seconds left on the "walk" signal. She pushed through a set of revolving doors to breathe in the welcoming aroma of fresh coffee. As ever, the smell conjured up a sense of home, of being a kid, and of memories of her parents chatting at the kitchen table, hands wrapped around their warm mugs. She didn't particularly care for the taste of the stuff, but the scent was pure bliss.

After collecting her order of cinnamon tea and cherry-almond scone, she settled herself at a cozy table far from the door, in a corner that allowed her to view the entire establishment at once. The perfect spot was always the one with no one behind her, no one beside her. The habit was one she'd developed from being with Charlie. She used to tease him about being paranoid, but she'd learned to appreciate the comfort of safe awareness.

Even better, this spot sat directly below the Virtu-Tech screen, making it easier for her to avoid watching its nonstop ads. Restaurants, bars, coffee shops, and even libraries were happy to run the company's commercials. Why wouldn't they be? Virtu-Tech paid a monthly stipend to any establishment promoting VR adventures. The ads with their smiling, cheerful spokespeople and constant reminders to upgrade were inescapable these days. Kenna was relieved to sit beneath the monitor. In places like this with piped-in music and busy conversation, ads were close-captioned, which meant she didn't have to listen to them, either.

As her tea bag steeped, she thought about her ransacked apartment and wondered if Charlie would have handled things differently. If it hadn't been for Patrick Danaher's cryptic note on her coffee table, she may have capitulated to Vanessa's insistence that she call the police. Kenna fingered her silver locket. No jewelry had been taken. All their pricey electronics remained in place. Even the gun she kept in her nightstand—her trusty Beretta—hadn't been snatched. The worst had been the mess of paperwork strewn everywhere. None of Kenna's important documents were missing. If any of Charlie's were, Kenna was unaware.

She pulled Patrick's note from her pocket and read it again. Clearly, he wanted to tell her something. She'd visit him tonight to find out what. That settled, she took a sip of her tea and sat back, doing her best to relax.

By setting tables close together, the café did its best to maximize seating capacity. Kenna broke off a corner of her scone and popped it into her mouth, happy to have snagged this table when she had. The place was beginning to fill up.

"That." Two tables away, a young man pointed to the monitor above Kenna's head as he addressed his companion. "The minute we hear when the Six will be available, I'm getting in line."

The woman, who may have been his girlfriend, shrugged. "I get upgrades shipped direct. They arrive a day or two after the rollout, but it's so much nicer than hanging outside a store in the early morning. Waste of time, if you ask me."

"I want to be the first to see what's new with the Sixes. I did that with the Five."

She shrugged again. "What's the big deal with these new ones? I didn't see much difference when we upgraded last time."

"That's because there weren't a lot of improvements to the experience. Virtu-Tech said they needed to work out some system bugs."

The woman sipped from her mug. "I'm glad they're free. Can you imagine if we would have to buy new implants every time an enhancement was announced?"

"I'd do it anyway," he said. "Totally worth it."

She laughed, wryly. "Yeah, I probably would, too."

Farther away, sitting alone in a booth near the café windows, a middle-aged man stared at the monitor ads, mouthing along as though he'd memorized them. Oblivious to the raging storm outside, he nodded occasionally, the soup on the table before him apparently forgotten.

Two young moms plunked their gear atop another nearby table. Parking their rain-soaked strollers against the wall, they stripped off wet jackets and huffed with relief when the three little kids between them were safely settled in high chairs and booster seats. Both women operated with brisk efficiency, handing the two older kids miniature tablets and placing a sippy cup in front of the toddler.

"My turn to get the coffee," the taller one said. "Anything special today?"

"Just the usual, thanks," the other one replied.

When the first mom stepped away to get in line, the second one gave the kids a perfunctory once-over, then fixed her gaze on the Virtu-Tech monitor. Her peace and quiet was cut short, however, when the toddler grabbed one of the older kids' tablets. The boy shrieked with indignation as the littlest child hugged the tablet to his chest.

"Give it back, honey," the mom said. Righting the sippy cup that had been knocked over in the fracas, she spoke coaxingly. "Come on, you have juice in here. You like juice."

The toddler shook his head. "No!"

The little boy kept bellowing. "Please, honey," the mom said to him. "I'll get it back. Be patient."

The toddler cried out when the mom tried to pry the tablet from his pink arms. "Mommy give you a different toy, okay? This one belongs to your brother."

The toddler pointed to his mother's purse. "Phone."

She sighed and dug out her phone, then pulled out a plastic frame that she wrapped around it like a safety bumper. "Here you go. Be careful with Mommy's toy, okay?"

The toddler relinquished the tablet as the other mom returned to the table with two cups of coffee and two frothy kid-size drinks. "Trouble?"

"Same as always. They always want what they don't have."

She sat down. "Isn't that the truth?"

The boy whose tablet had been swiped pointed to a spot behind his right ear. "And I'm gonna get my implant for my birthday, right, Mom?"

"We'll see," she said.

Both moms rolled their eyes.

"You promised."

"I didn't promise. I said I'd look into it."

Her friend leaned forward. "You know they're bringing out a whole new bunch of educational VR programs designed to give students an advantage in school. It may not be the worst thing."

"True," she said.

"Can I, Mom? Can I? You and Dad always say how much fun it is. And how much you learn."

"How much you *learn*?" The second mom raised her eyebrows and lifted her cup to her lips. "I'd like to hear more about that."

"Ha, ha," her friend said. "Get your mind out of the gutter. What I've learned is that there are too many things in life I don't want to worry about. I just want to go through my life happy."

When more people filled in the tables between them, Kenna lost track of their conversation. Because Stewart maintained a strict over-eighteen rule for participation at AdventureSome, Kenna had forgotten that kids were often fitted for implants, too. She stared out over the rim of her mug at the sea of café patrons. Could she find one customer *not* talking about VR? Or *not* mesmerized by the ads running on the monitor above?

Three young men, no older than twenty, had occupied a nearby booth since before Kenna had arrived. They'd kept their heads low and spoken quietly. She hadn't heard a word of their conversation, nor had she tried very hard to listen in. But now, as they shrugged on backpacks, and pulled up their hoods, their voices grew more animated.

"Can you imagine how much power that would give us?" one said. "My uncle is an envoy."

"Envoy school is supposed to be super hard, though."

Kenna's ears perked up and she leaned forward to hear better.

"Hey, if we flunk out, I'll bet we can buy an envoy implant. There's got to be a way, right? Like a black market or something?"

The boys were halfway to the door before she could stop them. Not that kids that age would have listened to her warning.

Envoy implants weren't simply pieces of equipment one could pick up and play with. Their distribution was tightly regulated because envoys were allowed enormous control over VR systems. Going in without training and without a properly fitted implant risked frying your brain.

Kenna watched the boys go, realizing how completely Virtu-Tech held the world in thrall and wondering why it had taken her so long to see it.

From her perch in the corner, she slowly, methodically, swept her gaze around the room, studying this random sample of strangers.

Nearly every person in the room appeared to be captivated by VR. Some gestured toward the ads as they conversed with one another. Some merely stared at the monitor as though spellbound. Many, wearing wistful expressions, absentmindedly fingered their implants.

Kenna glanced down at her half-finished scone. She bunched it up in her napkin, threw it away, and headed out into the storm.

TWENTY-FOUR

The moment Virtu-Tech's meeting broke up, Patrick Danaher got to his feet. He needed to get things moving or there'd be hell to pay when his brother got back.

He opened Werner's office door to look out over the staff beyond. Each of the three technicians had five monitors to manage, and each worked in one quadrant of a high-tech square. Two women, one man. All kept their eyes focused on the busy screens, switching and updating as information became available on new implants, upgrades, and virtual reality consumption data. Not one of them had any appreciation for the power Virtu-Tech controlled, and even less about plans for that power's use.

The fourth quadrant position sat empty. Patrick sometimes logged in from there.

He pulled on his windbreaker as he crossed the room. "I'm out for the afternoon," he said to the group as he made his way to the far door.

One of the other employees, Janet, looked up. Her face was blue-gray from the surrounding screens of sizzling pixels; she always kept the tip of her tongue perched between her lips while she concentrated. Now she half turned toward him, her eyes still scanning the data stream. "What's going on?" she asked.

"Can't talk about it."

That garnered him a raised eyebrow. "Ohhhh," she said, stringing the word out into two syllables.

"Let me know if that Tate guy shows up or calls in."

"You got it."

He made his way down to the Chicago headquarters main floor, then stepped out into the gray afternoon downpour. Lousy weather. Perfect. Yanking up his hood, he dug out his phone and dialed.

"It's me," he said, when the other person answered. "Get everyone together. I'll be there as soon as I can."

After disconnecting, he placed another call. "Simon," he said when the other man answered. "Timeline has changed. We're moving in today."

TWENTY-FIVE

A faraway loudspeaker announced the first boarding call for Werner's flight, but his attention remained on his cell phone screen, where Tate, visibly flabbergasted, protested his innocence.

"I swear I don't know what you're talking about."

Werner watched closely, gauging Tate's reaction for any measure of deceit. En route to Chicago after having endured yet another lengthy dressing-down in Celia's office, this was Werner's first opportunity to contact his assistant away from the eyes and ears of Virtu-Tech minions.

"You're telling me that, since I left, you haven't been to the warehouse where we stored the 6.0 upgrades?" he asked. "Not once?"

Tate's face curled up into a snarl. He looked out to his right for a moment as though to collect his composure before returning to meet Werner's inquisitive stare. "How could I? I've been following our target, like you wanted me to."

"So you say. You haven't come up with much."

Tate's face contorted yet again. "You don't seriously believe I'd have anything to do with sabotage, do you?"

"Not so loud." Werner's eyes flicked up to reassure himself that no one nearby could hear.

"You might be interested to know that somebody trashed her apartment the other day."

"That was Danaher and his team," Werner said.

"Danaher." Tate snorted. "Yeah, so what did they come up with?"

Werner didn't feel like explaining that he hadn't had a chance to talk with Patrick yet. "Enough," he said. "I'll tell you more later."

"He's the one you ought to keep an eye on," Tate said. "I don't trust him."

Werner shook his head, feeling every one of his years and then some. "It may not matter anymore. Celia is ready to shut me out of the Chicago operation if I don't produce something positive soon."

"She can't do that," Tate said.

Werner shot him a disdainful glare. "Don't be stupid. Of course she can." He thought for a moment. "And she will if I don't find out who switched our upgrades." He knew Patrick wouldn't lie about Tate's signature on the warehouse receipt. "Trust me, I *will* find out how the Sixes disappeared."

"Yeah, well"—Tate frowned—"I got nothing."

Tate seemed to be telling the truth, but then how had the dissidents gotten in without his help? Werner rubbed his face. He came to a decision.

"I'll tell Celia that one of the dissidents started talking to you," Werner said. "That you're working to get more. That'll buy me some time."

"But," Tate said, "I've been stuck following this envoy around. I haven't been able to get any intelligence on the dissident faction."

"All that matters is that Celia believes it."

"Where does that leave me?"

"Keep following that Kenna Ward. Find out whatever you can."

Tate groaned. "I'm tired of babysitting."

"You're tired of coming up empty, you mean," Werner said. "She's an envoy. That means she's smart. Time to up your game."

TWENTY-SIX

Mellow Mary, as Kenna had always thought of the computer voice, dispassionately announced: "Challenge number nine complete. Please indicate when ready to continue."

Jason shed his shirt; a sheen of perspiration glistened over his torso. "You sure you want to finish?"

Bent in half, hands on her knees, Kenna breathed deep. "Yeah."

"You don't look so good. We should've stopped at eight."

She lifted her head to face him. "And have to start from the beginning on our next attempt? No, thanks."

Jason ran the back of his hand over his forehead, wiping away sweat. He blinked several times. "You don't think Stewart would actually make us start all over again, do you? He seems like a pretty easygoing guy."

"Yeah, right." Kenna's most recent conversation with Stewart had been anything but. When Kenna had arrived at AdventureSome after her appointment with Dr. Baxter, she'd found Stewart agitated. He wanted to know why she hadn't mentioned the break-in at her apartment. Silently cursing Vanessa's big mouth, Kenna told the truth: she hadn't discovered anything missing. "I want to put all the negative behind me."

That's when he'd dropped the bombshell. Dr. Baxter had called Stewart this morning to advise him of Kenna's tenuous hold on her envoy credentials. "Based on Dr. Baxter's recommendations, I can't let you back into VR," he'd told her. "You can go through the exercises with Jason, but no more individual capsule time for you until you get a clean bill of health."

Kenna had argued that Dr. Baxter was out of line. Health privacy laws should have prevented her from talking with Stewart about Kenna's mental health. A valid point, Stewart had conceded. Except for the fact that Kenna had signed away those rights when she took on the envoy position. A damaged envoy posed real danger to unwary participants.

Kenna took another deep breath. *Had my appointment been only this morning?*

Now, Kenna stood. She rolled her shoulders and closed her eyes for several seconds, centering herself before she answered Jason. She decided that she *would* make it through this last challenge today. And she'd return to the jungle tonight, too.

You can't stop me, Stewart.

"I don't care if he would have let us complete one exercise per day and call it done. I'm not about to walk away from it now. Not when we're this close."

"Suit yourself," Jason said.

They stood for a long moment, two people in a bright white, empty room. No sights, no sound. Nothing but their uneven breaths, echoing against the shiny blank walls.

"Any idea what this next one is going to be?" he asked.

"No clue," she said. "When I went through exercises with…" She stopped herself. She'd been about to say "with Charlie," but the words caught in her chest and stuck there.

Jason arched an eyebrow, his face unreadable. "Oh," he said, stringing the word out. He nodded, as though confirming something in his mind. "That's why you keep beating me. You've done some of these before."

Fury broke through Kenna's logjam of emotions. "For your information, Mr. Flaxibar," she said, feeling the rush of hot blood to her face and the lights sparking behind her eyes, signaling an imminent loss of control, "this program changes each go-round. They have like...*three hundred thousand* different challenges that they can throw at you, and guess what? Not one of the ones we went through is a repeat for me, okay?"

She spun away from him, striding to the room's far corner, needing to release some of the pressure that'd built up, yet again. With her hands flat against two walls, she stared into the corner and took several deep breaths before turning to face him again. "What I was about to say," she continued in a quiet voice that carried across the twenty feet that separated them, "is that subsequent exercises are always based on how well you did up until now."

He maintained a blank expression. "How well *I* did?"

"How well *we* did. As a team."

"And how well, in your estimation, have we done?"

Kenna considered that. "We've done well," she finally admitted.

"As well as you did last time?"

"Don't go there."

"Fair enough," he said. The look he shot her was back-to-business, and she returned to his side of the room.

"I'm ready anytime you are," she said.

He nodded. "Program," he called out, "begin."

TWENTY-SEVEN

Patrick felt a peculiar sense of déjà vu as he strode into the shabby hotel room. "The timetable's been changed," he said as he glanced around. "Where's Aaron?"

"On his way," Maya said. "He said something about scouting new territory."

"What the hell does that mean?" Patrick waved a hand in front of his face. "Forget it. I'll deal with him later."

They were perched in almost the same positions they'd occupied last time. But now the heavy aroma of half-eaten food and too many people in one room hung in the air. Patrick kept his back to the hotel dresser. Once again he had bad news to share.

"We're switching upgrade implants tonight."

"Tonight?" all three chorused.

"Now, as a matter of fact."

"But—" Maya said.

"No time to explain. Just know that our suspicions will become reality if we don't get this done today." Patrick handed each of them a burner phone. "I've programmed all our numbers in. These are good to go. We're going to run this just like we discussed, except we're doing it now. Edgar, you get in touch with Aaron. Have him meet the three of you at the truck and give him his phone. As soon as you're all in position, call me. I'll handle security."

"Wait a minute. What happened?"

"Too much." Patrick was already headed back out the door. He glanced at his watch, then up at Maya, who'd asked the question. "Be ready to move in fifteen minutes. Or less. Once we get this done, I promise I'll explain everything."

◆

Patrick pushed back his rain-soaked hood as he stared through the warehouse security office's glass door. Leaning back in his chair, Ben rested his feet on the desk and his arms drooped limp at his sides. The man's eyes were closed, his jaw slack.

Three live screens played out views of the front door, the street downstairs, and the interior of the adjacent warehouse. Patrick held his breath as Ben's chin quivered. "C'mon," he whispered to himself.

As if in response, his group's white panel semitrailer lumbered across the middle screen. A moment later another truck cab followed.

Patrick gave a sigh of relief. He rapped on the glass door, letting himself in before the security guard had a chance to react. The small office smelled of strong coffee, greasy food, and stale sweat. "How's it going, Ben?"

"Mr. Danaher!" Ben wiped spittle from his lip. "What brings you out here, Mr. Danaher? No problem, I hope?"

Patrick pushed his damp hair back with a big hand. "Well, I'm afraid there is. Remember when I was here yesterday to check on the inventory?"

Ben nodded and blinked.

"I didn't want to say anything at the time. Not until I was sure…"

"What is it?" Ben asked, fully alert now.

"The shipment's been tampered with."

"No," Ben said in a low whisper. Then: "It didn't happen on my shift, did it?"

It's about *to happen on your shift.*

"No way to tell. I just talked with Trutenko. He's flying back from DC and will need to take a look for himself when he gets in."

Ben's wrinkled brow deepened. "What do you mean by 'tampered with'?"

Patrick dissembled. "The supply we have here is a bunch of fakes." He reached into his pocket and retrieved two 2.0s. Holding them up, he said. "I just ran some security checks on these." He handed them over as he sidled next to the observation desk and slipped Ben's cell phone into a frequency-blocking sleeve in his pocket. This baby needed to stay silent until it could be disposed of.

"Fakes?" Ben said, examining the devices as though he'd be able to determine their validity by simply looking at them. "You and Trutenko were here when they came in. Didn't you check them?"

In his other pants' pocket Patrick's phone vibrated, letting him know the team was in position. He connected the call so that they could listen in and track his and Ben's movements. "Of course we did. Tuesday. But we think the switch occurred on Wednesday. When the hauler came for the defective 2.0s."

"I don't understand."

"They took the Sixes instead."

"No way." Ben scratched his neck. "I was here for that. They took the right ones."

Patrick shrugged. "You sure? Because the ones I checked yesterday were Twos."

Turning his head from side to side, Ben concentrated. "Not possible."

"Come on," Patrick said. "Let's go down to the warehouse and have a look."

Ben turned back toward the desk.

Patrick started for the doorway. "You coming?"

"Yeah," Ben said slowly. "I want to grab my phone, though."

"Go ahead."

"I can't find it." He made a complete turn as he scanned the room. "It's got to be here somewhere."

Patrick pantomimed helping him look.

"Ah, screw it," Ben said. "I'll get it later."

The two men stepped out of the office into the small vestibule. A metal door to their immediate left led to stairs to the warehouse. Thunder rattled the walls around them.

"That's some storm we're having," Ben said.

"You should try driving in it," Patrick said. He pulled the door to the office shut behind him, giving it a good slam.

"Whoa," Ben said, startled. "Easy there, cowboy."

Patrick shrugged. "Sorry," he said, hoping the team heard it.

Ben led the way to the entry control box next to the door. He fumbled for his ID card, finally pulling it up from a chain around his neck.

Patrick waited for the sensor to recognize Ben's clearance. Two seconds later, the warehouse door unlocked with a metallic *clunk*. Patrick opened the door, then said, "Hang on. I just thought of something."

Ben stopped. "What?"

Patrick scratched at his temple. "We should probably watch the video of the transaction first. Maybe that will shed some light on how they were switched."

"You're right," Ben said. "Why didn't I think of that?"

Knowing that the records of the entire last year had been recently purged, Patrick patted Ben on the back. "We'll get whoever did this."

That's when the power went out.

"Holy geez." Ben loped past Patrick to get back into the security office. There was enough ambient light to see the guy fumble for his keys as he made his way back into the booth and all its dark monitors.

Still standing in the doorway, Patrick said, "The backup generators will kick in. Just hold on."

The two men waited in the darkness.

Finally Patrick asked, "Shouldn't they?"

Ben stood in the center of the small room with his arms akimbo. "Yeah, they should," he said, his shadowed face revealing confusion and dismay. "How could the generators be out, too?"

"I'm telling you, it's a helluva storm out there. Lightning must have fried everything." Patrick held on to the open door with one hand, wedging his body between it and the jamb. "Let me go down there, see what's up with the generators."

"I should do that." Ben reached for the telephone. "I gotta call this in to corporate security." Ben started to dial but held up the phone and shook his head. "Damn landline," he said, clicking the flash button over and over. "Where the hell is my phone?" He dug around his desk again, searching for it in the dark.

"When it rains, it pours," Patrick said insipidly. "You stay here. Look for your phone. I'll go to the warehouse."

"Hang on." Ben searched his desk until he found a flashlight. He snapped it on, then checked its glow by pointing it at the desk, giving himself one more shot at finding his phone. Reluctantly he handed the flashlight over. "You'll need this."

"Thanks." Patrick started through the doorway, then thought of something. "Wait," he said.

"What?"

Patrick hesitated. "You carrying?"

"Yeah."

"Let me have it." He sensed rather than saw Ben's puzzlement.

"What do you need it for?"

"What if there's more going on down there than we realize?" Patrick asked. "I'll be by myself, working in the dark." *And the last thing I need is to have you stumble on my team with a loaded gun.*

"Sure, yeah." Ben hustled to close the distance between them, drawing his firearm from his belt. "You know how to use one of these?"

Patrick took the semiautomatic from the guard's hands and shoved it into his jacket pocket. "Yeah. Thanks, buddy."

"You be careful."

Patrick pulled the heavy door shut behind him.

His team would be outside the easternmost section of the structure, waiting. He double-timed it down the dozen or so metal stairs, the flashlight's pale beam leading him to the cement floor, where he broke into a careful trot. Overhead skylights allowed barely enough illumination to avoid running into walls or equipment.

It was possible for Ben to figure out that they'd intentionally knocked out the power and were controlling the phones and cameras. Ben might even find some way to reinitiate the generators. If the team had been able to pick Aaron up along the way, Patrick would feel better about the logistics. The kid was a master at thwarting security.

He let himself into section D and made his way past a tandem trailer to a massive overhead door. Opening the side compartment next to it, Patrick reached in and yanked a lever, switching the door's mechanism from electric to manual. He moved to the door's center, grasped the metal handle, and twisted it open. He then bent his knees and braced against the floor.

"Ho!" he grunted, levering his weight to raise the door. Three sets of hands appeared at the bottom and the strain melted away.

The hollow metal squeaked as it scraped upward. Seconds later, he faced Maya, Sabra, and Edgar. All soaking wet; all wearing night-vision goggles and exhilarated expressions. Behind them, two truck cabs. One with a tandem trailer attached.

"Where's Aaron?" Patrick asked.

Edgar gestured toward the side of the building. "Monitoring the power." He handed Patrick an extra set of goggles.

"Excellent. Let's move." The moment he donned the goggles, Patrick twisted his face away from the flashlight's beam. Too bright, too sudden. He clicked off and pocketed it.

Edgar hooked up the empty cab tractor to the tandem trailer parked inside the warehouse. The moment he was clear of the structure, Sabra backed the team's truck into the large cavern exactly where the first trailer had been. Identical in size and color, the team's trailer was wet from the rain. Maya slung a screwdriver out from her back pocket and began switching license plates while the rest of them dried the sides and top of the trailer as much as possible. The team operated in spectral pools of luminescent green, working like efficient ghosts.

If all went according to plan, in a few short minutes the defective 2.0s would be left here and the team would take off with their cab hooked up to the trailer filled with Celia's 6.0s. Virtu-Tech's entire Midwest supply.

Patrick pulled out his set of keys. He held them up high, examining them slowly through his thick lenses. As he removed the numbered locks from the first truck and switched them onto the second, he checked his watch. They'd been at this for eight minutes. Only about halfway done. If Ben decided to walk the perimeter and found the overhead door open, they'd be screwed. With any luck, the thunderstorm would keep the guy inside.

When Aaron grabbed Patrick by the shoulder, he jumped, startled. His jacket swung out, whacking Aaron's arm with a heavy *thunk*.

Aaron grabbed the fabric and held tight. "What's this?"

"Aaron," Patrick said, surprised. "Good job with the power outage."

"I asked you a question."

Patrick tried to turn, but Aaron held him in place.

"It's exactly what you think it is," Patrick said. "A gun."

"Yeah." Aaron's eyes glittered. "Why do you have it?"

All movement around them stopped. "Keep going," Patrick said over his shoulder. "We can't slow down. We can't get caught."

"So why do you get to have a gun?" Aaron asked, more quietly this time.

Maya and Sabra began moving again, much slower now, their eyes on the scene playing out before them. Edgar moved closer to the two men. "What's the problem?"

Aaron answered Edgar but didn't take his eyes or hands away from Patrick. "I just don't want to get a bullet in the back of the head from some corporate spy."

Patrick didn't need this kind of delay and especially didn't appreciate being restrained. "If I were a corporate spy, would I be here right now?" His words came out fast and furious as he tried shrugging Aaron's hands off. "The guard gave it to me. In case I ran into trouble down here. Okay?"

Aaron nodded—but didn't move away. "So why did plans change?" he asked. "I thought we were supposed to make this switch sometime next week."

"Everything hit the fan at corporate. If you'd made the meeting I called just before this, you'd know that."

"Don't bullshit me, man."

"You think I'm bullshitting you?" Even though Patrick knew Ben wouldn't be able to hear them from his security office, he still harbored fear that the guy would exercise some initiative and take that perimeter walk. "Then get your sorry ass out of here. I don't have time for this. We've got work to do."

Maya and Sabra had stopped moving again. Gripping her tools in one hand perched at her hip, Maya ran the other through her dark hair. "Maybe if you gave us the whole story, Pat? Why did everything change all of a sudden?"

Half turned, with Aaron's pressure on his shoulder and back, Patrick grimaced. "Get your goddamn hands off me."

Aaron glanced sideways at Sabra, who nodded.

Released, Patrick turned around, blowing out a breath of frustration. They didn't have time to waste, but if they didn't trust him, he needed to fix that before they moved forward. Otherwise—

"The security guard isn't going to sit on his butt for too much longer. I'm supposed to be checking the backup generator. He's going to want to get the power going again, and he might even decide to come down here and have a look for himself. Especially since he knows I'm down here, alone, and I've got his gun." He turned to Edgar. "You want to hold the gun? You tell me right now. I'll give it to you until it's time for me to head back to Ben." Patrick kept his hands up. "You want that? You tell me. It's yours."

"Just tell us what we want to know, Pat," Edgar said.

Patrick waited a beat. They all stared at him, their faces a mixture of suspicion and hope. They wanted to believe him. He needed them to know he was on their side.

"At the Virtu-Tech meeting this afternoon," he said, "Celia Newell came this close"—he held up his index finger and thumb a millimeter apart—"to giving the order to go. Today."

Sabra's mouth opened. "But I thought we had at least another month."

"Yeah," Patrick said. "So did I. But the other five territories are ready. They want to kick the initiative into gear now and let everyone else catch up as future upgrades are distributed. I lied. I told them that we didn't have any Sixes here."

Aaron's stance had relaxed, slightly. "They bought that?"

"They had to. Werner argued, but he couldn't prove me wrong. I blamed it on that new assistant he hired. And my brother is due back here tonight. We have to move, otherwise all our strategy is going to be dead in the water."

The fivesome stood, the quiet settling among them like an uneasy truce.

A flash of lightning obliterated their vision with a green flash, punctuated by the roll of accompanying thunder. "Come on," Aaron said, "Let's get back to work."

When they were done, Patrick pulled Aaron over. "Good job with the power," he said. "I mean that. You're going to restore it as soon as we're clear?"

Aaron nodded.

"Where were you anyway, when I called?" Patrick asked. "They told me you were scouting new territory."

Aaron smiled for the first time all day. In the green glow of the night goggles, it was a welcome sight. "I took a look around Virtu-Tech's headquarters," he said. "Doing a quick perusal of their security system, just in case."

TWENTY-EIGHT

It didn't take Kenna long to set up this time. Without anyone running tech, she got in faster, though a whole lot less securely.

The potential consequences of her actions were on her mind even as she watched the Virtu-Tech logo appear at the program's startup. Stewart could fire her. He could arrange it so that she never worked in VR again. But she wasn't about to wait until self-important Dr. Baxter gave the okay. Any day now, whoever created that werewolf program could delete it and then where would she be? She pushed her fears aside as the infinity-shaped symbol faded and her scenario began.

She had assembled all the components in place exactly as she had before. Additionally, she'd outfitted herself with an armed nine-millimeter Beretta. Going in unmonitored and untethered was bad enough. This time she wasn't taking chances.

Once the scene crystallized before her, with the warm sun on her arms and the plants' hot chlorophyll heavy in the air, she hurried to the rope bridge and issued a directive, ordering the werewolf to appear.

Nothing.

Kenna blew out a breath and tried again. She specified everything exactly as she'd done before.

Still nothing.

He *had* to be here. There was no way he couldn't be.

Kenna studied the scene. She held control of the global database. She was able to access all files, all scenarios. The werewolf had to be where she'd left him. The only way he could be missing was if someone had moved his file.

And then it hit her.

Jason. Damn that meddling son-of-a-bitch.

Like a waterfall, the realization of what he must have done cascaded over her, making her furious, yet hopeful at the same time. Vanessa had casually mentioned that she'd told Jason about Kenna's quest. And she'd done that right before he spent time in a capsule, purportedly to work out before their exercises. He could have moved the file by saving it in a new location. Could it be that simple?

If he *had* moved the file, it still had to be here somewhere. She just needed to locate it. But to do that, she needed time.

So much for getting in touch with Patrick Danaher tonight.

✦

As she wandered through a gray maze of file locations, Kenna blinked her weary eyes. The long day's aggravation was getting the best of her. With millions of locations to choose from, the task could be impossible, but Kenna was determined to find this werewolf and she wasn't about to give up now.

She'd been able to narrow her choices to files accessed that day. It cut out a lot but still left much to sift through. She'd searched through and been disappointed to find nothing in files that had "Jason" or "J" as part of their file name.

Kenna commanded the program to expand the thumbnail descriptions. Whereas a file on a computer might offer the first five lines of text, in VR, an expansion provided a small visual of a program's opening scenes. Not much, but it was all she had to go on at the moment.

When she finally narrowed her choices to about a dozen, one in particular caught her eye.

Nighttime setting. Full moon.

A woman dressed in eighteenth-century clothing wearing a dark hooded cloak stood frozen midstride as she crossed a misty moor. Her head was turned to stare over her shoulder, her expression one of fear as her long blond tendrils curled out from the hood and twisted across her face.

Kenna's neck tingled.

Oh yeah. This had to be it.

Jason hadn't simply moved the file. He'd borrowed it.

With no way of calculating how much time had elapsed since she'd first logged in, Kenna knew that if she had any hope of success, she'd have to get in and out fast.

The program's opening sequence beckoned with motionless drama. She considered copying it, but better information would be gleaned by inspecting its matrix in action. Assuming this was where the creature lurked, Kenna realized she'd have to go in and examine it here rather than move it back to the Hun jungle program. Plus, Jason would notice if the monster was missing. She had no intention of leaving any evidence that she'd been here tonight.

Have it your way.

Resigned, Kenna took a deep breath and started the program. A chilly wind immediately kicked up, bringing with it the wet scent of decay. The girl in front of her broke into a run.

Kenna took off after her.

"Wait," she called. "Stop."

The girl turned as she ran, her expression one of fearful shock when she caught sight of Kenna. The gap between them was widening rather than narrowing, as Kenna's feet sank with each step into boggy ground. How was it that the blonde could scamper so lightly across this swamp?

It was cold here. Kenna fought off a bone-deep shiver as the damp breeze chilled her sweating body, ballooning her wet shirt for a brief moment before pressing it against her clammy skin. Her clothing had changed. She wore what for this time period would probably be underwear. Lightweight cotton camisole and to-the-knee cotton knickers. Button shoes with narrow heels. Again, she cursed Jason. "Cloak," she said aloud, "wool, hood, black," and one appeared on her bent arm. *Damn.* "I meant I wanted to wear it," she complained to the program as she swung it around her back.

With the next squish of her shoes into the soft mud, Kenna swore aloud. She pulled up the hood and fastened the neck clasp while she called out another program change. The girl was half a football field ahead of her now, and Kenna knew without a doubt that the werewolf would be close behind. She couldn't let the story's victim get away.

"Parameter modification," she said, raising her voice to be heard over the mournful wail of the wind. "Adjust the ground. Pavement."

The girl's fleeing figure disappeared into fog as heavy breathing sounded nearby.

Kenna pulled her feet out from the sucking mud and kept moving, repeating her parameter change, wondering why the scenario hadn't complied with her demand.

Exasperated, Kenna cursed herself. Jason must have locked out anachronistic changes to the scenario. It was a common practice among VR adventure seekers who didn't want people messing with their setups. If Kenna had thought of that, she could have copied the program before entering and provided herself with permissions to make any and all changes she saw fit. But now, she was stuck working within whatever limitations Jason had dreamed up here. Could the little twerp have made this more difficult?

An immense shadow lurked within a tangle of trees about a hundred feet behind her. As another low wind moaned, Kenna watched the forest that framed this wide meadow. The werewolf was in there, all right. And a fat lot of good it would do her to face the beast with her feet stuck in muck.

Her hand groped her side for reassurance that her pistol was still there. When her fingertips touched the firearm's metal however, she knew something was wrong. Pulling it out, she realized that it had automatically changed to fit the time-frame parameters. She stared at the ancient, muzzle-loaded pistol. On the order of a flintlock. Just what era was this supposed to be anyway? She'd have only one shot before ordering a reload and waiting for the program to comply. Have to make it count.

The trees behind her rustled, and even at this distance, she could hear the deep growling sounds of the monster in the woods.

Kenna tugged her right foot up. It made a sucking sound as it emerged from the spongy mud, and her left foot sank in farther. Ankle-deep now, she was trapped in this damn mire. Another low growl echoed, louder this time.

She fingered her cloak and considered options that would be consistent within the time frame of this story. "Okay, fine," she said aloud. "Change the ground to cobblestone."

The land beneath her feet solidified, lifting her up. Though uneven, it provided welcome traction.

In that instant, the purple sky exploded as a flood of bats burst from the trees. Their silhouettes swarmed against the backdrop of the full moon, heralding the werewolf's lunge.

Howling, teeth bared, the creature raced toward her, its four legs pounding the ground with a racehorse's gallop while the bats *whup-whupped,* encircling her in a tornado of leathery wings. Instinctively, she covered her head, ducking to avoid their onslaught. Though not a single one touched her, the air current from their mass exodus forced Kenna's eyes shut as she rolled to the ground, hearing and feeling the earth pound beneath the werewolf's feet.

It stopped short, barely six feet before her, its nose tilted upward, flaring, sniffing. Blasts of warm air shot out with each exhalation, curling up and away in the cold night. When it continued to search and sniff, she realized the creature's eyesight was poor.

She crawled backward with ginger movements, placing hands and knees on the uneven bricks of the cobblestone to silently extend the space between herself and the man-wolf.

And yet...

She studied it from her low position. Though the moonlight cast gray shadows dulling the beast into monochrome, she could tell it was the same bright yellow fur, the same pale color eyes.

Yet they were different. When the beast had gone after the warriors in the original scenario, it had turned and looked at her. And when it did, its expression held cunning, intelligence, and what she'd sworn at the time was sentience.

But not now. Now the monster looked merely wild and hungry, oblivious to its surroundings.

Kenna backed farther away, breathing through her mouth to minimize the sound. She was confused—wondering if somehow her memory had endowed the creature with a sentience it hadn't ever possessed. Could Dr. Baxter be right about Kenna seeing things that weren't there?

Crouched, ready to boost herself to run, Kenna engaged the recording mechanism to tag the monster's vitals. Once she had the information uploaded, she could find out where its program had originated.

Okay, big boy. Smile for the camera.

As though it had heard her thoughts, the werewolf's massive head turned. Its long jutting jaw opened. Saliva strung out from both sides, landing on the uneven ground with soft *plops.*

Nostrils widening, it sniffed at the air.

Kenna willed herself not to move. The enormous flaring nose, still shooting out warm air like a locomotive, inched closer—so close that she could feel the blasts against her bare arms, smell the fetid expulsions. A chill breeze swept along her arms, rippling goose bumps to a state of high alert. Involuntarily, she shivered.

The triangular ears perked up and the creature hunched back, drawing up its shoulders, lifting itself high, its growl directed at prey it obviously couldn't quite see. The monster's lips spread thin, baring pointed teeth. Its eyes were wild, pitching back and forth in a mad attempt to locate her.

Kenna reminded herself that none of this was real. She merely needed to collect every byte of information before letting this nasty fellow go.

Once she had that, she didn't need to ever meet this monster in person again. Schematic designs in VR were like DNA in people. It might take her a while, but she'd find a match and when she did, she'd track it to find out who designed this beast—and whoever had killed Charlie.

A scream, high-pitched and too close, jarred the quiet night so unexpectedly that Kenna couldn't process it until the blond girl was almost on top of her. Emerging as a blur from Kenna's far right, the girl shoved Kenna to the ground. In her rush, she tumbled on top of Kenna, all the while shouting in an unintelligible language. Kenna's left shoulder took the brunt of the fall. The blonde scrambled to cover Kenna, as though to protect her, her hood falling back to expose her waist-length hair. What the hell kind of fantasy had Jason come up with?

Kenna struggled to push herself up, her ruminations on Jason's fetishes cut short when the werewolf pounced, landing atop the two girls, knocking Kenna's shoulder into the stone ground a second time. Sharp knives of pain seared across her back. Still pressed against the rutted cobbles, Kenna cried out in frustration, wedging her hands between herself and the young woman, pushing her off.

The girl screamed as the creature's jaw clamped around her hair, yanking her head back. With his huge front claws pressing the girl from behind, her body arched backward in a grotesque U. The girl's face stretched in a silent, horrific mask of torture and she made no sound beyond whimpering mewls that came from the back of her throat.

The girl's hair still tight in its teeth, the werewolf shook her head like a puppy playing with a toy, and the moment the weight lifted enough for Kenna to edge herself out, the girl's back gave way with a sickening crack.

Howling, the werewolf lifted its head skyward, dropping its prize, allowing the girl's head to hit the ground: the sound of a club hitting a ripe watermelon. Kenna rolled away, revolted. Face down, she choked back sudden nausea, and repeated the envoy mantra. "'Nothing is real,'" she mouthed silently. "'Everything is perfectly safe.'"

Scrambling to get to her feet as the werewolf continued its baleful howl at the moon, she hobbled as far away as she could get. Her eyes teared up from the sharp, unyielding throb in her head. Blood dripped from the side of her face to puddle on the ground.

She pulled the gun with her right hand, reaching around her side with her left to check her readings on the progress of this matrix's upload. Her left arm pulsed, protesting movement as her skin pressed against the filmy fabric of her shirt. Her shoulder joint began to swell.

Only half the being's program had recorded thus far. This was taking forever.

With the beast's howls coming more slowly now, she limped away, blinking through the hot pain that shot up her back like fire against raw skin.

How could she *feel* so much? This was sensory overload, yet she'd set the parameters for normal. There should be no reason why she experienced this level of pain.

Unless...

Could she be facing mortal absorption?

She shook her head, refusing to believe that.

"Nothing is real. Everything is perfectly safe."

Her heel skidded in the slippery blood beneath her feet. She fell to her knees, crying out again when the blow jarred her body.

Her left hand groped instinctively for her signal medallion, even as her fingers wrapped around her silver heart pendant. She had no one on the outside monitoring her vital signs. When she'd initiated this scheme tonight, she'd been so sure she'd simply walk in, capture the werewolf's program, and get the hell back out.

Damn that Jason, she thought for the dozenth time. When I get out of here, I'm going to kick his ass.

If I get out of here.

The only way to get the information she needed was to follow the scenario to a resolution. Kenna had no doubt that killing the werewolf would resolve the storyline and grant her escape, but she needed him moving and alive to finish her upload. Only slightly past the halfway point now.

The werewolf stepped off the blond girl's back and began to sniff the ground, probably smelling Kenna's blood.

Rising hatred bubbled up from Kenna's gut, lodging itself hot in the back of her throat. The creature that killed Charlie now wanted to kill her, too. The hell if she was going to let that happen.

Schematics be damned. She turned and sighted the werewolf down the barrel of the pistol. Clenching her teeth, she cocked the hammer back and curled her finger around the trigger. Her brain screamed: Kill the sucker.

The barrel wobbled in her shaking hands.

She hated this werewolf. Hated it with every cell of her being.

Stop. This is only a clever mixture of pixels and synapses and light and smoke and mirrors. It isn't real.

She couldn't hate it.

But it had killed Charlie.

Moving closer, its pale eyes shifted, searching warily, as if to see what it knew was there but could only smell and sense.

"Die," she said.

She increased pressure on the trigger, ready to blow the werewolf's head to kingdom come.

She inhaled, stopped, then gently removed her finger from the trigger and dropped the gun to her side.

"Nothing is real. Everything is perfectly safe."

But her shoulder didn't feel perfectly safe.

When Kenna shook her head, it felt as though she were banging it against a wall. She wouldn't kill the monster. She couldn't kill it. Then they—whoever they were—would win.

Bringing the gun up again, two-handed, she sighted the werewolf's front leg as it loomed closer. Maybe a dead werewolf wouldn't be any good, but an incapacitated one could serve her purposes just as well.

She fired, wincing at the sound and recoil of the blast. It jerked her shoulder. Exploding powder lit up the darkness.

The creature fell back, letting loose a call of frenzied pain that sent shivers up the back of Kenna's neck. She stood her ground, watching as the beast struggled to pull its bulk up to stand again, tucking its head down, whimpering as it did.

Was this really only an oversize wolf, protecting its territory? Was she being ridiculous to believe that a mythical creature might lead her to Charlie's killers? Her conscience jolted at the sight of the beast licking its wound, and she wondered, not for the first time, what the hell was going on.

The whimpers grew softer as the pink tongue worked at the front paw's bloody gash.

Her own injury, the pulsating open wound on the side of her head, and the sight of the damage she just inflicted constricted her throat and brought hot pressure to her eyes.

Charlie.

A vision of his face floated into her mind, his expression concerned, his head shaking from side to side.

"'Nothing is real,'" she said, but her voice trembled. "'Everything is perfectly safe.'"

She lifted her head at a hoarse growl.

The werewolf charged, its mouth wide, its breath steaming, its forepaw amazingly healed.

She pulled the gun up again, realizing too late that she'd used her only bullet. Remembering her training from envoy school, she thought fast. "Program!" she screamed as the monster bore down on her. "Reload!"

As the VR system processed her command, she stumbled backward. Keeping the gun pointed dead center of the creature's head, she knew the matrix hadn't fully recorded, but she'd take what she got. Staying here any longer could be fatal. For her body and her mind.

Her eyes flicked down to the gun's chamber an arm's length away. The werewolf, screaming, lunged. Though the bullet's appearance and her loading technique had taken no more than a few seconds, the sequence crawled in hideously slow motion.

She fired at the moment the beast's jaws clamped. The explosion from the firearm rocked her back, and her arm scraped against sharp teeth, sending the pistol skittering to the ground.

The werewolf fell at her feet, its legs twitching, swinging its head back and forth as it howled.

Kenna backed farther away. Her entire body shook with cold, fear, and a sense of dread she'd never before experienced in a VR scenario. "'Nothing is real,'" she started to say, when she spotted an odd patch of color beneath the creature's fur.

Curious, she inched forward, coming within five feet of the creature, its body shuddering with wracking spasms from the wound in its chest, its breathing wet and labored. She must have gotten it in the heart. Blood pumped out, fountaining from the site, puddling around the stones beneath it.

Lying on its side, the werewolf arched its back, stretching its neck till she could see the tendons of its throat through the taut fur.

The colored patch grew more distinct.

Furry animals were not blue.

She stepped closer to examine the patch, and the werewolf closed its eyes, going perfectly still. The odd thing was, it seemed as though it had closed its eyes on purpose. Animals didn't do that, either.

Fixing her recorder on its relaxed form, she watched as the meter told her that the entire matrix was less than a minute away from completion. She crouched, pushing the blue-tinged fur aside to explore what looked like a tattoo on the beast's skin.

A blue tattoo.

She couldn't make out the design, but now that the creature was dead, it would disappear at any moment. She had no time to waste. Remembering the era, she called out for a straight razor, and one appeared in her hand.

Careful not to damage the tattooed skin, she began to shave away the fur. But the yellow fur was coarse, and it took too long.

Cold fingers of apprehension danced up the back of her neck.

This creature should have dissolved by now. Scenarios never went on very long past resolution. Was another person involved? Would another character emerge from the woods to play a key role in this story?

With her left hand on the beast's shoulder, and her right hand poised above, she let her eyes wander to the bloody hole in the werewolf's chest.

Disbelief paralyzed her: even as the wound stopped bleeding, it began to seal. Healing itself.

"No," she said. Too late.

With a sharp intake of breath that roared beneath Kenna's hand, the werewolf opened its eyes and leaped to its feet.

Knocked to her butt, Kenna crab-crawled backward, ignoring the stabbing pain from the razor tucked into her palm.

The werewolf growled, coming around to face Kenna. It could smell her. It could see her.

The fingers of her left hand fumbled across the clammy ground searching for the gun, her brain doing its best to make sense of this.

The long snout came within inches of her nose. As though the creature wanted to taunt her before killing her, its growl steamed hot and wet against her face. The rancid smell of its breath churned her stomach. Frozen to the spot with fear, she choked back the rush of bile—unable to even turn her head to retch. Kenna's heart pulsed in her ears; her head hammered in terror. Get away, she told herself. Get away. She slashed out defensively with the razor, its shiny blade shimmering in the moonlight. The werewolf jumped back.

How could it be afraid of this little blade?

The realization hit Kenna with clarity that left her breathless. A *silver* blade.

On her hands and knees now, she switched the blade to her left hand and searched for the gun with her right, screaming a command for a silver bullet. Her fingers wrapped around the gun's barrel. The werewolf turned toward the sound of her voice.

Nothing appeared.

"Now!" she screamed. "Give me a goddamn silver bullet!"

Still nothing.

She didn't have time to think—to try to reason why a silver bullet couldn't be conjured up in this scenario. Grabbing at the locket hanging from the silver chain around her neck, Kenna yanked it off. Righting the pistol, she shouted for gunpowder and firing cap, and took the precious seconds she needed to load the weapon and point it toward the beast. She sucked in a breath.

It leaped.

She fired.

What took a mere second expanded to feel like hours as the shiny projectile exploded from the chamber.

The werewolf fell back again, its scream different this time, louder. Frenzied.

No twitching, no spasms. It simply lay there, staring up at the moon. And as it howled at the sky, Kenna got to her feet.

With a brief glance at the recorder, satisfied that she'd gathered all the data she needed, she raced to the creature's side. She didn't ever want to meet this thing again, no matter how controlled the circumstances. She needed to find this tattoo fast.

Switching the razor back to her right hand and blinking away the burning pain in her left, she worked as fast to shave away the monster's fur.

Seconds later, she'd cleared a wide enough swath to recognize the pattern on the tattooed skin.

With a staggered step backward, the razor fell from her grip onto the cobblestone ground. Its metallic ping rang like a bell in the open air.

Kenna stood there a long time, her breath coming out in ragged gusts. She stared.

A bright blue infinity symbol with Virtu on one side, and Tech on the other, was tattooed onto the animal's skin.

TWENTY-NINE

L ight faded to darkness and gradually back to light as the
Virtu-Tech icon shimmered and dissolved.

Kenna blinked, coming aware of her surroundings
as though waking from a deep sleep. It took long minutes
for her mind to process what her eyes were seeing, skewed as
her view was. Lying more or less on her side, she'd fallen and
twisted so that her face pressed hard against the VR capsule's
chilly tiled floor.

Turning, she tried to pull herself up onto all fours but
stopped, waiting for the pounding in her head to subside before
moving again. The headgear she'd donned before entering the
scene was slightly askew. Her temples throbbed as she eased to sit,
her right hand instinctively grabbing her left shoulder, rubbing
it to ease the knot of pain. This would be one nasty bruise.

She tugged the blinder off, crying out at the unexpected
pain. Her fingers reached up to find a sensitive gash on the left
near her crown. The dried blood must have adhered her broken
skin to the equipment. Ripped anew, bubbling sticky-warm
blood leaked down her hand.

Blood smears streaked the tile floor beneath her. Now
she understood why it had felt as though she'd pounded her
head against a wall. In a way, that's exactly what she had been
doing. Wincing, she sat back on her heels and gingerly began
the disconnecting process.

Gritty and drained, Kenna stood, knowing she still had to clean up the place—get it back to normal so that no one would know she'd been here. She swept her surroundings with a weary gaze. She'd never felt this drained before, never so wholly lost track of time before.

All that mattered now was tracing that werewolf back through the matrix until it led her to whoever killed Charlie. Then she'd have all the time in the world to avenge his death.

After Kenna verified that she'd been able to record the pertinent werewolf information, she transferred the data to a memory stick, pocketed it, and then made certain to delete any record of her recent adventure from the system's hard drive. She waited till verification beeped.

Across the room a digital readout broadcast the time in red numerals—0453. Nearly five in the morning.

She couldn't put her full weight on her right leg. The same calf that'd been speared by the Hun warriors had been pierced by the werewolf's claw.

But that didn't really happen, Kenna told herself.

Still, it sure felt as though it had.

Grabbing paper towels from one of the washrooms, she mopped up the remaining blood from her head wound, bundled the sheets up, and shoved them into her pockets.

Time to go.

THIRTY

R eady to get back in there today?" Jason asked Kenna
when she walked in that morning. A second later, he
said, "You feeling all right?"

"I'm fine." Kenna ran her fingers through her hair, pulling
it up and out of her face. "Lot on my mind. Is Vanessa here yet?"

"Haven't seen her." Jason half rose from his seat. "Let
me finish my coffee and my Flaxibar and we can get started."

"No exercises for me today," she said.

He narrowed his eyes. "What happened?"

When she sat down without answering, he tried again.
"Something amiss?" he asked.

*Yeah, you borrowed a part of my program and didn't put it back,
you jerk.*

"Amiss?" She rubbed the back of her neck. "Stewart and
Vanessa mentioned that you've been running VR scenarios
on your own."

"Is that a problem?"

"Not if you're getting in extra practice."

"What else would I be doing?"

"You tell me."

He squinted at her. "If you mean—"

Stewart came in, interrupting Jason. "Good to see you
two getting along," he said. "We'll be up to full strength in
no time. I'm sure of it."

Kenna leaned forward. "How come Vanessa isn't in yet?" she asked with a glance at the office clock. "She's usually here by now."

"Taking a half day, she said," Stewart answered. "She'll be here this afternoon. Out late with the new beau again last night," he said with a wry grin. "Let's hope this one is an improvement over the last guy."

When Stewart retreated to his office, Kenna stood. "What were you about to say?" she asked Jason. "Before Stewart came in?"

With a glance around as though to ensure no one was listening, Jason leaned forward. "I didn't mean any harm," he said quietly.

"Really?" she said. "Then what were you up to?"

"I don't know how you figured it out," he went on. "I made sure to delete any changes I made to the program before I left."

"You stole the werewolf element."

"I didn't. I copied it."

Kenna shook her head.

"Look," he said in a voice barely above a whisper, "it was probably out of line for me to take a look at your program. I'm sorry."

"You're sorry?" she repeated. "For invading my privacy? For stealing an element and transferring it into some wacky rescue fantasy you wanted to play out? What language was your blond friend speaking, anyway? I couldn't understand a word."

He scratched the top of his bald head. "I swear I copied it."

Kenna blinked. He seemed to be telling the truth about that.

"You're a tough person to figure out," Jason said. "Maybe it's a poor excuse, but it's the only one I have. I wanted to understand you better. I thought it'd help if I knew what happened in there."

"That's none of your business."

"Yeah, I know. But back home we jumped in and out of each other's programs all the time. If you didn't want anyone else to mess with it, you locked it with a password."

"That's not how we operate here."

"I understand that now."

Kenna thought again about what he'd said. "You're being straight with me when you said you tried to copy the werewolf?"

"Yeah, why wouldn't I be straight with you?"

Kenna held out both hands. "Seriously?"

"Give me a break," he said. "I honestly believed I'd copied the werewolf. I wouldn't have touched it otherwise. I didn't want you to know I'd been in there."

"Okay," she said. "I'm going home."

"But you just got here."

Kenna would wait for Vanessa's return to trace the werewolf's matrix. Vanessa possessed tech skills Kenna could never hope to match. Not only that, but there was no way she'd initiate such a venture with nosy Jason hanging around.

"I'll be back later," she said.

"And then we can get to our final exercises?" Jason asked.

"I thought I made it clear: not today."

"I am sorry." Jason stared up at her. "Truly."

"Tell Vanessa to wait for me. I'll be back this afternoon."

THIRTY-ONE

Werner Trutenko paced his office, heels snapping hard across the floor. Patrick watched, knowing that immediately outside this room, the three-person crew was scrambling in a futile effort to locate a record of the warehouse pickup earlier this week.

"Do you think he was in on it?" Werner asked.

Arms folded, Patrick leaned into the far corner. "Who, Ben?" he asked. "Not a chance."

"Fire him."

"But I'm sure he wasn't involved."

"Then he's incompetent. Get rid of him."

With regret, Patrick nodded.

Werner held up his hand. "Perhaps we need to have Tate interrogate him first."

"I don't think that would do any good," Patrick said.

"How the hell could all the 6.0s have disappeared?"

Even though the glass door was shut, the three technicians' heads shot up at Werner's outburst. Behind him, Patrick gestured for them all to get back to work, which they did, their expressions wary.

"Like I said during your meeting with Celia, the switch must have taken place when the recycling company picked up those defective 2.0s. They apparently took the Sixes instead. I'm working on it."

"Well, hurry up," he said. "Celia seems determined to chop off my head."

"Don't let her."

"And how do you suggest I do that?"

Patrick narrowed his eyes. "Have you ever considered beating her to the punch?"

"What do you mean?"

Careful now. Patrick lowered his voice. "Think about it: Once Sub Rosa is fully implemented, there will be no stopping that woman. You believe she's doing this for the greater good. I say she's in it for herself. Stop her now, before we lose the chance to stop her at all."

"You don't understand. Remember when we started this—"

"I *do* remember," Patrick said. "But I'm not sure you do. Step back and really look at what's happening. The initiative is not going the way anyone expected. People have *died*. Because of us. That was never part of the plan. This is chaos."

"Chaos is exactly my point," Werner said. "And yes, a few situations have gotten out of hand, but it truly is all for the greater good. Sub Rosa has the potential to bring order back to the world."

"It won't. Not the direction Celia is taking it. Werner, listen to your gut. I know it's telling you the truth."

Werner shook his head.

Patrick continued, "The other directors respect you. Why not work with them to scale back? To abandon Sub Rosa and redirect our efforts back into academia and medicine, the way Simon and Vefa originally intended?"

"The world isn't ready for enlightenment. They'll fight it, like they do everything else that's good for them. Sub Rosa is the only way to retrain their brains."

"Train them? Or paralyze them? There's a difference, you know."

"We can't allow the world to be run by VR addicts."

"We helped *create* those addicts."

Werner wagged his head from side to side. "What we did was help identify the simple-minded lemmings of this world. Those who rely on simulated entertainment to satisfy their foolish desires. We need the true geniuses of this world—like Simon, for instance—to envision our better existence. How can society's intelligentsia succeed when every idea they propose is shut down by large groups with small minds and loud mouths?"

"But who decides what's right?" Patrick asked. "Celia?"

"Patience, Pat. Turning the ship takes time. This is but a temporary maneuver. We're doing all we can to clear the way for leaders and visionaries to reclaim access to our resources. Those of us who eschew VR as entertainment fully intend to work with—and for—these geniuses in our midst. They will be free to invent and create and inspire. Society will flourish. You and I will be proud of ourselves once we attain these goals."

"You still believe that?"

"Of course I do. And so do you," Werner said. "If you didn't, you wouldn't be here. Feeble brains not only crave easy entertainment, they're also incredibly pliable. We see that at Virtu-Tech every day. Our goal is to herd them into compliance."

"More like 'into submission.'"

"A crude term." Werner made a so-so motion. "But apt. While the easily amused dunces dally in their ridiculous VR adventures, those with intelligence, strength, imagination, and resilience will be free to create a working utopia—or as close to one as we'll find here on earth. Finally, we'll see a world of people who do more than simply exist. A world of people who are *worthy*."

"A master race, in other words," Patrick said.

"What's gotten into you today?"

Patrick clenched both fists. It would not do to tip his hand. Not even to his own brother. He rubbed his forehead. "Just stress talking," he said. "I've had more than my fair share of Celia of late."

"Those who seek to stop us—these dissidents—are more than welcome to join our 'master race' as you so amusingly term it. If they're enlightened enough to reject the mindlessness of VR, then perhaps we *want* them on our team. That's the difference. We're inclusive to those who are eager to better themselves. We will welcome them into the fold once we've established structure. Once we're ready."

"Celia will never be ready. She doesn't want anyone else making decisions. She won't stop until she's the only power left standing."

"Would that be so bad?" Werner dropped his bulk into his office chair and crossed his arms. He stared up at Patrick for a long few seconds. "Think about the mess this world is today."

Not understanding, Patrick shook his head.

"Our mother," he said. "Would you trust her to make sensible decisions?"

"Why are you bringing up Mom? I don't see the relevance."

"You will." Werner pointed to the chair opposite him. "Sit."

Patrick sat.

"Both of our fathers were spectacular losers. You know that, even if you were too young to see as clearly as I did. Our mother's carelessness left me—and then you—hungry, not just for food, but also for kindness, hope, dignity. We were left to our own devices, you and I."

Patrick drew a sharp breath.

"We could have faltered," Werner said quietly, forestalling an interruption. "We could have turned out exactly like her—two more stupid little fools waiting for technology to solve their problems."

"Werner," Patrick began, "I know that you had it much harder than I did. And you know I appreciate all you've done for me—"

"What we've done *together.*" Werner said. "We were smart enough to fight our way out of oblivion. That's why we—and people like us—need to take control. Because the ignorant people in this world are running the show."

"And you truly believe this is the best way to do that?"

Werner's animated expression fell. "It's the only way."

"Tell me about Tate."

Werner seemed to snap himself out of a reverie. "Why?"

"Until Tate got involved, things were running smoothly."

The idea worked its way across Werner's features. He shook his head. "No. Tate killed Charles Russell. He wouldn't do that if he was one of them."

Patrick winced. He missed Charlie. "But Russell died before you got the information you needed, right?"

Werner worked his jaw.

Pressing, Patrick added, "What's his name? His full name? I only know him as Tate. Give me what you have on him, and I'll start an investigation."

"I don't believe Tate is the issue here," he said. "Celia recruited him herself. And he's handling a situation for us right now. He couldn't have switched the implants. It's impossible."

"What sort of situation is he handling?" Patrick lifted his index fingers. "I ought to be aware of his activities."

"No need to investigate him," Werner said, looking away for a moment. "He's busy following that envoy."

Werner's revelation didn't register immediately.

"Who?" Patrick heard his own question as though from a distance.

"Russell's fiancée, Kenna Ward."

"Following her?" Patrick didn't move. "Why?"

"To see if she'll lead us to the dissidents. So far, he's come up empty."

"Probably because"—Patrick tried to keep his voice from betraying his rising panic—"there's no indication that she's involved at all. None. I told you that. I went through all of Charlie's..." In his agitation, he caught himself using the more familiar form of his friend's name. ". . .Charles Russell's documents myself. You know everything I found in them. Russell considered bringing her in later but hadn't before he was killed. She's completely oblivious."

"Just because you couldn't find proof doesn't mean none exists," Werner said. "Thanks to the latest trouble in our warehouse, Celia is doubting my leadership." A glimmer of fear sparkled behind his set expression. "You're right about one thing: She's ruthless. Determined to succeed at all costs."

"Werner, do you hear yourself?"

"It's out of my hands now," Werner said. "Tate will do whatever's necessary to get to the truth."

"I don't trust him," Patrick said. "Call him off."

Werner shook his head. "If he truly had a hand in the mystery of these missing Sixes, we'll find out soon enough. I'll wait until I get his report on interrogating this envoy."

"He killed Charlie. What's to stop him from murdering Kenna?"

Werner looked away.

THIRTY-TWO

Celia Newell looked up when her assistant Drew came in to let her know that two of her guests had arrived. The young man stood across the chilly office, hand on the doorknob, waiting for direction. Celia sucked in her cheeks, biting back her impatience. "What about Adrian Tate? Is he here yet?"

"Landed and on his way," Drew said.

"Let me know when he arrives." She locked eyes with the young man as she waved the air. "Send Glen and Simon in."

The moment Drew turned, Glen brushed past him and strode across the carpet, twisting briefly to make sure he'd outpaced his companion.

"We've got trouble," he said quietly. "Simon wants out."

Celia raised her eyebrows. "He's not happy?"

"He's had a pang of conscience."

"Can't you handle him?"

He opened his mouth, closed it again, then said, "He's threatening the whole project," he said. "The guy is out of control. I thought if you talk with him—"

As if on cue, Simon Huntington entered. Though short in stature, with his mass of silver ringlets and a pair of ancient-looking gold-rimmed spectacles on his aquiline nose, he looked every inch the genius he was. His shoulders tense, his glare penetrating and direct, he made his way to Celia's desk, his body practically zinging with defiance.

"Simon," Celia said, standing. "How are you, my dear?"

The old man shook his head. He held her gaze for several seconds before directing his attention to the portrait of Vefa Noonan on the wall.

"It was our dream—your father's and mine," he said, "to revolutionize the world. Unite it through the exploration of fantasy. Take inspiration to a new level by allowing everyone to realize his or her dreams, albeit briefly."

"And how fortunate you are to see it come to fruition," Celia said.

"Fortunate?" The old man's expression soured. "Vefa is fortunate, perhaps. Because he isn't here to see what you've done to our creation."

Now it was Celia's turn to frown. "Simon, whatever's bothering you, get on with it. I have work to do."

"Concerning your most recent endeavors, no doubt." He bounced a fist against his lips as though struggling to control himself. "Don't think I haven't figured out what has been going on. What you're planning."

She raised her eyebrows in a display of placid disinterest. "Suppose you tell me what you think that is."

"Look, Simon," Glen began, "I've been trying to tell you. It's not like you think."

"Shut up," the old man snapped. He turned back to Celia. "Vefa and I had a vision. We saw where the world was going. We jumped on opportunity and created something no one ever believed possible. When he died, he left it in our hands. Yours and mine. It was to be his legacy." His gaze held hers. "And look at us now. Look what we've done with the gift he gave us—the gift he foolishly shared with you."

She sighed. "Simon, you've been well compensated for your work at Virtu-Tech. If you're not happy here, I'll be glad to release you from any further obligations and provide you a healthy settlement."

Simon trembled with rage. "How dare you say that to me?" He thumped a withered hand against his chest. "We built this company, Vefa and I. I won't stand by and see our dream corrupted."

Glen leaned in, palm extended. Before he could speak, the old man swatted him away.

"You and I both know you're not going to be satisfied with brown soap or candy bars made of flaxseed," Simon said quietly.

"I'm not?" she asked.

"Don't patronize me." The old man's mouth twisted downward. "If it weren't for this glitch in Chicago, you'd already have everything in place. Then, God help us all."

"How is it you've heard about the glitch in Chicago? I don't recall mentioning that to you." Turning to Glen, she asked, "That tidbit hasn't made the news, has it?"

"No," Glen said. "No one outside the meeting should have been aware."

"Interesting," Celia said.

"It doesn't matter how I found out."

"Oh, my precious, sweet man. It most certainly does. I've done my best to ignore the rumors I've been hearing about you: conspiring with the dissidents; you working to undercut my every move. I did it because my father loved you like a brother. He would have urged patience." She waved toward Vefa Noonan's portrait. "But, like you, he was a foolish man. My patience has reached its limit. You've become rather annoying in your refusal to appreciate Virtu-Tech's potential."

"Its *potential*?" Simon repeated, incredulous.

"What do you want, Simon? A bigger pension and a retirement villa on a remote island? Fine, I'll see that you get what's coming to you. Just walk away. This no longer concerns you."

The old man shook with fury. His arm shot out, his index finger jabbing at the air in front of her desk. "I will not be a party to this anymore. I went along with it, testing the limits for what I thought was the greater good. We envisioned this as a way to blend diverse populations and help them find common ground. Virtu-Tech was meant to boost our brains' evolution. It was designed for the betterment of humankind."

"Our aspirations are not so dissimilar, Simon. I wish you could see that."

"A human's free will is his life. Can you not understand that?"

"What *you* don't understand is that people happily trade that freedom for a promise of security. Happens every day." She smiled. "Virtu-Tech can provide that. Permanently."

"With mind control."

Glen cough-laughed. "It's not mind control, not really," he said. "We may influence sales of consumer goods. A little bit. No real harm done."

Simon turned to him. "Are you that obtuse? Celia doesn't care about your soaps and your candy bars. She has her eye on a much bigger prize."

Celia raised a hand. "Simon, please. Not now."

The elderly man glared at Glen. "She intends to rig the elections. She will be the next president of the United States. Didn't you know that? And from there what will she reach for next?"

Glen sucked in his surprise. His face lost all color.

"Oh, Simon." Celia chuckled. "That would be unethical. Immoral."

"When has that ever stopped you?"

"How noble you are," she said with exaggerated sarcasm. "But have you forgotten? You've enjoyed a worry-free lifestyle at the company's expense since my father's death."

"Not any longer," he said. "This cannot be allowed to happen. There are people with the power to stop you before this goes any further."

"No one has that power," she said. "Virtu-Tech can't be touched. Not any longer."

"I will make the authorities believe me."

Celia blinked twice, waiting. When the old man's arm lowered, she asked, "Is there anything else?"

Before he could speak, Glen stepped forward. "Simon, you've been under strain. You and I should talk; you can explain these crazy accusations you're making. We can get through this, believe me."

Simon glared at him. "Are you naive? Or simply stupid?"

Clearly shaken, Glen tried again. "What you need is a few days off. To think things through."

"An excellent idea," Celia said. She picked up her phone, pressed a button, and murmured into it. A few seconds later Drew opened the door.

"Is Adrian Tate here yet?" she asked.

"He just walked in." He stepped aside to allow the newcomer to pass.

"Tate," Celia said, holding her open palm toward the old man. "Mr. Huntington is leaving us. Could you see to it that his retirement process is expedited, please?"

Tate nodded. The old man shot a quick look in Celia's direction. "I'm not going away quietly."

As he moved toward the door, Tate grabbed him by the arm. "What?" Simon cried out. "Let go of me."

Without a word, Tate yanked Simon backward. He used one hand to ensnare the older man's head and wrapped his other arm around his neck. Tate's face tightened briefly as Simon—arms flailing—struggled to breathe. When the old man's body slumped to the carpeted floor like a broken puppet's, Tate took a step back.

"Looks like I got here right in time," Tate said with a grin.

"Yes, thank you. That's one problem we won't have to deal with today," she said. "You'll see to our esteemed founder's full retirement, yes?"

He hefted the man's motionless form over his shoulder. "Geez, this guy's heavy." As he made his unsteady way toward the office's back doorway, he turned. "You got a preference on cause of death? Stroke, heart attack?"

"Surprise me."

As soon as Tate left, Celia turned to Glen, whose mouth had gone slack. "But you can't just— He can't— Won't there be an investigation?"

"Simon often disappears for months at a time," Celia said. "Trust me, no one will miss him. And by the time they do, it will be too late to tie it to us. Quit worrying."

He continued to stare across the office.

"Glen?"

He made eye contact.

"You aren't going to be problem number two, are you?" Celia asked.

"No." His voice cracked. "Of course not."

"Good," she said. "Now go see about straightening out the Chicago mess. We need to put the final phase of the initiative into action."

THIRTY-THREE

Hold on a minute," Vanessa said that evening when she and Kenna were finally alone in AdventureSome's offices. "The werewolf program wouldn't copy?"

"Now do you understand?" Kenna asked. "This isn't normal."

Vanessa ran a hand through her hair. "The only elements in VR that can't be copied are the ones copyrighted by Virtu-Tech. They do that so people have to pay to access them."

"Right."

Squinting across the office at some middle distance, Vanessa continued to reason aloud. "But purchased elements can't be moved, either. Plus, access expires after a relatively short length of time."

"Uh-huh." Kenna could be patient now that Vanessa was beginning to grasp what she had sensed all along.

"We have to assume that Jason knows how to copy. That he didn't simply make a mistake."

"I think that's a safe assumption," Kenna said. "I may not like the guy, but I respect his skills. He knows what he's doing in there."

"That means," Vanessa said as she turned to her keyboard and began tapping, "we're looking at a whole different type of component. A feature we've not encountered before."

"Exactly," Kenna said. "Can you isolate it? Can you trace it back to its source?"

Working faster now, Vanessa tightened her jaw. "They haven't designed a program I can't navigate." Data from Kenna's thumb drive finished uploading. "If the monster is still out there, I'll find him."

Kenna paced. "What happens when the person who created the werewolf goes to look for it and it's not there?"

Vanessa hummed. "Good question." She lifted her fingers from her keyboard and stared ahead. "I'd say it depends on what we discover when we trace it. Virtu-Tech automatically prevents copying from the moment a new element of theirs is released. What they don't do, however, is prevent copying from their end."

"So?" Kenna asked. "How does that matter?"

"Their designers work cooperatively. That means that anything created by a team member needs to be accessible to all of them. If this came out of Virtu-Tech, then chances are anyone working from their systems can retrieve the werewolf at any time. They have access to it from their own system, meaning they don't need to search for its most recent appearance, the way you did."

"And if this didn't originate from Virtu-Tech?"

"Then somebody else has acquired some sophisticated technology." Vanessa returned to the keyboard. "Let's deal with that question later. Right now, I'm on the hunt for your monster."

Twenty minutes later, Vanessa sat back.

"You found it?"

"Not yet." Vanessa ran her fingers through her hair again. "But I've engineered a program to isolate its identifying markers. I've got it running now, but results could take a while."

Kenna sat in a rolling chair across the aisle from Vanessa. "So we wait?"

"So we wait," Vanessa agreed.

Kenna stared at the display on Vanessa's monitor, but she was too far to make out any of the rapidly updating information. Dragging her gaze away, she tried to take her mind off the search. "Stewart mentioned a new man in your life," Kenna said. "How's that going?"

Vanessa laughed, though not cheerfully. "Not sure yet. He's a good listener. Almost too good. I feel like he's deeply interested in everything I have to say."

"That's not the worst thing."

"But he's overly interested, if that makes any sense," Vanessa said. "I wish I knew more about him."

"What do you know?" Kenna asked.

"His job takes him out of town from time to time. As a matter of fact, he's in DC today. He's headed back tonight."

"What does he do?"

"Sales."

"Of what?"

"I didn't ask. Probably should have." Vanessa shrugged. "He's good-looking, fit, and generous with compliments. We've seen each other only a couple of times, and he can be very charming."

"I'm sensing a 'but.'"

Vanessa wrinkled her nose. "He always wants to stay in. I wouldn't mind going out. We haven't actually been on a real date yet. No dinner, no walk around the park, no movie."

"Vanessa." Kenna tilted her head. "Is this turning into another booty-call relationship? You swore you were done with those."

She grimaced. "It's not like I don't enjoy myself, you know. And he's really pretty good in bed. Attentive." She made a so-so motion with her head. "Most of the time."

"If you've only gotten together twice," Kenna said, "there's no 'most of the time.' He's either attentive or not. Which is it?"

"I know. I know. I stink at this, don't I?" Vanessa glanced back at the monitor before continuing. "This is why I wasn't going to tell you about him. Not until I knew where the relationship was going. I'm embarrassed to admit that I've fallen into the booty-call trap again. You're so much stronger than I am. I hate confrontation."

"This shouldn't *be* confrontation," Kenna said. "When you're in a relationship, you should be able to express your needs without it becoming a problem."

"I know that on a logical level." Vanessa picked at her fingernails. "But knowing what's right and actually doing what's right are not the same thing. It's hard."

"Watch out for yourself, Vanessa. Don't let anyone take advantage."

Vanessa nodded. "Don't hate me for putting it this way," she said, "but what I really want is what you and Charlie had."

Kenna's heart lurched. She didn't trust herself to speak.

"I wish I knew how to get there."

Vanessa's monitor dinged. In a flash, she returned to studying it, fingers flying across her keyboard.

"What is it?" Kenna asked. "Did you find it?"

"Hang on."

Kenna got up and began pacing again. She stole glances over Vanessa's back to study the screen but only saw diagrams and images she couldn't decipher.

Picking up the pace, Vanessa leaned closer—like a person hunched over a steering wheel—staring in at the digital road ahead. She made noises as she worked but Kenna couldn't discern whether they were expressions of aggravation or optimism.

A long minute later, Vanessa pushed back in her rolling chair, arms extended in exultation. "Woo-hoo!" she hollered. "I nailed you, you wily bastard."

"Yes!" Kenna cheered. "Where?" she asked. "Where did he come from?"

"He's a Virtu-Tech creation. No doubt about it." Vanessa pointed. "And he was born in the building right down the street. Chicago headquarters."

"How did he get into Charlie's scenario?" Kenna asked.

"That, I can't tell you. I've been insisting that technology for remote access doesn't exist." She tapped her station. "But after seeing this and knowing what happened to you in there, I'm starting to have my doubts."

THIRTY-FOUR

Patrick opened his front door. "Kenna?" he said, his voice high in disbelief. "My god! Get inside." He shut the door quickly.

When he started toward her, looking ready to wrap her in a bear hug, Kenna stepped back.

"What is wrong with you?" she asked.

The hallway light threw a warm yellow glow across the foyer of the Danaher home. So unexpected was Patrick's reaction, Kenna wanted to retreat into the darkness again.

He shook his head as though trying to speak; nothing came out but choked emotion.

"What?" she asked.

"We have to talk," he said in a husky voice.

He looked older than she remembered. She wondered what stress Patrick was under to cause him to look so drained.

"I'm glad you're here," he said.

The foyer was tight with a small living room/dining room combination to her left and beyond it a swinging door that led to the kitchen. The place was cozy, full of warm colors and soft furniture.

"Kenna! Is that you?" Patrick's wife, Mallory, pushed through the swinging door, making eye contact as she made her slow way across the room. A toddler gripped her index finger in his fist, walking alongside with unsure steps. "We were so very sorry to hear about Charlie. How heartbreaking. Are you all right?" As she reached Kenna, she asked, "Is there anything we can do for you?" and pulled her into a one-armed hug.

"Thanks, I'm hanging in there," Kenna said, feeling awkward.

Releasing Kenna, Mallory flashed a glance at her husband, a look filled with unabashed affection. "Don't just stand there, honey, offer Kenna a seat." She shook her head good-naturedly. "I can only imagine how much you two have to discuss, so I'll stay out of your way. I can't say the same for little Ryan here, though."

As if on cue, the towheaded toddler reached his arms to his father. "Uppies," he said, blue eyes bright, expectant.

Patrick scooped him up, nuzzling against the boy's soft cheek.

"Would you like anything to drink?" Mallory asked.

"I'm not staying long," Kenna said.

Patrick's eyes clouded. "I can understand that. Come on," he said. "We'll talk in the family room."

"Like, about what happened in my apartment?"

"That, and a few other things," he said.

✦

"Charlie orchestrated all this?" Kenna asked. "Without telling me?"

They sat in wing-back chairs, facing each other in front of a dark fireplace. The family room was small, comfortable, and warm. Kenna stretched her feet out toward the dead hearth. Despite the fact that no fire crackled in its depths, it felt good—homey—to be here, and for a heartbeat she remembered what it was like to relax.

Patrick shifted his son in his arms. "The dissident faction wouldn't have half the information it does if it weren't for Charlie." Ryan pulled his thumb into his mouth as he rested his head against his father's chest. "Charlie hacked into Virtu-

Tech's mainframe and uncovered a lot of intelligence I wasn't privy to. He brought it all to my attention, knowing I had some influence there. That's when I knew we had to act. But in his zeal to collapse the initiative, Charlie went in too deep." He paused and their eyes locked. "And when Virtu-Tech discovered Charlie's interference, they set a trap for him." Patrick was quick to reassure her. "No matter how hard they tried, he didn't give anything up—he died protecting us all."

She nodded. Knowing Charlie died a hero did little to ease the grief twisting like a knife in her heart, making tiny, painful cuts with each new shred of information. "That's when I found him?"

Patrick nodded enough to answer but not enough to disturb his son, whose eyes were slowly closing.

Kenna looked away. She should have gotten to Charlie sooner.

Patrick shifted his son in his arms again. Little Ryan had fallen asleep, his blond head turned inward, one little fist curled around Patrick's collar. Patrick leaned his cheek against his son's head. Ryan's mouth worked at the thumb, then twitched into a smile before going slack again.

"It's past his bedtime, isn't it?" she asked, with a glance out at the dark windows.

"Way past." Patrick sighed. "But how much longer do you think I'll be able to hold him like this? Pretty soon he's going to be too big for his old dad."

When he looked down at Ryan, Kenna's chest tightened. How long, indeed. She and Charlie always assumed children were in their future. Now, they had no future at all. No longer did she imagine herself with a little one on her hip. She looked away.

"Why didn't Charlie tell me any of this?" she asked.

Patrick seemed to have forgotten she was there. He gave a thoughtful shake of his head. "He planned to. There's no doubt about that. He was waiting for proof, though. Solid evidence before you got involved. Charlie knew what we were up against. Knew the danger. There's too much at stake."

Kenna sat back. "Because Virtu-Tech is controlling consumer purchases?"

Patrick nodded. "That and more. By creating Sub Rosa they've introduced a state of mind where people do little more than exist. In Sub Rosa, everyone is utterly agreeable. There are no conflicts, no controversy. Because no one cares. The higher functions of the brain are suppressed. Everyone does precisely what Virtu-Tech 'suggests' they do. They 'consent' to everything. It will be the end of free will."

"But I've never had any urge to buy that soap you talked about, and I wouldn't eat a Flaxibar if I was starving."

"That's the thing," Patrick said. "Because you're an envoy, your implants are different. Envoys are, by design, immune. At least for now. Celia has halted production on future envoy implants. She intends for your class of participants to become obsolete."

"I haven't heard about that."

"You wouldn't have. No one, beyond Celia's inner circle is aware of the order."

So that was the real reason for the shortage of envoys. And yet, her new partner, Jason, had been eating a Flaxibar when they picked him up. According to Patrick, he should be immune to suggestion. Kenna shook her head, not understanding.

Patrick shifted Ryan's weight. "We both know that Virtu-Tech owns proprietary rights to the most sophisticated VR technology, right?"

Kenna nodded.

"And people everywhere are addicted to VR." He rolled his lips. "But, as you and I also know, these addicted folks sometimes get into trouble when they become mortally absorbed. Hence, these people need protection. Virtu-Tech doesn't have a choice. If VR starts to get a bad rap—if people start getting injured or die during these supposedly 'safe' adventures—the government will step in and shut them down.

"Virtu-Tech can't afford that liability. And the only way to protect themselves is to hire people—like you, like Charlie—who are less susceptible to their subliminal suggestions."

Patrick stared out at the window. Kenna turned and saw them both reflected back in the dark glass.

"Once this final initiative is executed, however, envoys will be phased out. As will the government as we know it," he said softly. "In effect they'll control everything."

Kenna didn't know what to say.

"Charlie's knowledge of the system and his infiltration of the Virtu-Tech conglomerate was invaluable," Patrick went on. "We're still working to get our counterinitiative in place before it's too late, but the company has begun to employ resources that we don't have access to. They're moving fast to close off all possible obstacles."

"What kind of resources?"

"An interface device that allows us into their VR worlds—to navigate in and manipulate it—while remaining undetected."

"They say that's not possible."

"Virtu-Tech has it—thanks to them duping Simon Huntington into cooperating. That's how they trapped Charlie."

"That's how they did it, then." She and Vanessa were right. "They hacked into Charlie's program?"

"Yes."

"What's the plan to stop them?"

"Four of our main operatives and I have been working on accessing Virtu-Tech's global database from the Chicago location. I've placed a program in the system that has begun working in the background to access all subroutines. Once we execute the program, every bit of information Virtu-Tech controls will—theoretically—be corrupted and the company's communication to consumers lost. But in order to effectively break the bond between the mother—Virtu-Tech—and the suckling infant"—he glanced again at his son with a wry smile—"we need to get in at the right time and execute the payload."

"What are you waiting for? If the program is in place, why not execute now?"

"The longer the program is allowed to work its way through the system collecting and infecting data, the better our chance of success when we let it loose. There's no guarantee this will work, but it's the best shot we have."

"That's crazy."

Mallory knocked and peeked around the corner. "Want me to take him?" she asked.

Patrick shook his head. "I'm fine," he said in a soft voice.

"Okay, then," she said. She flashed them both a smile and turned away.

"It's enormous," Patrick said, picking up the conversation.

"Let me play devil's advocate here for a minute, okay?" Kenna said. "I mean, I need to understand this. So what if people buy the wrong items for a couple of months while the final details of the—dissident, is it?—plan is worked out? Shouldn't we wait to move until we're confident we can succeed? Isn't it better to get everything in place—to get all our ducks in a row—*before* we move?"

Patrick smiled.

"What?" she asked.

"You used the words 'we' and 'our,'" he said.

She had said that, hadn't she? Because Charlie died for this. And she was beginning to understand why. She met Patrick's inquisitive look with a stare of resolve. "Yeah," she said. "I did."

He gave an abbreviated nod. "Good."

She held up the index fingers of both hands, holding him off from further commentary until she had it all clear. "If I understand, you guys are going to basically destroy an entire industry? This is huge. Let me counter my last question: If it's better to let the program work in the background, why not hold off until we're sure it will succeed?"

"Because very soon *all* our choices will be gone," he said. "Celia Newell has nearly every piece in place. She intended to go live with the final phase of this initiative as soon as all areas rolled out the new 6.0s. A few weeks of brainwashing and the country will be under her spell, buying whatever she wants. Voting for whomever she wants." The corners of his mouth drew downward. "VR users will have conceded all autonomy. Which is exactly the plan behind Sub Rosa."

Kenna stared away for a long moment. "And when is the right time to execute the payload?"

"We could use six months. We have less than a month."

"What's happening in a month?"

"Less than that." he said. "They've already ordered a rush production of Sixes to replace the ones we stole. They'll be ready in a couple of weeks. Worse, primaries begin next month. If Celia isn't stopped, we'll have new leadership in the White House come November. She and her protégé, Nick Rejar, will be our new president and vice president. Once they're in charge—once all of Celia's handpicked congressmen are in office—VR will have a free ride. There will be no need for envoys, because the government will sanction Virtu-Tech's version of VR no matter the consequences, no matter how many people die."

"Celia as president?" Kenna said. "No way. She hasn't campaigned or anything. She has no experience. All she's known for is her position at Virtu-Tech…And I've never even heard of this Nick Rejar."

"Right, and a month ago nobody bought Flaxibars."

Kenna rubbed her temples as Patrick continued.

"Right now, Celia is simply a candidate with a strong business résumé. But she will take the primary and then win the nomination by a landslide. Come November, she'll be elected our next president. I've seen this VR system work. Virtu-Tech doesn't intend to imitate reality—it intends to *create* reality." He looked at his son, then to her. "This is big. Bigger than Charlie's death. Bigger than you or me."

Stunned, Kenna remained silent. This couldn't be real. This couldn't be happening. And yet, everything Patrick said made sense—it resonated with the shattering clarity of unexpected truth.

"This is all so unbelievable." She reflected again—this was what caused Charlie to put his life on the line. What better reason? "You've verified all this?" she asked, knowing the answer even as she asked the question.

"I have a contact—Simon Huntington."

"The inventor of VR?" Kenna asked. "I thought you said he was responsible for creating that remote interface device."

"He was, to his great regret. He despises what the company has become since Celia took the reins. He's been against consumer manipulation from the start, and now that he's been made aware of her plans, he's racked with guilt." Patrick's face tightened again. "He's an older guy, brilliant—unpredictable. He's been feeding us information to slow Virtu-Tech's assault on free thought, but even he didn't see the scope of Celia's plans until recently."

"Are you sure we can trust him?"

"Completely." He stared off into the wall for a moment, then took a deep breath. "In the spirit of trust, there's something important that I haven't told you—haven't told very many people, as a matter of fact. Werner Trutenko—"

"The man in charge of Chicago?"

Patrick nodded. "What I haven't told you—what no one else at Virtu-Tech knows—is that he's my brother."

"What?"

Ryan lifted his head, blinked.

Kenna got to her feet. "You tell me this now? You get me to buy in on all this crazy talk and then you sit there and oh so calmly mention that it was your *brother* who had Charlie killed? And you didn't stop him? What is wrong with you?"

Patrick didn't budge. He rubbed Ryan's back and cooed softly until the little boy rested his head again. "Please, Kenna," he said, directing his gaze to the chair she'd vacated. "Hear me out."

Shaken, she stared out the window, wildly uncertain about absolutely everything.

"Please."

She weighed her options, sat.

"Werner is actually only my half brother, not that the distinction matters. Our mom was—I could say she was flighty, but that would be too kind. She was an incompetent parent, atrociously so. Werner's father was a bully and a thug."

"A rough childhood doesn't excuse murder."

"Of course it doesn't. What Werner did to Charlie was unconscionable."

"Then why are you giving me his background?"

Patrick gave an abbreviated shrug. "I started at Virtu-Tech believing, as Simon did, that we could harness this amazing technology to open people's minds. Give them experiences they might not otherwise be able to achieve. We thought that it would encourage people to continue expanding their horizons in real life. To learn, to strive, to explore."

"Seriously?"

"Yeah, I know. With these past few upgrades, we're seeing more isolation, not less. We should have anticipated that." He frowned. "We were guilty of hubris."

Kenna lifted her hands. Where was this going?

"Back when Simon helmed it, I believed in Virtu-Tech. I only stay on now because it offers our best shot at keeping Celia from corrupting us all. No one there knows that Werner and I are brothers. He trusts me, and, from the very start, we saw no need to share our blood relation. Now we keep it to ourselves because—well, such information in the wrong hands could hurt us."

"But you're telling me."

"Charlie was my friend. He died trying to save us all. I trusted him. He trusted you. I need to give you reason to trust me."

Kenna blew out a breath.

"If Celia fires Werner, I'm her best candidate to replace him. We need to get him out from under her thumb. He's lost himself. He's become fearful, angry, and cruel. I not only want to save the world, I want my brother back."

"If Celia's truly guilty of everything you suspect, will she let him go so easily?" Kenna thought about Charlie. "I mean... with everything he knows, will she allow him to...stay alive?"

"I think so. Alone, Werner couldn't stop her if he tried."

"But the dissident faction can?"

"God, I hope so. We need to take the entire network down. That's entirely possible, especially if she promotes me into Werner's position. I have to protect our future." He passed a large hand over the back of Ryan's head. "For him."

THIRTY-FIVE

S itting at his desk with the door closed, Werner dialed. "Where are you?" he asked when Tate's image appeared on his phone screen.

The tall man spread his arms in frustrated abdication. "Why?"

"I've been trying to reach you all day."

"Took a trip to DC. You got a problem with that?"

"When you don't tell me about it beforehand, yes," Werner said. "Why are you in DC?"

"You sure you want to know?"

Tate's demeanor was off. Brash as ever, he carried himself with a heightened degree of impudence. Werner read the question as a taunt.

"Of course I should know. We have a lot of work ahead of us and I count on you being readily available."

"Yeah, well," Tate said with a head swagger, "look what happened when I counted on you."

"What are you talking about?" Werner focused on Tate's setting. "Are you at Virtu-Tech headquarters?"

"You promised me I'd get another shot at becoming an envoy. You haven't done squat about that."

"Not yet."

"Yeah? When?"

Taken aback, Werner hesitated. He couldn't tell Tate

about Celia's ban on future envoys. "Soon. I told you. We can't move forward on your career prospects until the 6.0s are fully distributed."

"What's so important about those Sixes?" Tate asked. "Why wait? Don't you trust me to tell me the whole story?"

"Where is all this coming from?" Werner asked. "What happened?"

"You blamed me for the missing Sixes."

"I asked you about the missing Sixes," Werner corrected. "That's not the same thing."

"Doesn't matter. Why should I trust you if you aren't going to support me?"

"I have every intention of getting you envoy status."

Doubt worked its way across Tate's features. "How come you haven't kept me updated about it, then?"

"I've had a lot on my mind." *That was an understatement.* After a calming breath, Werner said, "We can talk more about this when you return to Chicago."

"I'll be back in town tonight."

"Good." Sensing that Tate had settled down enough for calm conversation, Werner tried again. "What took you out to DC?"

"Special assignment."

"For Virtu-Tech?"

When Tate nodded, Werner spotted it again. An increased level of smugness.

"What kind of assignment?"

"Celia wanted me to do a little housecleaning, if you catch my drift."

Werner sat forward. "Explain."

"Well," Tate said, drawing the word out as he massaged his chin. "Not really sure that Celia wants me to be telling stories out of school, but the news will hit today or tomorrow anyway. Can't really see the harm in giving you a little advance notice."

"Get on with it, man."

Tate glanced both ways, as though to ensure no one was listening. "That old guy, Huntington, passed out in her office. Celia asked me to make sure he was properly taken care of." He grinned again. "If you take my meaning."

Werner's gut rolled over on itself. "Simon? He's—"

"Dead, yeah."

Drawing a sharp breath, Werner steepled his fingers in front of his mouth.

"You've got a weird look on your face," Tate said.

Werner stared away. "Call me when you get back," he finally said. "In the meantime, stay out of trouble."

After they hung up, Werner slammed his desk with a fist. The techs working outside his office glanced up at the jolt. Werner ignored them. He sighed, rubbing his eye sockets with the heels of his hands. Emotions warred for his head and heart.

Werner stared out over the busy office, wryly noting each time a tech shot a panicked glance his way. They'd been tasked with running diagnostics on the security system in an attempt to ascertain what had gone wrong at the warehouse. Their job was to determine who switched the 6.0s and when it had happened.

With a miserable laugh, Werner resigned himself to the fact that they would undoubtedly come up empty. Why should today be any different? No matter how meticulously he planned, no matter how excruciatingly accurate his calculations, everything in his life always went wrong.

Except for Patrick, that is. His one shining success.

He rubbed the stubble on his chin and down the front of his neck. Too warm in here. Too close. The office grew smaller, tighter. Shaking off sudden light-headedness, he got to his feet and strode out the office door. If the techs looked up, he didn't notice. He had to get away.

THIRTY-SIX

Vanessa held the headset tight as she concentrated, replaying the recording for the fifteenth time in a row. There it was. A little bit of static. Same place every time. And definitely part of the original recording.

She marked the time on the recording at 02:11. Two minutes and eleven seconds after Charlie's final VR scenario began someone had accessed the program. Whoever it was had embedded information into the stream. That code could provide clues they needed to uncover the hostile program's designers. Vanessa scribbled notes.

She removed the headset, sat back, and stared at the control panel before her. All the rooms were empty; Kenna had left Vanessa alone at AdventureSome an hour ago, saying that she needed to meet with one of Charlie's friends. Vanessa had opted to stick around a little longer. She had an idea about how to search for a remote-access program but didn't want to get Kenna's hopes up.

Vanessa pressed her fingertips hard against her temples for a long moment. Finding the werewolf had been only the first step. Now that they'd located the mythical monster—a mere avatar for a living, breathing, human being—they needed to determine how best to identify that human and confront him.

Vanessa jotted down a few more notes to discuss with Kenna tomorrow. They would figure this out together, of that she had no doubt. They hadn't known what they were looking for when they'd started this investigation—all Kenna had insisted was that something wasn't right. Now, it seemed they may have found it.

The remote hack—and, at this point, there was no doubt that that's what they were dealing with—was a sophisticated incursion. The stream Vanessa listened to over and over was five degrees separated from the original. Each data stream consisted of a half-dozen other streams, each of them dedicated to key ingredients for delivery of high-quality VR. After Kenna left, Vanessa had gone through every one but kept coming back to this one. That little hiccup, two minutes and eleven seconds in, had caught her attention and sent tingles of anticipation up her spine. She scribbled down every bit of information she uncovered and wished Kenna would have stayed after all.

Stewart would be home, though, she thought, and reached for her cell phone. Her excitement at finding a clue to a remote system was too much for her to wait. She had to tell someone.

As she started to dial, however, the tiny instrument rang out a tune Vanessa had programmed to alert her to Adrian's calls.

"Hello?" she said, hearing the smile in her voice.

"Hey, beautiful," he said. "It's Adrian. You busy tonight?"

She stared at the notes she'd written and thought about her phone call to Stewart. "A little," she said coyly.

"Yeah?" The word came out disappointed. "Okay then, I guess I'll catch you another time."

"No, wait," she said quickly. "Are you back from DC?"

"Hopped off the plane this minute and couldn't wait to hear your voice."

"I'm really glad you're back." Thinking about the conversation she'd had with Kenna, she decided to be up-front about what she wanted. "Want to meet for drinks? I have so much to talk with you about."

"I'm kind of wiped tonight." She could almost picture him shrug. "I was thinking I'd swing by your place. If you're up for extracurriculars, that is."

Vanessa bit her lip. He hadn't outright refused to see her; he'd merely expressed a preference. It was now up to her to decide if she wanted to see him on his terms. Adrian was probably exhausted from traveling. And why not let him see how agreeable she could be. She'd worry about the state of their relationship later. "Sure," she said. "What time?"

"I'm on the way now. 'Bout a half hour."

Vanessa looked at the clock. It would take her at least twenty minutes to get there even if she left this minute. And she needed to tidy her apartment, change the sheets. Standing up, she stuffed her notes into her desk drawer. "Sure. I'm on my way home, too."

THIRTY-SEVEN

Werner pulled the brim of a baseball cap down almost to his brow. He wore a dark windbreaker, dark pants, and the look of a man in a hurry as he stepped through the automatic doors of Super V. The biggest and busiest Virtu-Tech franchise in the city, it offered deep discounts on annual memberships, and state-of-the art privacy options.

While there were no hard rules in place prohibiting him from accessing personal programs, as a principal member of Celia's administration he understood that VR interactions were to be kept to a minimum. Any and all necessary time in a capsule should be limited to interfaces that propelled the company's initiative or otherwise provided education. Celia's team was to remain pure-brained, at all costs. She believed that only flawed individuals fell under VR's spell, and she would not tolerate such weakness in her organization.

None of that mattered to Werner. Not today. He'd followed every rule. Forsaken his own needs in order to further those of his team. It was far past time for him to encounter something real.

Real.

He might have laughed if it wasn't so sad.

✦

Werner was seventeen, a high school senior again—wearing threadbare blue jeans and a faded Darth Vader T-shirt. Out of school early that day for teacher institute day or some other bogus reason. Heading home.

No one else was out along this shabby street. Of course not. He didn't need them to be. He strolled slowly. Every home he passed was precisely as he remembered. The blue cottage with warped siding, its front yard encircled by a rusted chain-link fence. The boarded-up bungalow with crumbling front steps. The A-frame a young couple had painted bright pink and green before they abandoned it. And next door to his own home, was the old Polish lady's brick three-flat—the only unspoiled structure on the block. It stuck out like a freshly manicured thumb on a coal miner's sooty hand.

Werner, little Patrick, and their mom occupied the first-floor apartment of a ramshackle two-flat. Owned by an off-site landlord who ignored calls about leaky pipes but generously offered discounts on rent in exchange for "quality time" with their mother, it was the only home Werner had ever known. His father, Patrick's father, and all the men who had come and gone in between had lived here for a time, too. Mom couldn't afford to move. Where would they go? Unless she found a man willing to take on an alcoholic with two kids, they were out of luck.

Werner stole a moment before opening the back door to feel the brisk breeze on his face, the weight of the backpack on his shoulders, and a final moment of peace before his world fell apart, again.

He opened the door. "Dad?" he said. "What are you doing here?"

A tall, muscular, red-faced man, Werner Senior bared his teeth in a semblance of a smile. "Is that how you greet your old man, boy?"

Werner's stomach twisted. His father's presence here was bad enough. Worse was that he held little Patrick in the crook of one arm and a glass of whiskey in his free hand. Paddy rubbed an eye socket with a chubby fist. One cheek was bright red. He must have just woken up from a nap.

"Where's Mom?" Werner asked.

"Getting dressed," his father said, gesturing toward the bedroom with his head. "Why are you home so early? She said you don't get in until three."

"Short day." Werner tried to peer around his father's bulky form. "Mom?" he called. "You okay?"

"She's fine. Sleeping off a little too much of this." His father winked as he hoisted his glass and took a deep gulp. "You know how she is."

"What are you doing here?" Werner asked again.

The elder Trutenko bounced Paddy, who glanced around expectantly. Probably looking for food. "How come you never told me about this little guy?"

"What about him?"

"Your momma seems to be keeping secrets from me. Now, I know this rug rat ain't mine, so I gotta ask, who's the daddy?"

"What difference does it make?" Werner stammered. Why did confronting his father always make him so nervous?

"Don't you mouth off to me, boy."

Werner worked his jaw. Drawing a deep breath, he dropped his backpack to the floor and reached for Paddy. "Here, I'll take him."

His father stepped back. "Not so fast. Who's the daddy?"

Werner wanted to tell him to put two and two together. But the last thing they needed was for him to beat up their red-haired landlord. Mr. Danaher would kick them to the street, son or no son.

The elder Trutenko swirled the whiskey in his glass before draining it and slamming it down on the kitchen table. "I'm waiting."

Werner was saved from answering by the appearance of his mother stumbling out of the bedroom. Barefoot and clad only in a T-shirt, she kept her face down as she made her way toward them, one hand plastered against the wall for support. Her hair was tousled and her well-worn T-shirt, emblazoned with a local bar's logo, was ripped.

"Whatcha doing home s'early?" she asked. Her words were slurred, but not the way they usually were when she had too much to drink.

Werner took a step toward her. "Mom, are you all right?"

When she looked up at him, he had his answer. Her bottom lip was fat and blood-crusted—the left half of her face, purple, swollen, scratched.

Werner started for her, but his father stepped into his way. "No, no. Not until you tell me more about this here toddler." Again, he jiggled the little boy. "Your momma couldn't seem to remember."

Patrick, possibly sensing the escalating tension in the room, began to whimper. He reached for his brother. "Woonoo?"

"Listen," Werner said. "He's...uh, mine. I got my girlfriend pregnant and, well, that's what happened."

The elder Trutenko curled his mouth to the side. "Oh yeah? This is your little brat?"

"You've been gone so long, you couldn't know anything about this," Werner said as he reached for Patrick again. "Yeah, he's mine. Hand him over."

His father cracked him across the face. Werner stumbled backward. "Don't you lie to me, boy. Your momma's been stepping out on me, and you're trying to protect her."

Werner cupped a hand across his mouth. Blood dripped between his fingers. His mother slunk along the wall, wide-eyed and silent.

Patrick's whimpers grew. "Woonoo," he cried. "Woonoo."

"Pause program," Werner said.

Like that, the room went silent. His mother, father, and little Patrick froze in place. Werner took his time, examining each of them. This was the moment. This was when he should have grabbed Patrick, gotten him out of harm's way, and beaten his father's face into dog meat.

And yet, he hadn't. He'd yielded to his teary-eyed mother begging him to let it go, just this once. It was her fault, she promised.

"It *was* your fault, Mom," he said to her image. "Even after you knew what a monster this man was, you allowed him back into your life. Into your *children's* lives."

None of the images moved.

"You were a terrible mother," he went on. "But you were all we had." He walked closer to his father and lifted Patrick out of his arms. The little boy came alive again.

"Woonoo!" he said, wrapping his soft arms around Werner's neck.

"I got you, buddy. You're okay now." He pointed to their mother. "You see? She chose booze over us." He pointed to his father. "She chose him over us."

Patrick rubbed his nose with the back of his hand.

Werner rubbed his little brother's back. "Like most of the brainless fools in the world today, she made terrible decisions that affected people around her. People she swore she cared about." Patrick blinked at him, confused. "Don't you see? This is why we have to take control. We can't allow society to be guided by people like her."

Patrick pointed. "Momma sad," he said. "Momma owwie face?"

"Yeah, buddy. Momma has an owwie on her face." He pointed toward his father. "Bad guy."

Patrick stared at the large man. "Bad guy?" he repeated.

"Yeah, you understand? He thinks he can control all of us. Even though he left us years ago, he believes he can step into our lives and order us all around. That's wrong. I have my life. You have yours." He glanced at their mother. "And even she has hers, such that it is. He needs to butt out."

Toddler Patrick disappeared from Werner's arms.

"Patrick?" He turned side to side. Their mother was still there, battered, teary, silent. His father still there, too, but motionless and looking ready to crush anyone in his path.

A second later, his brother reappeared, this time as an adult.

Werner took a step backward. "What the hell?"

Patrick raised both hands. "Don't worry, I'm still just an image. You created me—or at least part of your brain did." Grinning, he glanced at his upraised hands and turned the palms inward. "All grown up now, am I?"

"I don't understand."

Patrick tilted his head. "Look, I only know what your mind wants me to process. Apparently, I'm here to argue with you."

"About what?"

Patrick pointed to Werner's father. "What did you just say a minute ago, when you were holding me? That he believes he has the right to control all of us? And how that's wrong?"

"Yes, why?"

"If you really believe everything you just said, how do you reconcile that with helping Celia with her mind-control plans?"

"You're just an image in a VR scenario. How do you know about that?"

"Werner," Patrick said, not unkindly, "your mind created me. I know everything you do."

Werner studied their mother and his father again. "She should have stood up to him."

"I know."

"She should have tried harder; she lived her whole life in the bottle."

"I know that, too," Patrick said.

"I couldn't protect her."

"You were a kid," Patrick said.

"I'm not a kid now. I have power. The power to protect the world from itself."

"The world needs to find its own way. How else can you expect humans to learn and evolve?" Patrick shook his head slowly. "But you're right: You do have power to protect the world. You can save us from Celia."

Werner sat on the floor. "You're telling me that I should abandon the Virtu-Tech initiative. You're telling me it's wrong."

"Technically," Patrick said, "you're telling yourself." He jerked a thumb. "Back in the real world, your flesh-and-blood brother tried, but you didn't want to listen. You hate that you've made mistakes. I understand that. But instead of recognizing how to make things right, you're doubling down on bad decisions and making things worse."

"But we're the good guys," Werner said. "Aren't we?"

"We were." Patrick drew a breath. "Not so much anymore."

"Patrick is working with the dissidents, isn't he?"

Patrick shrugged. "I'm just an image. I don't know. But I have my suspicions. Which means so do you."

Werner dropped his head into his hands. "End program."

THIRTY-EIGHT

Vanessa left the bedroom lights on this time. When Adrian climbed on top of her, she noticed a blue tattoo near his left shoulder.

"What's this?"

Ignoring the question, he grunted, spread her legs, and pushed inside.

Vanessa stiffened at the sudden onslaught. It hurt. He hadn't so much as even tried to make her ready. She struggled to force her body to relax as he began moving. A puff of air shot into her face with each thrust and the pungent tang of body odor assailed her nose. His eyes were clenched, and he moved into a too-fast rhythm. In no time, she'd be raw.

"Could you," she kept her voice low, but it wavered. "Could you slow down, just a little?"

Pale eyes flipped open to stare down at her. His face, unusually pallid, took on a grotesque, furious expression— but he didn't stop his hurried thrusts. "I only need a couple more minutes," he said, then closed his eyes again. "Enjoy it."

Chastised, she bit her lip and looked away. She wondered why he kept his eyes closed. Maybe he was picturing someone else. The thought made her want to shove him away, but his angry outburst made her afraid. She kept silent and turned her head.

Julie Hyzy

Vanessa took a deep breath when he rolled off. She took a better look at him. The blond hair flat against his head and the sheen of grease on his skin made it obvious he hadn't showered today. She wrinkled her nose.

"Yessss." He sprawled across the bed. Lacing his fingers behind his head, he stared at the ceiling for a half minute before closing his eyes. "It's been a helluva day," he said.

The throbbing pain, his casual disregard for her comfort, and the fact that he'd never so much as offered to take her out anywhere, to dinner, to a concert…to anything… suddenly bubbled up in a flash of indignation. "So who were you thinking about just then?" she asked him, knowing she sounded petulant. *Wanting* him to hear the sarcasm in her voice.

He opened one eye and looked at her sideways. "I was thinking about my girl," he said, turning to face her. He propped his right elbow on the pillow and rested his head in his hand. A smile broke out over his relaxed features and he ran a hand along her bare belly. "You're my girl, aren't you?"

Hardly mollified, Vanessa nonetheless mirrored his position. As she faced him, the blue tattoo caught her eye again. She touched his arm. "What's this?" she asked as she boosted herself up to see.

Adrian's face split into a grin. "That," he said, his voice a notch higher than before, "is my badge of honor."

Vanessa knelt next to him, tilting her head to make the design out better. The bright blue infinity sign with the company name split between the two bubbles surprised her. "This is the Virtu-Tech logo," she said. "Why in the world would you have that tattooed onto your skin?"

The wide grin drooped a little. "Why do you think? I'm damn proud of what I do. This tattoo," he said, lifting his head enough to allow the fingers of his right hand to reach around and finger the design, "represents all the work I did to get where I am today."

"You never told me you worked for them."

Settling his head back onto his right hand, Tate nodded. "Must have forgotten to mention it." He chuckled as though he remembered the punch line to a joke he hadn't told her yet. His eyes clouded as he continued. "I dropped out of envoy school to join them. Best decision I ever made."

Vanessa had never heard of anyone dropping out of envoy school of their own volition, but she let that slide.

"And so you took up with these guys?" she asked, touching the tattoo again.

"Yep," he said. "Soon as I was on board, I celebrated by getting myself this tattoo. I look at it in the mirror to remind myself of all I've accomplished."

She nodded, eased herself back down. "What do you do for them?"

"What do I do? Everything," he said, lifting both eyebrows and glancing away long enough for Vanessa to imagine that he was revisiting some recent memory. His free hand wandered down his body to scratch. "I'm damn good, too."

"I bet you are," she said, suppressing a shudder from the memory of their recent coupling. Maybe over time she could get him to be more attentive, get him to slow down. Or maybe she should dump him and be done with it.

"Take these damn dissidents for example," he said. He was suddenly animated, more alert than ever. "You know what they've been up to, don't you?"

"I know what I've read. They're protesting Virtu-Tech's monopoly. They're calling for a boycott," she said. "But there's only a handful of them out there. I doubt they'll have much impact."

"Nah, that's nothing. I mean the real stuff."

Vanessa shook her head, not understanding. She stared up at him. "What real stuff?"

"They've been blowing up VR centers across the country. People are getting hurt. Some are even dying. Why? Just because the dissidents believe that VR is bad for you. Is that a good enough reason to go around killing people?"

"Whoa." Vanessa shook her head again. Her voice edged with sharp skepticism before she could quell it. "I haven't heard about any VR centers being blown up."

"Yeah, well, the media keeps stuff like that quiet."

"Give me a break. These dissidents are passive folks. Nobody's gotten killed because of them. Nobody even gets hurt. The whole point of the movement is to protest violence and the simulated brutality in VR scenarios. Sure, they've tried to hack into VR systems, but so far they haven't had much luck," Vanessa's words trailed away as she remembered the blip of static in Charlie's final scenario. "Except..."

"What?" he asked.

"Probably nothing," she said. "It's just that I found something today that makes me think our place was recently hacked."

"Yeah?"

"It happened during the scene where Cha—one of our envoys—was killed." She grimaced. "I mean, I tried to trace it down, but it looks like whoever got into our system came through Virtu-Tech's mainframe first."

Adrian had a peculiar look on his face. Vanessa couldn't read him.

He pursed his lips for a moment. "You say you found this today?"

"Yeah," she answered, wishing she hadn't mentioned a word of it. "A couple of minutes before you called."

"Good."

"Good?"

"I'd hate for you to talk to the wrong people about this." Adrian continued looking at her in that peculiar way. "You could get into trouble."

She decided to change the subject. "So why did you drop out of envoy school?"

"It was boring," he said. "I'm smarter than they are, and they knew it. I needed a bigger challenge, so I figured I'd work in the private sector. Best decision I ever made."

His gaze had wandered somewhere over her shoulder, but now he brought his attention back to her.

Vanessa sat up. "Sounds like fun," she said. Yawning, she glanced over at the clock. "I have a busy day tomorrow, so maybe we ought to call it a night."

"Kicking me out?" he asked.

For the first time, Vanessa felt as though she held the upper hand. "I wouldn't put it that way."

He rolled off the bed and got to his feet. "All right. Have it your way." He picked up his underwear and threw it out the bedroom door.

"What are you doing?" she asked.

"You said you have a busy day tomorrow, right?"

"Right."

Next, he picked up his khaki pants, then changed his mind, dropping them to the floor by his bare feet. The pants hit the ground with the sound of a landing brick.

"What do you have in there?" she asked.

Tate stood for a long moment, staring down, apparently deep in thought. He picked up the pants but didn't put them on. Still naked, he remained motionless, intent, as though he were working out a problem in his mind. Finished, he lifted his face, and grinned at her. It wasn't a pleasant look, but Vanessa didn't understand it, so she smiled back. "What's in there?" she asked again, trying to sound playful.

"In here?" He shoved his right hand into the pants pocket. "Yeah."

"Who else knows about this hacker trail you found?"

Vanessa stopped herself from mentioning Kenna. Her gut shot the lie up to her lips. "Nobody. Why?"

He shook his head, slowly, from side to side. "I can't have you tracing that down," he said.

"What's going on?"

He grinned again, and just as Vanessa wondered how a person could look so crazed when smiling, he pulled a thick-barreled revolver out and pointed it at her.

Vanessa screamed.

"Shut up," he said.

She screamed again, pulling the covers tighter as though they'd protect her. Frozen, she couldn't run, she couldn't breathe, she couldn't even think.

"*Shhhh,*" Adrian said, moving closer. He moved onto the bed with one knee and grabbed a pillow with his free hand. "You've got nothing to worry about."

Close now, he shoved the pillow against Vanessa's bare chest, pushing her up against the grooved headboard. She was acutely aware of its hard and uneven surface against her back even as she stared at the firearm's barrel pointed straight at her. Instant sweat popped from every pore on her body. Streams leaked down her face from her forehead, stinging her eyes.

With the gun tight into the pillow's center against her breast, Adrian yanked Vanessa's protective sheets away and straddled her.

For a wild, hopeful second, Vanessa thought maybe this was some weird game he liked to play, and if she went along he'd finish and let her go and she'd never have to see him again. The gun couldn't be loaded. It couldn't be. This had to be some sort of twisted, sick fantasy.

Adrian tilted his head in a friendly way. With a grunt of pleasure, he smiled again. "Do you really think I'd hurt you?" he asked.

Vanessa whimpered.

"Do you?"

She shook her head, whispered, "No?"

"Guess again," he said, and squeezed the trigger home.

THIRTY-NINE

himes sounded a third time, and Stewart's head popped up, his attention pulled from the confusing configuration Vanessa had left. He glanced at his watch, then leaned far to the right of where he sat, glancing over to his own console to double-check on Kenna and Jason's progress.

They may not necessarily like each other but, according to the readout, they were making good progress on the team-building drill.

Stewart reached across both consoles to silence the chimes, then returned to the confusing array of connections in front of him.

What the hell had Vanessa been doing last night? She wouldn't have reconfigured the system so strangely without a good reason.

He knew she and Kenna had been working on Charlie's final VR scenario. Stewart scratched his head. Vanessa generally left an e-mail or voice recording letting him know what was up, but there was nothing from her this morning. And the state of disarray she'd left was unlike her. Unless, Stewart reasoned, she'd planned to be back early this morning to continue her work.

Stewart stood up and stretched, enjoying the satisfying pops of his spine snapping into place. He took a deep breath, contented. Life was starting to get back to normal again. He'd been worried about Kenna more than he cared to admit. The girl had suffered so much in her life. And yet, every hit she took only served to make her stronger.

He walked around his own console to take another reading on Kenna and Jason's progress. They were doing well. Alert to any hint of distress, techs kept a close eye on the duo, too. Charlie's death at his facility had taken a toll, and Stewart hated the fact that he was constantly afraid that he might lose another one of his kids. He wondered, not for the first time, if this VR business wasn't all it was cracked up to be.

Stewart paced the control room. White walls, stark lighting, giant gray workstations, and tall gray consoles against the walls. Equipment everywhere: flat, ugly, harsh. Depressingly necessary for making customers' dreams come true.

Stewart strolled to the room's far end. Windowed, it looked down over the ground-floor mainframe that ran every VR adventure for their clients. He stared at the mechanical monstrosity. It took an enormous amount of power to maintain detailed adventures, and yet Virtu-Tech promised smaller units were on their way. They'd take up far less square footage and allow for more VR capsules and stations. Continual upgrades...

Virtu-Tech. Always looking to squeeze another buck out of the fantasizing, eager—not to mention, paying—public. Like a low-lying storm cloud, it remained above the masses, hovering, powerful...threatening...omnipotent.

He shook his head to dispel the negativity. Things were finally back to normal. He needed to chill.

Stewart wondered at that. Entertainment came solely from VR adventures nowadays. Few souls really "did" anything anymore when it was just so much easier to participate virtually. Almost no one walked along the lakefront. Or skied. Or read books. Why should they passively read, when they could, virtually, live the story?

Every single day, people trotted off to work to pay for future VR adventures. Each night, they'd return home to sleep before starting the cycle all over again. He wondered about future generations and what the effect of all this would ultimately be.

Maybe he should retire.

A fourth chime sounded. Kenna and Jason would be halfway through the program soon. Marching right along… they seemed to be able to work together. He hoped he hadn't pushed Kenna too soon.

Stewart scratched his head again. Time to focus on something positive, he reminded himself, returning to Vanessa's console. She must have found something—there had to be a good reason why she'd left things a mess like this.

He glanced up at the clock again. It was nearly eleven in the morning. Pretty late for Vanessa, even if she had worked through the night. Maybe he should give her a call.

FORTY

Stewart noticed Vanessa's car in the lot of her apartment building as he headed to her door. Metal steps sang out as he took them, two at a time, fighting his rising panic. It was not like her to forget to call.

He crossed the walkway lining the ordered doors on his left. The sun's rays, bright against the apartment walls, made the gold door numbers glow. He strode to hers, knocked, waited, and knocked again.

Knowing the attempt was futile, he nonetheless brought his right eye to the peephole and tried to see in. The doorknob didn't turn when he tried it, which gave him a measure of relief. Doors were always left open when something bad was inside. He knocked again, harder this time.

"Hey," someone said from his left. "Whatcha looking for?"

Stewart hadn't heard the man come up. Dark, with an uneven unibrow, he was short, heavy, wearing a sleeveless T-shirt over dirty blue jeans. He carried a brown paper bag in the crook of his right elbow, but as his eyes narrowed, he switched the bag to his left and raised his chin. "Who are you?" he asked, before Stewart could say a word.

"My employee," Stewart started to say, but then amended, "my friend didn't show up for work today."

The dark guy shot a glance down at the parking lot, scanning. "Her car's still here."

Stewart nodded. "You know Vanessa?"

The unibrow bunched together, creating a furry V on his forehead. "She's been my neighbor for two years. Nice girl. Always says hello." The suspicion in his eyes shifted to one of concern. "What, you think something's wrong?"

Stewart stared at Vanessa's door, as if it had the answers. "I don't know."

"She had company pretty late last night," the guy said. "Her boyfriend didn't leave till like two in the morning. Maybe she's sleeping."

Stewart stared at him. "That's not like her." Something was very wrong here, but he couldn't put his finger on it.

"Yeah." The guy twisted his left wrist to see his watch. "It is pretty late. Want me to get the landlord?"

Stewart nodded, then paced the walkway as the guy hurried away.

He knocked at Vanessa's door twice more, as hard as he could. "Vanessa?" he called, his face close to the jamb. "Open up."

Still toting the brown paper bag, the dark guy returned, accompanied by an attractive, skinny woman of about thirty-five with hair in a pixie cut, wearing a wide leather tool belt that hung loosely at her narrow hips.

"What's going on? Mark tells me you want to get into a tenant's apartment." Her words came fast as she shook her head. "Can't let you in. My people have a right to privacy."

"Come on, Margie," Mark said. "Look at the guy. He's no stalker. And"—pointing with his free hand—"Ness's car is still down there. You know there's gotta be something weird going on when she doesn't go to work."

Margie stared out over the lot and wrinkled her nose. She blew out a breath and addressed Stewart. "Show me some ID."

Practically bouncing on the balls of his feet now, Stewart pulled out his wallet and let her inspect whatever she wanted. She twisted her mouth in apparent satisfaction and handed it back.

"You'll let me in, then?"

She held up a hand. "I'll go in." Dragging a chain out from a pocket of her belt, she sorted through the sequentially numbered keys. Her mouth was set in a tight line when she pulled up the right one. "Wait out here," she said.

Margie knocked again, calling in a loud voice for Vanessa to open the door. She waited, her head tilted as though listening for sounds of movement.

"I knocked already," Stewart said, "about ten times."

Margie's look told him she would not be rushed. "Vanessa?" she called again, "please open your door. Or I'll have to come in." She slowed the pace of her words. "Okay, Vanessa?" she yelled again. "I'm coming in now."

Stewart kept his top teeth tight on his bottom lip, clamped hard enough to hurt. The feeling that had come over him earlier—a gut-level knowledge that something was wrong—had kicked into high gear. His ears rang with panic. Margie moved in super slow motion, inserting the key into the dead bolt, then trying to turn it.

She glanced over her shoulder with a look of puzzlement. "The dead bolt isn't set," she said.

"Hurry up," Stewart whispered. "Please."

Mark placed his brown bag down on the concrete walkway, his eyes focused on the door as Margie turned the key in the knob. "Vanessa," she called as the metal tumblers clicked open. She pushed at the door. "You here?"

As Margie made her way into the living room, Stewart followed with Mark close behind. She shot them both a warning look and pointed with her chin. "Outside."

Stewart brushed past her toward the short passage that led to the bath and bedroom.

The bathroom was open—lights off. It was empty. He strode past, becoming aware of an unfamiliar smell, something different—not overly strong, but definitely unpleasant. He glanced at the kitchen on the right on his way to the back bedroom, listening for some sense of habitation. Nothing.

"Vanessa?" His voice came out panicked, but it didn't matter. If she was still asleep, she deserved to be startled awake for the worry she'd caused. "Vanessa, are you—"

The words died on his lips as he stopped, two steps into her bedroom.

Mark came up behind him. "Holy mother of God."

FORTY-ONE

M ellow Mary's familiar, disembodied voice ran through the instructions that Kenna and Jason were required to follow.

"You will have one hour to complete this final challenge. At the end of the elapsed time, if your team has not successfully navigated a conclusion, you will be awarded a failing grade for this section."

"Only an hour?" Jason said aloud.

"Higher standards are what set us apart from bargain companies, like Super-V," Kenna said.

". . . nothing at all," Mellow Mary continued. "If items are required, they will be provided as necessary." And as she said that, all the VR-created apparatus Kenna had equipped herself with disappeared. Across the white room from her, Jason's gear vanished, too. He cocked an eyebrow at her.

Mary continued. "Technical staffers will monitor your vital signs. Your body may undergo stress in this scenario, but the staff will not end this program unless your blood pressure drops below sixty over thirty, unless cardiac failure is imminent, or unless you clearly speak the end-program code words."

Jason's eyebrows shot up before he shook off his surprise. "Mind games," he said.

"Countdown to the challenge begins momentarily," Mary said. "Please stand together in the center of the room." A few background noises—clicks and hums—and then she returned. "Countdown commences. Ten...nine...eight..."

Kenna and Jason moved to the center of the room, instinctively positioning themselves back-to-back. The last challenge had them in a darkened room, using laser-beam pistols to shoot multicolored moving lights without getting shot themselves. They'd covered each other while taking out as many targets as possible. Together they'd scored a ninety-one. Though individual scores weren't recorded in team-building scenarios, Kenna was pretty sure she'd outshot Jason.

Mary droned on. "Five...four..."

"Scared?" Jason asked.

"It's VR," Kenna answered over her shoulder. "What's there to be afraid of?"

"Well," Jason said, as Mary got down to the final two numbers, "with all you've been through, I wouldn't blame you if you were a little tense."

"Now who's trying to play mind games?" she asked.

Mary said, "Begin."

All the lights went out. The pitch-black room was utterly silent.

Jason was the first to speak. "You there?"

She felt the tips of his fingers against her hip. "I'm here," she said, brushing them away.

"Just making sure."

Kenna said nothing. She stared at nothing. Heard nothing.

Tense, she waited for something to spring out of the surrounding blackness to attack them.

Nothing.

"What do you think?" Jason asked.

Kenna tried to pick up some sense of danger, some imminent threat, but came up empty. "Maybe they plan to let us sit here until one of us tries to kill the other."

Kenna tilted her head at the sound of her own voice.

"They'd have to give us a lot longer than an hour," Jason's voice edged with humor—and something else.

Kenna ignored that. "Keep talking."

"What do you want me to say?"

She blinked a few times. She shut her eyes for a count of ten, then opened them again, hoping to pick up a source of light in the room's depths. "I think we're in a tunnel," she said. "There's an echo. A slight one."

Jason called out, "Echo!" and the word bounced around twice before disappearing in the dark. "I think you're right," he said.

He bumped her from behind and they stood, backs touching. She didn't move away this time, knowing that if they were in a tunnel, or a labyrinth of some sort, they should strive to avoid being separated.

"Give me your hand," she said.

She gripped his right with her left, feeling his sturdy warmth even as they extended away from each other. Kenna reached her right hand out, fingertips extended, searching. "Anything?" she asked him.

He tugged her hand. "Let's count our steps and move this way," he said.

Keeping a taut hold between themselves, they inched their way Jason's direction. A half step later, Jason said, "Ooof," then, "I found the wall."

Holding onto each other, Kenna stood firm. "I won't move," she said. "Go as far as you can."

They maintained a loosened grip as Jason explored. She felt like the pinpoint of a drafter's compass—stuck holding down the center while the pencil leg circled around.

"Feels like cement. Cool to the touch," he said.

"Like a cave?"

"Too smooth," he said.

They were silent another long moment. Kenna strained to hear something, anything, but all there was, was Jason's gentle breathing and her own.

"So what do you think?" she asked. "A maze of some sort?"

He grumbled.

"What?" she asked, frustrated. She didn't enjoy being the compass point. She wanted to do something.

"Not a maze," he said finally.

"Then what?"

She felt him shrug. "It's round...a hole."

"Oh, that helps a lot."

He sighed. "Fine. Cylindrical, approximately twelve feet in diameter, give or take a few inches. Concrete sides, concrete floor." He let go of her hand. "Looks like we won't get lost after all."

Kenna angled her head up, still seeing nothing, reaching her hands out ahead of her to touch the wall. Unused to such pervasive darkness, she blinked several times. Even when she and Charlie would get up at ungodly hours to maximize vacation days, stumbling into the kitchen without turning on the lights, she welcomed the sense of her eyes adjusting to the dark. Here, there was nothing.

The smooth concrete, cold to Kenna's touch, appeared to have no nooks, no hidden devices, no secret latches for opening an escape hatch. She crouched, feeling the walls from the floor to as far up as she could reach. Making her way around the circular environment, she tried to cover as much area as she could as quickly as possible.

"I can't seem to find—*uhpff*," she said, as she and Jason collided. She stumbled backward; his strangled curse let her know that he'd almost lost his balance, too. Her next words came out sharp. "What were you doing?"

"A methodical search along the walls."

"Wall," she corrected. "Singular."

She couldn't see him, but she would've bet he rolled his eyes. Let him.

"There should be some way out, some key we're not seeing," he said.

"I agree."

"I'm looking for it by searching the—*wall*—counterclockwise."

"Some team we are," Kenna said. "I was doing the same thing, only clockwise."

His hand tapped her shoulder, then worked its way down her arm to grab her hand. "C'mon," he said. "We're missing something here."

"You can let go," she said, tugging her hand away. He held fast to the tips of her fingers.

"And risk you plowing into me again?" he said. "No, thanks. I want you where I can keep an eye on you."

Despite herself, she laughed.

"Whoa! The iron maiden has a sense of humor?" he said. "Who would have guessed?"

His gentle jibe stung. Frowning in his direction, she tugged her hand to pull it free, but he held fast.

"Uh-uh," he said. "Not till we come up with a plan of action."

"Hard to accomplish much when I don't have both hands free."

Kenna heard him give a resigned grumble. He dropped her hand, and she let it fall to her side.

He made a few more noises: pacing, from the sound of it. Slowly.

"What are you thinking?" she asked.

"You know how the prior challenges had 'steps,' to let us know we were on the right track?"

Kenna nodded.

Jason must have sensed her concurrence because he continued, "Whenever we hit a certain target, or whenever we made a correct choice, the program rewarded us in some way."

Kenna picked up his thought. "And we've been in this hole for a little while now, and there's been no change."

"Exactly."

"How tall are you?" he asked.

"Five foot four."

"I'm six two," he said.

"And we're surrounded by solid stone," she said. "No way out but up."

"How do we know there isn't a stone ceiling preventing us from escape?"

"Only one way to find out," she said. She sought his bulk in the darkness, realizing that he was facing her. With both hands on his shoulders, she said, "Give me a boost."

They tried reaching the top with Kenna sitting on Jason's shoulders, then with Kenna standing on them. No matter how high she stretched, her fingers encountered nothing beyond the vertical concrete wall. Sweaty and frustrated, she stood on tiptoe, feeling Jason's slight flinch when her foot dug in.

"Sorry," she said.

"S'okay," he said, but his voice was tight. "Anything?"

"No, just more wall."

His hands clasped around her ankles. "Skinny thing, aren't you?"

"Hey, how about you boost me up, cheerleader-style?" she asked. "I'll get as high as I can."

"You sure?" he asked. "I mean, you're small enough that I should be able to hold you high for a few seconds, but hurry it up, okay?"

"Yeah. Count of three?"

His hands moved from around her ankles to beneath her feet. She locked her legs and tensed, facing upward into the abyss, ready to go. "One...two...," he said, and she felt herself lower slightly as he bent his knees, readying himself for the boost. "Three."

Her fingers skimmed along the concrete as she moved upward. Scrambling with her hands, she crawled them high above her head, searching with blind desperation for any opening, even a crevice. But the wall continued upward, with no apparent end. "Damn," she said, as sweat, beading from her hairline, dripped into her eyes. She blinked the sting away and swore again. "Damn it all to hell," she said, as Jason brought her back down to his shoulders. His hands walked up the backs of her calves, and in moments she was back down on the ground.

He released a long noisy breath. When she felt its warmth against her face, she instinctively stepped back.

"Well," he said after an extended period of deep breathing, "we never expected this one to be easy, did we?"

"No." Kenna sat on the floor. Knees up, she wrapped her arms around them, and put her head down. Jason sat next to her.

"Sorry," he said, when his leg knocked into hers.

She scooched over a few inches, lifting her head. "We're missing something."

"You hungry?"

"A little. Why?"

"During one of the other challenges, you said, 'You won't

like me if I get hungry.' So I figure maybe we wait long enough, get you hungry enough, you'll turn into the Incredible Envoy and knock these walls down and get us both out."

Kenna laughed. "Sorry to disappoint you. I don't get super strong when I'm hungry, just super cranky."

"More than normal?" Jason asked. "I can't wait for that."

Again, the sting. She stood. "Come on, let's figure this damn thing out."

Kenna explored the wall from floor to about waist-height; Jason searched as high as he could reach. They ran their hands up and down the concrete. While it had seemed smooth at first, the constant chafing against their hands started to wear at their fingertips.

Jason had pulled off his shirt and left it on the floor at their starting point so they knew where their circular exploration should end. A few minutes into the search, Kenna said, "Hey."

"What?"

Kenna stood, her surprised fingers exploring cold metal. "I found something. It's—" Despite the dark, she instinctively closed her eyes, focusing on her tactile sense. "It's steel, I think. It feels like a handle of some sort. An indentation in the wall."

"A handle?" Jason said.

"It's about eight inches square, about six inches deep." She stopped talking when Jason's fingers joined hers. They encountered, recessed into the hollow, a vertical rubber handhold.

"Feels like a grip," he said.

Kenna nodded. "Let's pull it."

"Stand back."

Kenna frowned at him in the dark. "I'll do it," she said. "You stand back."

They'd gotten better at avoiding collisions in the dark, and now, as he stepped away, Kenna wrapped her fingers around the rubber grip. A lot like an extra-thick bicycle handle—but solid—set on a low hinge. She wrapped her fingers around the thing and yanked downward. Smooth, it moved with the clunk of a bolt sliding into place.

The moment the grip went horizontal, lights flooded the area.

Jason blinked, raising an arm to shield his eyes. Kenna did the same.

"Let there be light," he said.

Still blinking, Kenna let her gaze travel around their enclosure and then wander upward. "I didn't expect the walls to be yellow," she said, fighting to keep her eyes open against the onslaught of brightness. In addition to an overhead lamp that illuminated them from above, the surround had six high-beam lamps set about five feet apart just below the top rim. They extended outward from the wall like cannon barrels, pointing their beams downward with stark streams of brilliance.

"We'll get used to it." He moved to inspect the handle.

Kenna blinked until she was able to focus fully.

Machinery kicked on, and they were enveloped by a sudden blast of cool air. "Nice," Jason said. "At least it'll counteract the heat lamps."

Hands on hips, Kenna stared up and shivered as the chill danced across her sweaty limbs. "Wow. We've got to be twenty feet deep," she said. "No way could we crawl out."

Jason fiddled with the handle. "Maybe we're not supposed to."

Making a small circuit of the area, facing upward, Kenna nodded. "Good point." She pondered that for several seconds.

"Or maybe…" She tilted her head, thoughtful. "We're envoys, right? And this is VR." Arranging herself dead center of the hole, she called out in an authoritative voice, "Program. Provide ladder."

No response.

Too specific, maybe. "Program," she tried again, an edge of condescension in her voice, "provide means of exit."

No response.

Jason joined her at the center. "Teamwork is the goal, right?" he asked. "Let's try it together."

Their voices joined, they ordered the program to respond, but still nothing happened.

Puzzled, Kenna pursed her lips and tried to think like a computer.

Jason stared upward next to her. "All right, *Fortranna*, what do we do now?"

She twisted to look at him. "What did you call me?"

"Fortranna. You know, from *The Mainframe Files*?" he asked. "You ever watch that?"

"God, yeah. Watched 'em by the hour when I was a kid. I love old movies and television shows. Even some of the crazy ones from the twentieth century."

"You did? So did I." Jason's voice was animated, and dimples appeared on either side of his wide smile. The dimple on his right was far deeper than the one on his left, and it gave his expression a cheerful crookedness. Kenna found herself smiling back. She glanced away.

Turning to him again, she asked, "Are you starting to feel a little claustrophobic?"

He didn't answer, but his eyes gave him away.

"Me too." Kenna reached for the horizontal handle. "Might as well get started," she said. "Any suggestions?"

"None that you haven't already considered, I'm sure."

Kenna wondered if he was being sarcastic, but his expression remained neutral. He directed his gaze toward the rubbered grip. "Let's see what we've got."

They levered the handle up and down, discovering that when it was slid back up into the vertical position, the lights went out. They tried forcing it downward past its horizontal stop, but there was no give whatsoever. They attempted wiggling it from side to side, with the same result.

"So it's no more than a switch," Jason said.

"I guess if we get too hot under all these lights, we can shut them off. Which brings us back to the first assumption—that we're stuck here until we're ready to kill each other." Kenna waved the air to indicate Mellow Mary's dire warnings. "Or one of us is in danger of heart failure."

"I don't think that's it," Jason said.

"Neither do I."

Kenna gripped the front of her T-shirt with two fingers, flapping it back and forth to air herself out. The initial cool rush of air had reduced to a light breeze no longer enough to combat the heat. "But it is getting miserable in here."

"Uh-oh," he said, clearly fighting a smile. "You're not getting hungry, are you? Maybe we should order up something to eat. Like a Flaxibar."

Flaxibars again. Kenna steeled herself. She kept getting pulled into this teamwork scenario when she needed to maintain her distance. Patrick had said that envoys were immune, but if there was one thing she'd learned recently it was that there were no guarantees. "We're in VR, remember. The food isn't real."

"But the act of consuming might be convincing enough to keep you from ripping off my head."

"Don't bet on it," she said. "Why do you eat those things, anyway?"

"Flaxibars? They're the best."

"They're disgusting. But wait—let me guess. You saw an ad for them not long ago and you just *had* to try one. Now you can't get enough of them." She studied his reaction. "Am I right?"

He shrugged. "No."

"Then what?"

"Why do you care?"

"Humor me."

He gave a sideways grimace. "My mom bought cases of them. Cases," he said, with emphasis, "when my brother and I were little. She thought they'd be good for us. Healthier than candy, you know? I hated them at first, but one day, back when I was sixteen or seventeen, I got a craving for one." He gave an embarrassed shrug. "Now I eat 'em all the time."

"Did you get your implant updated to 5.0?" she asked.

He screwed up his face, evidently confused by the non sequitur. "Why should I? I've got an envoy implant—why would I want a consumer-grade one?"

"Just asking."

He shook his head. "You don't make sense sometimes."

Kenna pondered his assertions as she stood before the handle, still horizontal, and pointing toward the cylinder's center. "How long you think we've been down here?" she asked.

"Half hour?"

Kenna's stomach growled. "Yeah." They'd tried to manipulate the rubber-handled grip every logical way. But they hadn't tried any illogical ways. She stood facing the handle, her right side to the wall, her left toward Jason. "Let's think out of the box."

"Don't you mean out of the hole?"

She rolled her eyes but didn't laugh. This Jason fellow was growing on her—but she didn't need new friends, didn't want to care about anyone, especially not this new partner.

Patrick had warned that once he took over Trutenko's position as a director for Virtu-Tech, he'd be calling on her to depart AdventureSome to work directly for him. That meant she'd need to abandon Stewart, Vanessa, and all her friends here. Though the sacrifice would be temporary, and for the greater good, it was hard enough to know she'd be turning her back on them. The last thing she needed was to add more people to that list.

Business as usual. That's what Patrick had told her. And to wait for his call.

"Stand in the center," she said.

Jason nodded, took two steps back.

Grunting, Kenna gripped the handle with both hands, bent her knees, and pushed.

The wall moved.

With a triumphant grin, she began walking counterclockwise. She took it slowly at first, amazed at how effortlessly the wall turned.

"Whoa," Jason said, with a look of amazement. "Excellent." He shuffled in place, turning to watch her progress.

"So we know two things," Kenna said as she continued. "This wall isn't solid concrete, and it turns. What do we do with that information?"

He studied her as she moved. "Go around a couple more times."

She did.

Although the act of pushing wasn't difficult, brightness blazed down from the overhead lamps, drenching her in heat. "What are you seeing?"

"The handle," he said. "Let go for a second."

She let go and stopped. But the handle didn't. It kept moving until coming to rest three-quarters of the way around the room.

"Check this out," he said, pointing. "The handle's slightly lower than it was before you began."

Kenna nodded, a little bit breathless from the heat. "You're right. The wall is spiraling down."

"Hmm." Jason grabbed the handle. "Does it spiral upward in reverse?" He put all his weight behind a clockwise push. The wall didn't budge.

"Down it is, then," Kenna said. "Let's do it."

Once the handle made it where they could lower it no further, they stopped pushing. The wall remained too high for either of them to scale, but they could, at least, see that there appeared to be an apparatus much like a jungle gym beyond the top lip.

"Here's the question," Jason said. "Do we lift the handle to make it flat again and try to spiral the wall farther down in the dark, or do I attempt to boost you up over the wall's ridge?"

Kenna studied the vertical obstruction. "I'm not thrilled with the idea of working in the dark. We may not be able to get the lights back on again."

"I agree." Jason turned to her. "Ready?"

"As I'll ever be."

As Kenna backed up as far as she could, Jason positioned himself near the wall, knees bent, hands linked. When he nodded, she raced forward, leaping with confidence, placing her right foot into Jason's ready hands.

She flew up—a fleeting freedom, birdlike and weightless— before grasping the top edge of the wall with her right hand, using what little leverage she had to swing her left arm up and over. Twisting like a gymnast stretching for the high bar, she strained every muscle in her body to swing her right leg up far enough to lodge her knee atop the hard wall.

Panting, she managed to croak, "All good."

"Take your time."

"Okay." She allowed herself to the count of ten to muster her strength. The drop on the wall's far side was less than two feet. Drawing a deep breath, she rolled off the top of the wall and scrambled to stand.

She waved to Jason, who stood at the center of the tall cylinder. He waved back.

"It's even hotter up here than it was down there," she shouted.

"What's up there?"

She turned. "Nothing." This second level appeared to be completely empty. She shielded her eyes against the bright lights, trying to see deep into the depths of the dark that surrounded the hole. Nothing at all. The area beyond was like a wide, unending warehouse. Minimal light, no movement, nothing.

Except for a box twenty yards away. She made her way toward it.

"Kenna? What's going on? Teamwork, remember?"

"Hang on," she said.

Like something a merchant ship might have had in its hold back in the 1800s, the box was wooden. About three feet by two by two, it was made of crisscross beams of gray wood, with a hinged lid.

Inside, Kenna expected to find a rope or something similar to help get Jason out of the hole. Instead, she found a glittering golden globe illuminated from within. Kenna reached in to lift it, surprised by its weight.

The moment she had it in her hands, the room disappeared. The cylinder she'd escaped dissolved, and Jason stood next to her, looking as perplexed as she felt.

"What did you do?" he asked as the room's walls morphed from a dark never-ending expanse into the familiar blankness of VR as it powers down.

"I picked this up," she started to say, but then the glass ball disappeared as well. Her words went quiet, fading into nothingness as Jason reached for her.

But he was gone.

And she was gone.

A moment later, she was back in the VR capsule, facing a tech who'd begun removing her headgear.

"What's going on?" Kenna asked.

FORTY-TWO

tewart stood outside Kenna's capsule. He appeared older and more careworn than she'd ever seen him before. "Hurry," he said to the tech.

With deft fingers, the man finished his work freeing Kenna. She worked out the aches in her arms and legs, all the while keeping her attention on Stewart.

"What happened?"

He gestured with his head. "In my office."

Kenna looked back at Jason's capsule. He, too, was in the process of being disengaged.

"Shouldn't we wait for him?"

Stewart wrapped an arm around Kenna. "Later."

Jason emerged, shouting. "But we're not done," he said. "We didn't complete that last challenge."

The tech who'd worked on Kenna answered him. "You guys got the seventy percent you needed. You passed."

"But I wanted to finish," he said. "I don't like leaving things undone."

The last thing Kenna saw before heading into Stewart's office was Jason fighting to follow.

The door closed with a vacuum-like *whoosh*. Stewart didn't sit. He paced, alternating his gaze between her and the far window overlooking the machinery. He stopped. Brought a fist to his lips. Began pacing again.

Unable to endure the tension any longer, Kenna crossed to grab Stewart by the shoulders. "What is it?" she demanded. When he hesitated still, she gripped tighter. "With everything that's happened lately, it can't be that bad."

But from the hollow expression on his face, she immediately doubted her words.

Stewart covered his eyes. "Vanessa," he said. "She's dead."

FORTY-THREE

J ason drove her home. They kept silent for the entire ride. Kenna stared out the passenger window, seeing nothing. The moment she made it through her front door, she bolted to the bathroom to vomit violently, not caring that the door was open and Jason was still there. Not caring about anything. The world had become a constant swirl of emotion and uncertainty. With both hands on the cold ceramic bowl and tears commingling with the sweat of exertion, she heaved again and again.

She sat on the floor, weak and heavy, unable to move.

"You okay?" Jason asked from the doorway.

She would never be okay again.

"Yeah."

He leaned in, flushed the toilet, and then ran his hand over her forehead, pushing damp hair out of her eyes. She sat back, like a sick child staring up at a concerned parent.

"I'm staying here tonight," he said.

Kenna's throat burned. She started to say, "The hell you are," but the words wouldn't come. She nodded.

Jason pulled her up from the floor with great care. He wet a washcloth, sat her on the edge of her bathtub, and wiped her face.

He ministered to her with no commentary whatsoever, keeping busy as he made her rinse, spit, and then gargle with mouthwash. He was amazingly efficient.

"You do this a lot?" she asked.

The crooked grin made a flash appearance.

"Usually I'm swearing up a blue streak at whoever got themselves plastered." He draped the wet washcloth over the bath faucet and crouched so that he and Kenna were eye level. There was no mistaking the emotion she saw there. Sympathy. He felt sorry for her. And for the first time in her life, she didn't want to push away from it. For the first time in her life, she didn't care if she appeared weak. Maybe it was because she didn't know this Jason well enough to care.

Kenna sighed. She didn't want to think about it tonight.

"I need to go to bed," she said.

Jason nodded and stood, pulling her up with both hands until she was standing, too. "You going to be able to make it?"

Kenna nodded.

"I'll sack out on the couch," he said. "You need anything, just call. I'll hear you."

Kenna tried to manage a smile, but the effort was too great. "Thanks," she said.

FORTY-FOUR

Mallory stopped brushing her teeth when the doorbell rang. "Who could it be at this hour?" she asked with a mouthful of foam. "It's after ten."

Patrick wasn't expecting anyone. "No idea," he said.

He padded to the front door. "Tate?" he said in surprise at the sight of the guy on his front porch. "What are you doing here?"

"Celia called a meeting. I'm bringing you in."

"You're taking me to DC? Now?"

"Taking you to headquarters here."

Patrick wanted this man as far away from his home and his family as possible. "Celia is in Chicago?"

"On her way."

"What happened?"

Tate blinked, as though considering how to answer. "There's a problem. With Werner Trutenko."

"What kind of problem?"

"He went missing," Tate said. "Get dressed."

FORTY-FIVE

When Kenna awoke, she didn't know why she had. Sitting upright in bed, she blinked away the stock-still feeling one gets when startled out of a deep sleep. Furniture shadows faded in and out as clouds slid past the moon. A glance at her nightstand told her that it was a little past four in the morning.

Had a dream awakened her? It felt more as though she'd been nagged by something she'd been trying to forget.

In an instant, the recollection of all that had happened recently came rushing back. She blew out a breath and closed her eyes. Vanessa. Dear God, she'd spoken with her only the day before.

And Jason here in the next room. Sleeping on the sofa.

Kenna started to lie back when an out-of-place sound broke the room's silence. In that moment she realized *that* was what had woken her up.

Scraping.

Kenna's heart skipped a beat. "Jason?" she called to her door. "What are you doing out there?"

The scraping came again. But not from her door. From her window. The right-hand one. Closest to where she slept.

Fury rose in her chest, propelling her off the bed. She yanked open the top drawer of her nightstand and wrapped her fingers around the comforting grip of her Beretta. Years of practice at the range made her methodical checks rote and reassuring. Safety off, she scrambled to crouch along the side of her bed. She focused on the right-hand window.

She decided against calling out to Jason again. Having just awakened, she'd have a hard enough time defending herself. If she had to shoot, she didn't want to have to worry about hitting him.

For a long moment there was not another sound. Kenna modulated her breath, trying in vain to relax her tight nerves. Just as she began to wonder if she'd imagined the noise, it came again. A shadow crossed the moonlit window.

She wanted to take out the intruder before he got inside, but her pale curtains distorted his shape. She may only get one shot. She didn't intend to waste it.

Sharp metallic sounds accompanied the movement. The window sash began to inch upward. Long feminine fingers wrapped around its base, squeezing, as though the hands that pushed it were trying to keep quiet. A second set of hands appeared. Dark hands. Male.

"I have a gun," Kenna shouted, speaking clearly—taking care to enunciate each syllable. "I know how to use it." Both pairs of hands froze in place. "Leave. Now. I'm calling the police."

"Wait, Kenna," The strained voice was female—and urgent. "We need to talk with you."

Kenna's finger instinctively moved off the trigger. "Identify yourself," she said. "Now. Don't come any closer."

Kenna's door flew open, banging against the back wall. Jason stood in the open area, his eyes wild as he scanned the room. Silhouetted in the pale doorway, he made a perfect target.

"You all right? I thought I heard—"

"Get down," Kenna whisper-shouted. She raised her voice to the window, trying to keep their attention on her. "I told you to identify yourself."

The voice that answered her was deep, male. Black. "Patrick Danaher—"

"The hell you are," she called out. Jason took up position next to her.

"—Danaher needs your help," the voice continued.

"Please." The female voice again. "We need to talk with you."

"Ever hear of a phone? A front door?"

"Couldn't risk being seen," the female voice said. "I'm coming in. Shoot me if you have to, but we don't have time to waste arguing."

As a blue-jeaned leg came over the sill, Jason crept across the room, taking up a position in the far-left corner. Kenna nodded. Once the intruders were inside, he'd be behind them. A tactical advantage they might not expect.

"Keep your hands where I can see them," Kenna shouted.

"We're not armed," the male said.

"Well, I am." Kenna said. "Don't forget it." She focused her attention on the space in front of her window. All the way in now, the girl held her hands up, her gaze flicking between Kenna's aim and her companion outside the window, who'd begun to work his way in behind her. The girl was slim, with shoulder-length dark hair and Polynesian features. She wore a backpack and an anxious expression.

The guy, when he finally made it through the opening, stood over six feet tall. He was black, muscular, and even from here, with his hands held in a supplicating way, Kenna could feel tension radiating from his taut form.

"Two steps forward," Kenna said. "Both of you."

They complied.

Out of the corner of her eye she was aware of Jason rounding behind them.

"And don't move," she added. "Now, identify yourselves."

"We don't have time for this shit," the man said, wagging his head from side to side. He started to move toward Kenna. "Listen, Patrick told us—"

Arms wide, Jason lunged, effectively blanketing the other man. The two grappled, elbows and knees hitting the wooden floor amid thuds and grunts of exertion. They rolled, knocking into Kenna's dresser, making the pictures atop it wobble and fall. The young woman moved into action—she grabbed at her companion's arm. "Aaron," she shouted. "Stop."

Just as Jason got all four of the other man's extremities against the floor in a wrestling hold, Kenna jammed the gun into his temple. He froze. She addressed the young woman. "Sit," she said, then turned her attention back to Aaron. "And you, don't move."

"Get this lunatic off me and I won't," he said.

Jason had just begun to release his grip, when Aaron attempted to shove him off. With a grunt of fury, Jason pounded his fist into the other man's side, causing him to double up.

"I told you not to move," Kenna said. She backed away, gesturing for Jason to join her as Aaron sat up and the woman joined him on the floor. "Okay," she said. "*Now*, I'm ready to talk."

Aaron ran the back of his hand against his lip. Even in the shadowed light, Kenna could see the venomous stare he shot at Jason. "I knew this was a mistake."

The young woman placed a restraining hand on his arm. "I'll handle this," she said. With her mouth set into a line, she took a deep breath then began. "Can we talk"—she tilted her head toward Jason, as if to dismiss him—"alone?"

Kenna bristled. "You break into my home and you want to set conditions?"

"We don't know him," she said. "We don't know if he can be trusted."

"Talk to both of us or get the hell out of here," Kenna said. "And talk fast."

The girl nodded, her expression grim. "My name is Maya," she said. She reached for her backpack.

"Hold it!" Kenna said.

The girl froze. "There's something in my bag you've got to see."

"Hand the backpack to him," Kenna said, indicating Jason.

She passed him the bag. Seconds later Jason pulled out a metal box, no bigger than a paperback.

"What is this?" he asked.

"Our only chance right now," she said. "Well, that, and… you. We're friends of Patrick Danaher's." Her dark eyes met Kenna's. "We need your help."

FORTY-SIX

Not quite together in step, the heels of the two men's shoes snapped a hard syncopated beat against the tile floor at Virtu-Tech's nearly silent headquarters. Tate's gaze held straight and steady, though his posture was uncharacteristically rigid. He smirked in a way that made Patrick worry for his brother's safety.

Although Celia didn't visit the Chicago offices very often, she maintained a private space on the building's top story and presumably that's where they were headed. Here, on the first floor, the place was hushed, soft mechanical sounds lost in the high-ceilinged space that—during the day—housed more than three hundred employees.

There were precious few doors in Virtu-Tech office buildings on this level—everyone remained closely monitored with low-ranking worker bees stationed at the building's center, surrounded by three-hundred-and-sixty degrees of plasma screens and a perimeter walkway for supervisors to oversee the group.

No wonder so many people turned to VR these days. Being inside one's own mind alone—escaping reality to experience one's own fantasies beyond the view of anyone else—held an allure few could resist.

The walkway was vacant now, all the screens dark. During the day, they provided an endless, cycling presentation of cheerful people spouting the benefits of VR. Even at work, one couldn't escape the constant stream of commercial advertising reminding employees of delightful virtual adventures, the ultimate reward for toiling at their mundane jobs all day.

Patrick remained silent as the two men made their way across the main floor, his thoughts consumed by his brother's welfare. Werner hadn't given any indication of abandoning Virtu-Tech's initiative. Rather, he'd argued its importance. Which means he wouldn't have walked away. Not of his own accord, at least. Something was wrong. The sooner Patrick got out of this meeting, the better.

A muted buzz echoed as the two men entered a restricted area. Tate slowed.

Ahead of them, an elevator descended to the first floor. Its doors opened to reveal Celia's assistant Nick, who didn't smile when he nodded hello.

The men stepped in, and Patrick started to reach for the fifth floor's button, but Nick said, "Three."

"Three?" That made no sense. The third floor held only VR chambers running experimental programs. He hesitated.

Tate reached past him and punched the number.

"I thought we were meeting Celia," Patrick said.

"You are." Nick crossed his hands at his waist. "On three."

Patrick pondered that for the elevator's short trip. What was going on? Simon had gone silent for the past few days—no response through their regular channels. While that behavior wasn't unusual, and it typically meant that he had secreted himself in his lab, his recent absence coupled with Werner's disappearance did not bode well.

FORTY-SEVEN

When the elevator door opened again, Celia welcomed the small group. Dismissing Nick, she led Patrick and Tate down a long corridor before stopping at the entrance to VR chamber two.

Celia scratched at the room's metal door, absently, like one might stroke a pet. The little shiver-squeals her movement produced made Patrick wonder if her nails were metal, too. He ignored the sudden gooseflesh on the back of his neck and forced himself to project a mien of calm detachment.

Her eyes turned down slightly at the corners, as did her mouth. She was the unhappiest-looking human he'd ever encountered.

"So satisfying," she said, "that you could join us today."

Her hand dropped from its caress of the metal doors, but the hairs on the back of Patrick's neck stood firm.

"Tate tells me that Werner's missing," he said. "Is that true?"

"Isn't that adorable." She wrinkled her nose. "You're actually worried about him, aren't you?"

"Of course," Patrick said. "He's an important part of our enterprise. As is Simon. I haven't heard from him recently, either. I'm concerned for them both."

Celia's brows came together, deepening the vertical lines between them.

"Simon?" Her sharp laugh was as grating as her fingernail shrieks. "He couldn't be here today." Her dark eyes sparkled. "Apparently you haven't heard...the unfortunate news."

"News?" Icy fingers of fear clenched Patrick's stomach. "What happened?"

"The dear man." Sighing deeply, Celia rotated her neck, scanning the ceiling above their heads as though seeking out spiderwebs. "He wasn't well. When old men aren't careful, they have accidents." She winked at Tate. "Poor Simon." She turned to open the silvery door. "I'm sure someone will miss him."

Patrick reached for the wall to steady himself. His mouth opened, but no words came out. Simon was his friend. Like Charlie had been. At every turn, the dissidents were crumbling while Virtu-Tech's power grew. He squeezed his eyes shut, wondering how he could handle it all with Simon gone. Simon...gone.

Forcing himself to get a grip, he focused on why he was here. To find out what had happened to Werner. He opened his eyes and did his best to muster strength.

Celia tilted her head. "Something wrong?" she asked.

"I will..." Patrick cleared his throat. "I will miss Simon."

That cold glint of humor shot from Celia's eyes again. "No, you won't, Mr. Danaher." She shrugged. "Not for long, anyway."

FORTY-EIGHT

Werner made his way to a local twenty-four-hour diner, where he sat in a booth with his back to the door. He sipped hot coffee, staring blindly at the menu, thinking of nothing but what had transpired in that VR capsule. Or, more accurately, in his mind.

The waitress returned to refill his mug. "What can I get for you?"

Shrugging, he pointed to a line on the menu.

"How do you want your eggs?"

"Doesn't matter."

She turned away without another word.

Werner stared without seeing. When his food arrived, he ate without tasting. If he backed out now, Celia would never understand.

Pushing away his plate, Werner drew out his cell phone and grimaced when he noted the time. *Too bad, Patrick. This can't wait until morning.*

The call went straight to voice mail.

Damn. Werner had never known his brother to shut his phone off overnight. He waited for the beep and said, "Call me."

He fingered the port behind his right ear. The one that had allowed him to revisit his old home. That he'd done so at a commercial enterprise—one without the protections offered by VR capsules at headquarters—spoke to his tumultuous state of mind. Such behavior was expressly forbidden. Virtu-Tech directors were expected to remain pure-brained, to eschew VR as entertainment and to avail themselves of "safe" VR systems, like the one at headquarters, for education and self-help purposes only.

Absentmindedly, he scrolled through his notifications of missed calls. Tate. Tate again. Tate a third time, less than an hour ago. For God's sake, what was up now? He'd left three increasingly insistent messages, all imploring Werner to call back right away. No matter what time it was.

Werner lamented ever hiring the man. Celia had convinced him that Tate was no more than a compliant wannabe who would do anything to advance himself. Short on smarts but long on suggestibility, Tate with his unquestioning obedience seemed like a perfect choice to help him flush out the dissident faction.

To be fair, that job should have gone to Patrick. But Werner had been unwilling to tap into his brother's talents. Deep down, he'd suspected Patrick was working with the opposition. So deep down, he hadn't admitted that fact to himself until this moment.

The waitress silently slipped his check onto the table.

There was no choice. He had to talk with Patrick tonight. Before it was too late for both of them. The hell with worrying if he'd wake his brother and family at this hour. Werner looked out over the empty diner tables. Harsh light, tinny music, nothing but reflection from the blackness of the window. Bleak. If he didn't reach his brother now, while he could summon the strength to make things right, he'd lose his nerve when the sun came up.

Sighing, Werner prepared to stand. When his phone rang, he sat back down, pulling his phone out of his pocket, desperate to see Patrick's name on the screen.

Tate.

Werner debated letting the call go to voice mail, but Tate would simply keep calling. May as well get this over with.

"About time you answered," Tate said. "Where the hell have you been?"

"It's late. What's so important?"

"Are you at the office?" Tate asked.

"Get to the point."

"I got news. The kind that has to be delivered face-to-face."

"In the morning, then," Werner said. "My office."

"No can do. You're gonna want to see me now. Trust me."

Werner didn't trust him, but he was tired of playing Tate's games. He provided his location, then added, "If you can be here in ten minutes, fine. But that's all you get."

When the waitress returned to fill Werner's coffee cup again, he handed her the bill and two twenties. "Keep the change," he said. "A man will be joining me here shortly. Please don't give him a menu or take an order. Just ignore him. I don't want to prolong this visit."

She tucked the two twenties behind the pens in her apron pocket. "You got it."

✦

Tate was right about one thing. He hadn't been very far. He swung into the booth across from Werner, his canny grin taking up almost as much space as the rest of him.

"You know how you told me to stay out of trouble?"

Werner ran a hand across the top of his head. More games. "Remember?" Tate asked.

Werner glared at him "I believe I also told you to get out."

Tate gave a one-shoulder shrug. "Well, I'm back."

"What is it, then?" Werner asked. "Make it quick. I have a lot to do tonight."

"Newsflash, it's morning."

Werner couldn't hide his impatience. "Get on with it."

"Geez," Tate said with exaggerated outrage. "What's got into you?"

As Werner drew a sharp breath, Tate waved the air with his hands. "Never mind. Believe me when I tell you I've got a cure for whatever's bugging you. Kind of a good-news / better-news situation."

"Fine." Werner folded his hands atop the table. "Dazzle me."

Tate scowled. "You're weird this morning."

Before Werner could respond, Tate jumped in. "All right, you remember I told you about that girl I've been pumping for information—the one from AdventureSome?"

"What about her?"

"She almost found us out."

"What are you talking about?"

"Settle down. Everything's okay." Tate grinned. "You know how we had to use the remote technology to access Charles Russell's program? And you know how the system glitches up a bit when you first get in?"

"What about it?"

"Don't know how she did it, but that girl almost traced the glitch back to us."

Werner leaned forward. "Explain."

"She was able to isolate the interference. Told me she planned to work on tracing it the next day—today—this morning. When she got back to AdventureSome."

"That's your good news?" Werner asked. "And when they complete the trace? Then what?"

"Don't worry." Tate sat back, thrusting his jaw forward. "That's where the better news comes in."

"Spit it out already."

"I made the problem go away." Tate pantomimed taking a shot while simultaneously popping his lips. "Permanently."

Werner flexed both hands, fisted them, then flexed and fisted again. He lowered his voice. "You killed her?"

Tate shrugged. "Had to. She was this close." He held his thumb and index finger a millimeter apart. "But she was the only one working on it. Didn't have a chance to talk with anybody else yet."

Werner stared away.

"Don't I at least get an attaboy?" Tate asked.

"You're telling me that you killed yet another person?"

"She would have uncovered the whole Sub Rosa initiative, believe me. Only a matter of time."

Werner sat up. "What do you know about Sub Rosa?"

"More than you think I do." Tate pointed both thumbs at his chest. "Remember when I went out to DC? I learned a few things."

Werner ran a hand across his brow. "You've killed three people."

"Not bad for a week's work." Tate chuckled. "And I'm not finished yet."

"Oh, yes you are."

"Say what?"

"Did we get any valuable information from Charles Russell before he died? No. Did you get anything from Kenna Ward? No. Now you've killed another person from AdventureSome and you think the authorities will chalk it up to sad coincidence?"

"Let 'em investigate. By the time they put the pieces together, Sub Rosa will be up and running." Tate scratched his shoulder.

"And we'll have everything we need to stop those dissidents once and for all. Smooth sailing ahead."

Werner rubbed his face. This was all spiraling out of control. Exactly like Patrick had predicted. Werner drew out his cell phone and glanced at its display. Still no reply, no messages. Had Patrick given up on him? Was that why he wouldn't respond?

"Tate?" Werner said.

"Yeah?"

"You're fired."

"You can't do that. Not after all I've done for you."

"I just did," Werner said. "Now go away and stay there."

Tate raised his hands in bewilderment. "What the hell is going on today anyway?"

"Go," Werner said. "I have work to do." He pulled up his cell phone and dialed his brother's number.

Tate didn't budge. He had the strangest look on his face.

"I told you to leave," Werner said as his call connected, once again, directly to Patrick's voice mail.

"Not happening," Tate said. "I'm too valuable. You can't expect me to walk away when——"

"Shut up," Werner said as Patrick's greeting ended and the standard beep sounded in his ear. "Patrick, it's Werner again. It's imperative you contact me as soon as you get this. The minute you get this. Understand?" He hung up.

Tate's face slowly rolled into a smirk. He pointed to the device in Werner's hand. "You trying to reach Patrick Danaher?" he asked.

Werner drew in a breath. "Leave, before I throw you out myself."

"Like you could." Tate said with a laugh. "But that's not what's funny. You trying to reach Danaher? Yeah, good luck with that."

"What do you mean?"

"Let's just say he's going to be tied up for a while."

Werner didn't like where this conversation was going. "Cut the games, Tate. What's going on?"

"Oh, so now you're interested in what I have to say, is that it? Once baby brother's well-being is on the line."

Tate's words roared like a bat to the head.

"What did you say? You're talking nonsense."

Tate leaned across the table. "How stupid do you think I am, Trutenko? Danaher has been undermining you every minute of every day. Yet somehow you're blind to it? I couldn't figure out why you never busted his chops the way you do mine. So I did some extracurricular investigating to see what dirt he had on you. Never pinned you two as brothers, though."

"You don't know—"

"I know enough." Clicking his tongue, he pantomimed shooting again, this time with both hands. "Should've seen Celia's face when she found out."

"Celia?"

"She didn't even believe me at first. I had to show her stuff I found before she took action." Tate shook his head. "*Tsk, tsk.* She's very disappointed in you, Werner."

He started to ask how Tate had uncovered their secret, but it didn't matter. What mattered now was that Celia knew of their blood relationship and she would consider Werner's omission an act of betrayal.

"He was gunning for you. Your brother, I mean," Tate said. "That much will probably save your ass with Celia. And here's the best news of the evening: We're taking care of that little loose end."

Werner felt slow and dumb. "Taking care?"

"We got Danaher where we want him," Tate said with a grin. "As long as he gives up the dissidents, we won't need to hurt him. Much."

FORTY-NINE

"Are you sure about this?" Stewart asked for the fourth time.

Kenna bit back her frustration. She couldn't snap at him. After all, she'd roused Stewart from home with very little in terms of explanation. He knew the basics, but there wasn't time to answer all his questions. Fortunately, he'd accepted everything she'd told him on her word alone, even including Maya's and Aaron's presence here.

Despite all the curveballs she'd thrown him tonight, Stewart remained steadfast. His bright blue eyes were rimmed red, pouched with pockets of swollen sorrow. He stared, silently begging for answers she didn't have.

As they worked together, Kenna was transported back to those precious few moments before going in to try to rescue Charlie. Those confident minutes when she was certain she'd get him out. She could never have imagined the defeat she'd experienced. The weight of failure clenched her heart.

"I'm sure," she finally answered.

Stewart completed the last step and reached for her headgear. "Come back to us, Kenna."

Kenna swallowed the bile that rose up at the back of her throat and pushed up a smile. "No problem," she said. She looked over to the capsule next to hers, where Aaron assisted getting Jason set up. "I've got a partner this time."

"I don't like it," Stewart said.

"Trust me."

"I do," he said. "But this new remote technology?" He glanced at the gizmo that Maya had rigged into the system. Stewart lowered his voice. "You're placing trust in people you don't know. Fanatics who broke into your home. And if that contraption works the way they claim, I may not be able to monitor you at all."

Kenna eyed the mechanism again. She had no idea if it would perform the way Maya and Aaron promised. But she had to believe. Her fate and Jason's rested in that interface device's virtual hands.

Back at Kenna's apartment, Maya had explained as much as she could. Patrick Danaher had been escorted from his home several hours earlier. It had taken concerted effort on the part of all dissident team members, but they'd managed to discover that he'd been taken to Virtu-Tech headquarters to undergo interrogation. Celia intended to break Patrick, using threats to his brother—Werner Trutenko—as leverage.

"They'll conduct his interrogation within VR," Maya had asserted. "How else to crush a person without leaving any physical evidence?"

Everything in Vanessa's notes seemed to confirm the dissidents' claims. An unknown person or entity *had* logged into Charlie's reality from outside AdventureSome. Remote access was no longer simply a fanciful possibility. If this gadget behaved as Maya promised, Kenna and Jason would be able to transport themselves into any VR running anywhere. And tonight they knew their target: Virtu-Tech's VR chambers. Maya had expertly run two simulations based on data Vanessa had uncovered. She pronounced the system good to go.

A thousand thoughts ran through Kenna's mind. She opened her mouth to speak, to try to make Stewart understand, but time was her enemy right now. Patrick's, too.

"Trust me," she said again.

Stewart closed his eyes for a long moment, then lowered the headgear over Kenna's eyes.

FIFTY

J ason?" Kenna called.

Surrounded by nothing, she sorted through her disorientation. Programs always began with a grayish cloud, vapors that dissipated within seconds of entry. But this time, the dense fog remained.

As Maya had explained the experimental device, she'd apologized for not being able to provide more detailed instruction. Apparently Aaron and a colleague had tried out the hacking unit, but without envoy implants—necessary to fully control one's own VR—the best they could accomplish was observing remote scenarios as though through thick glass. Neither was capable of gaining full access to the scenario. That was why they needed Kenna.

And Kenna needed Jason.

How she could have come to trust him so quickly, she didn't understand. Right now, however, it didn't matter. All that mattered was linking up with him inside and then finding Patrick. Once they reached him, the dissidents could move forward with their plans to cripple Virtu-Tech's empire.

A tall order.

"Jason?" she called again.

The vapors around her glimmered, sparkling rainbows everywhere. It wasn't an artsy aberration, it was the program itself reaching out through the infinite electrons, searching for a place to land. She had no inkling how long it would take Maya to establish the link with Virtu-Tech.

Kenna heard her name and turned, realizing almost immediately that there hadn't been any real sound. She'd heard Jason's voice in her mind.

"Where are you?" she asked.

He took a long time to respond. "Look down at your feet," he said. She did.

They weren't there.

Kenna tried touching her chest, her legs, her face. But her hands, or what she thought were her hands, came up empty. "Why isn't the program giving us visuals yet?"

"I think we *are* the program."

Kenna stared down at where her body should be, unable to wrap her mind around what she didn't see. The twinkles of rainbow glitter began to take on a sinister air. This was like being caught in a searing snowstorm, blinded by unyielding light.

"Hang on."

Jason speaking to her from within her own brain was both reassuring and invasive. She waited while he paused an interminable length of time.

"Okay, try this," he said. "I'm..." He swore. "I'm having some...luck...Shit. Damn."

This was the opposite of claustrophobia. Kenna wanted to break out of this boundless space and reclaim her finite existence. In this vast state of nonbeing, she felt crushed by expansiveness.

Jason's voice whispered in her mind again. "Concentrate," he said. "It's starting to work. Concentrate on yourself. I'm starting to see..."

He broke off again.

Kenna closed her eyes and almost laughed at the ridiculous endeavor. Though her body felt as though it complied with her conscious and autonomic actions, she could discern no physical reaction. Eyes open or closed, there remained only this blanket of sparkling white.

"It's working," Jason said. "Start with your hands."

Kenna did. She raised her hands in front of her face, or at least where it felt her face should be.

"I'm trying," she said, seeing nothing.

No. Not nothing.

A shadow at first. Then, as Kenna's mind struggled to re-create what her hands looked like, how they narrowed at the wrist attached to tanned arms, the appendages began to materialize. Jason spoke again, but she ignored him as her upper body re-created itself. She moved down, staring at where her feet should be. As they came into focus, she exclaimed her satisfaction.

"Kenna?" Jason asked.

"All here."

"Okay, now try concentrating on me," he said. "And I'll do the same for you."

She focused on Jason's appearance, his quirks—forming his image in her mind.

A hand rested on her shoulder. She spun.

"Nice to see you again," Jason said.

Elated, she grabbed Jason's upper arm. Immediately embarrassed, she jerked her hand back.

"Now what?" she asked, twisting to take in their surroundings. Blank white nothingness as far as the eye could see.

"You have that control they gave us?"

"I hope so," she said, reaching into her back pocket. She came up with the VR equivalent of the device the dissidents had provided them. "Good old Stewart," she said, hefting it and examining its keypad. "The gear came through perfectly. Now let's see if Maya can get it to work."

"It's supposed to home in on the target signal, right?" Jason asked as Kenna fiddled with the control's center dial. The bronze gadget, a replica of the one pulled from Maya's backpack, had a nickel-size dial at the top and ten soft-touch numbered buttons set deep enough into the front to prevent accidental commands. The contraption looked very much like the primitive television remote controls on display in the broadcast history museum.

"Yeah. And it should maintain enough of a connection between the target VR and our base to be able to manipulate the program's parameters." She turned the dial, making tiny clockwise ticks.

A high-pitched buzzing caused Kenna to clap her free hand to her ear. It didn't help. The sound was in her head.

She tried turning the knob back counterclockwise but the sound continued.

Jason winced, twisting away.

"You hear that, too?" she shouted.

He nodded, grimacing.

Kenna hunched over the control, one shoulder pressed against her ear in a futile attempt to stem the pain from the screaming noise. She fiddled with the dial, typing the code Maya had given them, hoping for relief. Jason paced away from her, his hands fisted above his head, his body bent.

"Silence!" Kenna shouted.

As suddenly as the sound had begun, it ceased.

"Oh," she said.

The sparkling white cloud disappeared.

In its place, Patrick sat strapped to a metal chair facing

her. His hands were cuffed behind him, his feet bound to the chair's front legs. He stared straight ahead, mouth set in a tight line.

The room was square, white. No windows, no doors. No visible means of illumination providing the room's bright light. No means of escape. Hospital-like, sterile, and cold.

"Patrick!" She took off running, vaguely aware of Jason following. Tucking the remote into her back pocket, she sprinted less than five steps when she rammed full force into an invisible barrier. Like metal clanged with a hammer, her body hummed in agonizing reverberation. Stunned, she tumbled backward.

"Whoa," Jason said, breaking her fall and lowering her to the ground.

Kenna's mouth hung slack until her breath returned. It required effort to wheeze, "What was that?"

Jason hit the barrier with the side of his fist, knocking and shouting to be heard through the invisible blockade. Patrick gave no indication of awareness.

"Must be some sort of parameter safeguard," he said. "Or firewall." His hands began to explore the unseen obstruction, his movements like that of a trapped mime.

"Obviously, we're not going to get through this with brute force." Kenna massaged her temples. "We need to think. This is a problem-solving exercise. Like our tests. Except the stakes are real."

Kenna pulled the dissidents' VR control back out of her pocket and studied its numbered keypad. Maya had given them only one code. Kenna typed it in again, then called to the program to respond. Cheered by the acknowledging beep, she ordered the program to release Patrick's bonds.

Nothing happened. She swore under her breath.

Jason stood next to her. "Tell it to lower this force field."

She tried.

Nothing.

"What good is this damn thing if it…" She didn't finish her sentence. Typing in the code again, she tried something else. "Program," she called out, "no lights."

Instantly their area went dark. But the sterile chamber remained bathed in illumination, its occupant still oblivious to his unseen audience.

"What good is this," she asked, "if it only works out here?"

Jason grabbed Kenna's arm. "But look at what you did. We can see where it ends." He tugged at her and began to trot along the border between light and dark. "There might be a way in after all."

Kenna followed as they made a quick circuit around the area. They circled behind Patrick, and she could practically hear his thoughts: *Nothing is real. Everything is perfectly safe.*

When the device in her hand vibrated, she glanced at it. One of the keypad digits flashed. Then another. She looked up long enough to see Patrick's garments disappear. Still strapped to the metal chair, he was now stripped to his shorts.

"Dang! I missed it," Kenna said. "That had to be some sort of control code from whoever is running this program. We could have used that information. Why did I look up? Why?"

"How many digits?"

"Not sure." Kenna tapped her chin with her fist. "One of the numbers was seven, but beyond that I couldn't tell you."

"We'll get in one way or another," Jason said. "We have to."

FIFTY-ONE

Werner banged the front door of AdventureSome. Inside, the lights were on, but the doors were locked. He'd rung the bell several times to no avail. He didn't care what time it was. He'd tried reaching Kenna Ward at her home first, assuming he'd be waking the young woman. How to explain what he needed? He had no idea.

There had been no answer at Kenna's. Desperate, he'd made his way here.

A disembodied voice came through the intercom: "We're closed."

Werner glanced around, finally locating the security camera. Facing it, he adopted an authoritarian tone. "Stewart Mathers? Is that you?"

"Who is this?"

"Werner Trutenko. From the Tribunal. It's urgent you allow me in."

FIFTY-TWO

When the device in Kenna's hand vibrated again, she looked down in time to watch the number seven flash and disappear, followed by the eight, and then the nine. With a quick, surprised glance at Jason, she asked, "Could it be that easy?"

Without waiting for an answer, she typed the three-number sequence in. "Come on," she whispered.

All ten digits flashed at once, which Kenna recognized as defeat. She shook the handheld control, ready to swear at it, but her attention was drawn back to Patrick's sterile chamber.

"Celia Newell?" Kenna exclaimed at her appearance. "What is she doing here?"

The leader of Virtu-Tech stood facing Patrick, hands clasped behind her back, head cocked slightly to one side, looking like a toddler encountering a ladybug for the first time—gentle and inquisitive. Yet the expression in her eyes conveyed she was anything but.

Walking slowly, she circled Patrick's chair. Her mouth moved in a way that suggested calm questioning. She'd speak, wait, and then speak again. Patrick kept his expression impenetrable, his gaze straight and steady. Celia continued to circle, in chillingly placid fashion, as she continued her silent interrogation.

"So, Celia Newell is hooked up to the system?" Jason asked. "Does that mean she's at Chicago's Virtu-Tech headquarters, too?"

"Could be," Kenna said. "That, or she's reaching in from a remote location the way we are."

"Just what we needed," he said. "More unknowns."

Inside the bright tableau, Celia shook her head, expressing dismay. She held her hands up as though in supplication. A second later, a curved, serrated hunting knife appeared in her right hand. A small brown vial in the other.

Kenna went back to trying number variations to break through the entry code. The entire keypad flashed after every failed attempt. "Must be a six-digit code," she said.

"How do you know?" Jason asked.

"The error message begins flashing the keypad after the sixth digit."

"But we know three of them," he said. "We're halfway there."

Kenna glanced up long enough to see Celia grab a handful of reddened skin from Patrick's inner thigh. In a move, so fast Kenna almost didn't see it, she sliced away a three-inch chunk of skin.

Patrick's back arched. His mouth opened to the ceiling in a wail so primal, Kenna could almost believe she heard it.

Kenna banged on the barrier again. "It isn't real!"

Jason gripped her shoulder. "Keep trying," he said. "We'll get there." A second later, he said, "Holy geez."

"What?" she asked. Palms against the invisible barrier, like a kid looking through a plate-glass window, she found herself unable to tear her gaze away. Celia had unscrewed the cap of the vial she held. "What's she got there?"

Jason shook his head. "I'm afraid to guess."

Frozen with uncertainty, Kenna watched as Celia positioned the vial over the bloodied shred of skin that had fallen to the floor. She tipped the container to spill a drop of its contents on top of it.

Instantly the flesh curled, twisting as it smoked and blackened.

She repositioned the vial over Patrick's freshly sliced thigh.

Patrick twisted, wrenching himself away from the woman, the legs of his chair bouncing off the floor from his effort. He kept at it until the chair fell over and his face slammed to the ground, his big legs working against his constraints.

"I'm guessing acid," Jason said. "Damn."

Kenna pounded her fists. Jason pounded his. Like terrified viewers of a silent horror film, they shouted at the scene, knowing their efforts were futile.

Using a device exactly like the one in Kenna's hand, Celia tapped in a code. Patrick's chair righted itself. New clamps appeared, securing the chair's legs to the floor. Celia nodded. She returned to her spot just over Patrick's open wound and poured.

Kenna cried out. She couldn't hear the sizzle of acid against Patrick's skin as the wound bubbled black. She couldn't smell the seared flesh. But as Patrick's body arched back and he pointed his face skyward in a silent scream of agony, she felt his pain. "No," she whispered. Her hand reached out to grab at Jason. "We have to stop her."

Celia turned her face from the burning skin, wrinkling her nose. She capped the bottle. Unruffled, she returned to her interrogation.

FIFTY-THREE

There is not a chance in hell you're getting in," Stewart said when he opened the door to AdventureSome. "You have no business here."

Trutenko slammed a meaty hand against the door's glass pane, obscuring most of the company's cheery logo with his thick fingers. "I have urgent business here," he thundered. "It's a matter of life and death. My brother's life."

Taken aback, Stewart hesitated. Aaron and Maya had taken off shortly after getting Kenna and Jason hooked up and explaining what Stewart needed to know to monitor the situation.

Before she'd gone in, Kenna had provided only the barest of details about what was happening, but she'd been very clear on one point: Virtu-Tech was the bad guy. And Stewart vividly remembered Werner Trutenko as the face of Virtu-Tech.

"Get out before I call the police."

"Please," Trutenko said. "I know you don't trust me. I can't blame you. But I have nowhere else to turn. My brother—" He sucked in a breath. "My brother is in danger."

Stewart shook his head. "I don't know your brother, but I can tell you he's not here. There are thousands of other VR establishments, some of them open twenty-four hours. Maybe your brother's there."

"No." Trutenko banged on the glass again. "I know the dissidents are here."

"No one is here."

"Please. Where can I find them?"

When Stewart tried to shut the door, Trutenko wedged his large frame between it and the jamb. "Virtu-Tech killed Charles Russell," he said. "I was there. I take full responsibility. I recently found out that your associate—the young woman Vanessa—was murdered. The killing must stop. I can help stop it. My brother has been working with the dissidents. But he's been found out."

"So your brother—"

"Is Patrick Danaher. Yes. He's in grave danger." Trutenko's voice cracked. "I need to contact the dissidents. I need their help to save him."

FIFTY-FOUR

Kenna continued seeking the correct three-digit prefix to the known code seven-eight-nine, frustrated by the three-second delay in the system between her attempts. "If I have to go through every single combination, I will."

"Hey," Jason said, interrupting her. "Who's this?"

Kenna sucked in a breath at the new arrival. "That's Tate." She stared down at the device in her hand. "Why didn't the code come up when he came in?"

Jason shook his head, then pointed. "He's got a device of his own. Maybe different codes signal different actions?"

Celia wasted no time. She advanced on Tate, her spine rigid, her cheeks flushed. Handing him the vial of acid, she spoke quickly, authoritatively, and then swept her hand between them in dismissal.

A second later, he was gone.

Kenna's device didn't react.

"I'll keep trying. One of these combinations has to work," she said.

Jason paced behind her. They were silent for several minutes.

"Oh my god," Jason said. "He's back."

"What—" She stopped. In the horrifying seconds it took for the scene to register, she swallowed her next words.

Tate wasn't alone.

He had one arm wrapped around Patrick's wife, Mallory. Bound and gagged, she struggled against her captor, her efforts useless against the tall man's brute strength. Tate's other hand gripped the back of little Ryan's striped polo shirt. Red-faced and screaming, the boy reached for his mother.

"No," Kenna screamed. "No!"

Jason dragged her to face him. "They aren't real," he said. He pulled her by her upper arms, twisting hard. "They aren't real."

Kenna fought. "What if they are?"

"They're not," he said with authority, but Kenna caught the flicker of doubt in his eyes.

"We have to get in there now," she said.

Around the invisible perimeter, Kenna paced behind Patrick as she tried again and again to come up with the proper commands. Something gnawed at her. The numbers—something about them—where had she'd seen them before? If she could get a moment, one solid moment, to clear her mind, she might be able to reach back and remember.

Tate dropped Mallory to the ground and let go of Ryan's shirt. The little boy ran to his mother, all arms and legs. Doing his best to wrap himself around her, he wound up knocking her sideways. Strands of hair stuck to the sides of her face, framing her swollen eyes. She lay on her right side, while little Ryan nuzzled against her, burying his head in her chest, his shoulders shaking. Mallory pressed her cheek against her son's head, in a vain attempt to comfort him.

Arms crossed, Celia watched Patrick.

Kenna shut her eyes, forcing herself to remember.

"What are you doing?" Jason asked.

"Quiet," she snapped.

She stared down at the floor, concentrating. "I know the code," she said half to herself. "I know it. It was in Vanessa's notes." Drawing herself inward, she went silent, fighting through the jumble of recollections, trying to focus. "I didn't recognize it for what it was," she said, her words coming out slowly. Talking it out might make her remember. "And now I...can't...come up with it."

"You will," Jason said.

At movement beyond the barrier, Kenna instinctively looked up.

Tate reached down to grab a handful of Mallory's hair. He yanked—like a kid dragging a stuffed toy—and tossed her toward Patrick. Hands and feet bound, she landed in a heap, facedown. Ryan scrambled over to her, his pudgy fingers working to pull the gag out of her mouth.

The silent horror film continued.

Patrick bared his teeth, stared upward, his eyes clenched shut.

"Good man," Jason said. "He knows none of this is real."

Kenna wondered how long Patrick would be able to hold out. How long before the unrelenting pressure took over. She had tried to convince Charlie that his wounds weren't real. What if Jason was wrong? What if Mallory and Ryan were trapped in VR capsules, too?

Tate hoisted Ryan by his ankles and held him aloft. Kenna turned her back.

"Vanessa," she whispered. "Come through for me, girlfriend."

A hacked connection, she'd said. Static.

Deep within the system, Vanessa had explained, she'd found a series of numbers that repeated themselves, beating a constant, steady rhythm beneath the program it carried. She'd speculated that these numbers were a code that led directly back to the hostile program. When Kenna had gone over Vanessa's notes, she'd assumed these numbers were unique to the original takeover. Now, she wasn't so sure. They were likely a master code that would allow them access inside.

Suddenly Kenna remembered that she'd first thought the scribbles Vanessa left represented a phone number. Almost a phone number. Missing a couple of digits.

Her head shot up. She stared ahead but she saw nothing except an image of the note with Vanessa's loopy handwriting.

"What?" Jason asked.

"Three, seven, six," she recited. "Seven, eight, nine."

"You got it?" His hand reached out to grab the control box, but Kenna pulled away and began inputting the numbers.

Jason faced the violence behind her. He winced.

"Don't turn around," he said. His face pale, he blew out a breath.

Kenna touched the final number and held her breath.

A tiny buzz replied.

She spun as the area filled with sound: Mallory sobbing, her cries muffled by the gag stuffed in her mouth; little Ryan calling out: "Mommy, Mommy," through hiccupy whimpers. Patrick stared at the ceiling, an inhuman groan emanating from deep within his gut.

Kenna knew he was trying to drown out the sounds of his VR family's suffering as his only salvation from immersion. If he allowed himself to succumb to Celia's mind games, he'd be lost exactly the way Charlie had.

Kenna called out for Jason to wait a split second after he bolted toward them. None of those in the disturbing tableau had reacted to their appearance.

Jason hit the barrier, as hard as she had.

"Shit," he shouted when he stood back up. He banged his fists against the invisible wall. He kicked.

"Jason."

A man possessed, he strode up and down the perimeter of their barricade, his face twisted in frustration.

"Only sound," Kenna said unnecessarily. "God, how do we get in?"

Tate came behind Patrick again. He grabbed Patrick's head, pointing his attention toward Celia, who now stood next to Mallory. "Watch," the blond man said.

Patrick shook him off, working his head out of Tate's fingers, pulling his chin to his chest.

"I said *watch*." He held Patrick's head in a vise grip, the index and middle fingers of both hands wrapped around the front of the man's face, pulling Patrick's eyes open.

"I have an idea," Kenna said, turning away.

Jason hit the wall again.

"I think we were close," she said, working fast.

"Oh, God," Jason said, his voice a low moan.

Kenna looked, then wished she hadn't.

Celia pulled Ryan off his mother and held the squirming toddler tightly around the waist. Bent as far as he could, Ryan reached out with chubby arms, his face red with exertion, screaming, "Mommy," but Celia didn't budge.

Celia addressed Patrick. "Don't try to convince yourself this isn't your family," she said in measured tones. "We have them in the VR chamber. They're strapped in exactly the way you are right now, experiencing all of this."

Ryan writhed so violently, Celia nearly lost her grip on the little boy. Grimacing, she clasped tighter and Ryan *whoof*ed into silence.

"Look at what I have here," she said. "A perfect little specimen for practicing new techniques."

Ryan's cries almost drowned out Celia. Little fingers reached up, ineffectually prying at Celia's hands. His face contorted in pain as he squirmed and stretched. "Mommy!"

Celia lowered Ryan so that his feet touched the ground, but she maintained a tight grip on his hair, preventing him from running to his mother. Reduced to a gentle sobbing, he nonetheless held out fat arms and cried.

"Before I do," Celia said, "is there anything you'd like to tell me about the dissidents' plans?"

"He's just a baby," Patrick said. "He doesn't understand that any of this…"

"Shit," Jason said, "he's getting immersed."

Kenna twisted the dial at the top of the control. The high-pitched keening began again, and just as she decided it was as loud and as shrill as it could be, she shouted to Jason. "Be ready."

Her voice dissolved in the piercing signal.

Jason nodded.

"Hurry," he mouthed.

Kenna reached for Jason's hand, placing it on her shoulder. She had no idea how this technology worked, but she thought a connection would help. She felt his muscles tense.

Just as the resonance reached a crescendo, Mellow Mary announced: "Warning. You are entering a scenario with inoperative safety protocols. Virtu-Tech cannot be responsible for personal injury. If you continue, you do so at your own risk. Please acknowledge."

"Fine," Jason shouted to the disembodied voice. "Just let us in!"

Waiting for a moment longer to be sure the resonance was strong, Kenna pressed Vanessa's code numbers quickly yet firmly—there would be no mistake. The instant she hit the final key, the shrill blast silenced, leaving Kenna with its echo pinballing her ears.

They were in.

FIFTY-FIVE

Mallory's eyes went wide with panic and relief. She tilted her head toward Ryan as if to beg Kenna to free him first. Kenna forced herself to ignore them. Mallory and Ryan were virtuals—at least she prayed they were.

Tate's head snapped up, his sweaty red face practically glowing against the yellow-blond of his hair. He launched himself at Kenna, closing the gap in three strides.

Jason charged from Kenna's left, tackling Tate. As the two men went down, Tate's control box clattered across the floor. Kenna bolted for it. Celia lunged, swinging at Kenna's head.

Ducking, Kenna shouldered her out of the way, focusing solely on grabbing the metal box. The gadget had settled near the back of Mallory's neck, where Ryan had wrapped himself around her, hugging her around the shoulders.

Celia kicked, sending Kenna sprawling hard atop of Mallory and knocking little Ryan off his mother. Even as Kenna reached for the dropped control, even though she knew he had to be a virtual, she reacted instinctively to see if the kid was all right.

Celia took advantage, throwing herself full-bodied onto Kenna's back, knocking the wind out of both of them.

Tate wrangled his arms around Jason's back, grimacing as he fought off relentless body punches. Tate wheezed with effort as he struggled onto his stomach, all the while fighting to get a hand into his pocket.

Jason kept at him, grunting, landing hit after hit like slamming meat with a two-by-four. With his teeth clenched against the onslaught, Tate's face was a specter of determination. He winced, his eyes squeezing tight with the fury of each punch, but he worked effort-whitened fingers into his pants pocket.

Bracing a knee to the ground, Tate managed enough leverage to push Jason off his back. Diving out of the range of Jason's tireless fists, he turned long enough for Kenna to see the triumph in his eyes. He'd drawn the vial of acid from his pocket.

Jason lunged. The two men rolled. Tate elbowed Jason in the gut, knocking him back, but giving Tate the precious split second he needed to uncap the vial. When Jason shot forward again, Tate whipped the bottle's contents at his face.

Panting, struggling to her feet, Kenna inputted the code into her controller again, shouting to be heard over the din. "Program!"

Celia's fingernails tore at Kenna's arms, leaving long streaks of red. "Give it to me."

"Change parameters," Kenna shouted.

Celia pinned her facedown, slamming her head against the floor. Without letting go of the control box, Kenna reached her free hand behind her head to jam fingers into Celia's eyes. She twisted away, but not off. Kenna couldn't move, couldn't breathe.

Panting, she ordered the program to change. "Get her off me," she said.

No response. She must have jammed one of the keypad buttons when they fell to the ground. There would be no way to gain control until she inputted the code again.

Celia's arms reached upward along hers, straining to grab hold of the remote, her breath hot against Kenna's left ear. Though a small woman, she packed a lot of muscle.

Pulling the remote under her chest, Kenna jammed the device between her breasts. Arms tight against her body, chin down, she closed herself off from the assault. Celia remained on top of her, legs straddling her hips, sharp fingernails working their way toward the control.

"I will...have it," she panted, digging deeper.

Kenna snapped her head back, striking Celia's cheek. Celia swore but held tight.

"Jason," Kenna shouted, her voice breathless and weak. "Jason!"

Celia snaked her fingers around the control. Kenna stiffened herself, digging her own fingers into the backs of Celia's hands, trying to draw blood.

Sparkles danced before Kenna's eyes, and she knew that at any moment, she'd lose consciousness. "Jason!"

Without warning, the paralyzing pressure lifted. Kenna sucked in a deep breath as she twisted to see Jason throw Celia across the room. His face was covered with blackened burns.

It hurt to breathe, but Kenna clambered to her feet, gripping the remote in her left hand. She began punching the code in with her right.

Shaking his head as though to clear it, Tate rose. He body-slammed Kenna from the left, taking her down hard. She heard rather than felt her bare arms skimming the floor, shredding her skin.

With only one more number to complete the code, she struggled to make the final entry. Drawing her knees up, she cocooned herself, protecting the device from Tate's next onslaught.

Her finger hit the button.

Nine.

"Program," she shouted. "Change parameters."

She thought she heard an acknowledging chirp. Clenching her teeth, she pulled her knees up again, curling her body against Tate's attack. He dragged her onto her back, where she was able to see that Jason, blood dripping from his head, burn marks spreading across his face, had the upper hand with Celia. He'd pinned her arms to the ground and was about to place his knee across her legs when he turned—for the briefest moment—to check on Kenna.

It was one moment too long. Celia rammed a knee into Jason's throat, sending him stumbling backward, hands grasping at his neck. Had she been able to leverage her weight behind the blow, she would have killed him. As it was, his eyes widened in panic as horrific high-pitched attempts to breathe screeched from his throat.

"Jason," Kenna shouted.

He fell to the ground, body convulsing.

Inches from Kenna, Tate's nose dripped blood from a bubbling gash over his right eye. Teeth bared like a dog, he growled as he wrestled for the control.

Kenna opened her mouth to shout for a weapon, but as Tate snatched the box away, he cracked an elbow into her jaw, silencing her command and gasping out one of his own.

The man's weight lifted off her as the program complied with the command.

Kenna scrambled on all fours, making her way to Jason, whose breathing was still too shallow, too fast. An inhuman whistle. On his side now, with both hands gripping his throat, blue tinge crept up his face. Red rimmed his irises as mortal absorption sucked him into its death grip.

She reached into Jason's shirt and dug for his emergency signal medallion. She resisted turning at the scuffling behind her. There was no room for error, she thought as her fingers gripped the silver metallic chain. She had to find it before—

Fingers dug into her shoulder, spun her around, and then backhanded her.

Kenna fell to the ground, then twisted onto her hands and knees. She looked up.

Celia stood above her, so close her tiny frame eclipsed the rest of the room. She smiled in triumph. "Did you really believe you could stop our plans?" Behind Kenna, Jason wheezed. "Clearly, you suffer delusions of grandeur."

Like a sinister ringmaster introducing the center ring attraction, Celia stepped aside, gesturing to direct Kenna's attention to the creature behind her.

Frozen to the spot, Kenna breathed, "My god."

The werewolf was bigger this time, its hairy limbs extending from torn clothes—half the size it'd been when she fought it the first time. She had no weapon. She had no backup. Jason couldn't help her now.

Jason.

His uneven keening pierced through her fear, propelling her into action. Without shifting her concentration, she whipped her right hand behind her, feeling Jason's face, moving her fingers down his chest till she could grasp his signal medallion.

Jason grabbed her arm, thrust it away, his voice a weak gasp. "No."

Standing on his two hind legs, the werewolf opened its extended muzzle. Saliva dripped from its yellow fangs. A growl came from deep within its belly as it started toward her, blond claws reaching.

Celia whipped her arm out in front of it, stopping the beast in its tracks.

The werewolf's head snapped to stare at Celia, its blue eyes blazing with anticipation. "Let me get rid of her now."

Holy crap, Kenna thought when she heard it speak.

"We need information on all the others first," Celia said.

Kenna grabbed for the medallion again. Jason clutched her arm.

His hold was strong, but it was a grip of desperation, rather than one of true strength. He was dying—they both knew it.

"You've got to live," she whispered, as her thumb jammed the medallion's button.

Jason disappeared.

FIFTY-SIX

The moment he was gone, Kenna stood. "I'll give you whatever you want." When her voice boomed, she hoped they wouldn't realize it was hysteria talking. All she could hope to do now was let bravado carry her through. She pointed to Patrick. "If you let him go."

Celia arched a brow. "Just Danaher?" she asked in feigned confusion. "What about the rest of the happy little family?"

"They're virtuals, and you know it," Kenna said, hoping to God she was right. She needed the control box, but Celia had tucked it away. Tate the werewolf had the other. Where he held it, she couldn't begin to guess.

"Are you sure about that?" Turning toward the Tate-wolf, Celia pointed toward Ryan.

Lightning fast, the wolf snatched the back of the little boy's striped shirt. He screamed. Elevating the kicking youngster, the Tate-wolf held him above his nose. The monster's mouth widened, his black-rimmed lips thick with drool.

Patrick turned his head away.

Celia grabbed Patrick's chin. "You will watch," she ordered. "See what you did. Your family is about to die, and it's all your fault." Spinning, she addressed the Tate-wolf. "Do it slowly. One piece at a time. Prolong it. I want Daddy to hear his little boy scream."

The Tate-wolf nodded. He swung Ryan by his shirt like a magician inducing a hypnotic trance with a pocket watch. "Danaher," Tate crooned. The beast's blue eyes focused on Mallory, and it licked its chops.

Eyes clenched, Patrick's lips moved. Kenna knew he must be telling himself that nothing is real.

Kenna scanned the bare area, desperate for any means of defeating the giant wolf when she spotted a bulge in Celia's breast pocket.

She lunged, taking the woman by surprise. Slamming an elbow into her temple and then wrenching her head backward, she threw Celia to the floor. Celia shouted, but Ryan's screams drowned her out.

Kenna turned Celia onto her back, beating her fists into the woman's face, invigorated as tissue gave way beneath her furious poundings. Blinded by determination, she couldn't tell if the bubbling blood gushed from Celia's nose or mouth. Her signal medallion necklace jangled out from her blouse; Kenna wrapped the metal chain around the woman's neck and wrenched it tourniquet tight.

Celia blinked blood. She braced an arm on the floor in an effort to boost herself, to loosen the metal chain around her neck. On her feet now, Kenna delivered a sharp kick to the woman's chin. She fell back, flat, swollen fingers twitching.

The Tate-wolf clawed at Mallory's clothing as little Ryan beat at the creature's back. Tate shook the child off, flinging him away.

He has to be a virtual. He has to be.

Still conscious, Celia rocked from side to side, fingers clawing at her neck. Her face, contorted with effort, began turning blue. Fingers slick with blood, Kenna needed three tries to retrieve the control box from Celia's pocket.

Kenna tapped in the first numbers of the VR code as Celia managed to snag a finger under the necklace. With wide, red eyes, she wriggled two more fingers under, choke-gasping for breath. Her fingers reached her signal medallion. Seconds later, the woman's battered form was gone.

"Damn!" Kenna shouted.

When she spun to face the Tate-wolf, she was taken aback by an unexpected appearance. Werner Trutenko stood in front of Patrick's chair, glaring up at the yellow-furred beast.

"Stand down, Tate."

Kenna tapped in the code. "Program," she commanded. "Delete virtuals."

Mallory and Ryan disappeared. Kenna whispered thanks under her breath.

"Get out of my way," the Tate-wolf said to Trutenko. The wolf's great claws whistled as they sliced through the air to carve crimson rivers into Trutenko's chest.

Trutenko doubled over, then fell to the ground.

"How much power you got now, big man? I've been dying to take you down, you stupid son of a—"

"Over here," Kenna shouted.

Hunched, the Tate-wolf twisted.

"This is for Charlie."

As the Tate-wolf advanced on her, she shouted again. "Program: weapon, Marlin Guide Gun."

Continuing her orders, she shouted. "Forty-five seventy."

Confusion traced across the Tate-wolf's deformed features. Canine-human, its blue eyes widened as the old-fashioned weapon appeared in Kenna's hands.

Bending her knees, she pointed the barrel at the beast's enormous body and barked her final command.

"Load with solid ammunition," she bellowed, drawing out the words, "in sterling...fucking...silver."

She cracked the lever forward and back, chambering the first round. Sighting the beast, she took a breath. Held it. Then squeezed the trigger. A jolt exploded into Tate's center mass as the recoil pounded her shoulder.

He slashed the air, screaming. Yet he kept moving toward her.

Cha-chunk. Another round chambered.

She sighted, held her breath.

Tate lunged.

She fired.

The rifle's barrel shot yellow flame.

Tate staggered back, clutching his belly. Black blood bubbled between its claws.

Cha-chunk. Another round.

She fired again.

Writhing, screeching, the Tate-wolf dropped to the ground.

Kenna strode forward and emptied the remaining rounds into Tate's chest, gut, and head.

"Take that, you filthy son of a bitch."

FIFTY-SEVEN

The two blue-shirted paramedics elevated Jason's gurney with a metallic snap. One spoke into his radio. "Adult male exhibiting symptoms of shock. Likely grade-three mortal absorption." He took a quick breath, even as they began to move out. "Vital signs weak, breathing labored. Patient is unconscious, cyanotic."

"Will he be okay?" Stewart asked, trying to read the seriousness of the situation from the older paramedic's face, but the man wouldn't make eye contact. Neither would the young guy.

The younger, short and Hispanic, dragged a clipboard out from under the gurney as his partner wheeled Jason toward the door and out to the waiting ambulance. "Next of kin?" he asked Stewart.

"I...I have that information on file. Just a minute."

Torn between distress over Jason's well-being and alarm for Kenna in the nearby capsule, Stewart hesitated.

Behind him, the console emitted a series of chirps alerting him to dangerous distortions in Kenna's vital signs. Stewart moved toward the control panel.

Halfway out the door, the veteran paramedic said, "We'll get the patient's info from you later." His voice was strained. "Let's go, José. The patient is in shock."

As the younger man hurried to join his partner, Stewart called out. "Please," he said. "What if Kenna needs help?"

José alternated glances between his partner and Stewart. The other medical tech raised his voice to be heard as he headed out the door. "We'll radio for another team for her."

Stewart had expected Kenna to emerge from the program any moment now. She should have returned with Jason.

The ambulance departed AdventureSome with a mournful wail. Stewart pressed his thumb and fingers into his eye sockets. His head throbbed, his eyes burned, and his stomach chugged sour. What was taking Kenna so long to disengage?

FIFTY-EIGHT

F eet planted wide, gun pointed downward, Kenna panted
over the dead beast. Her entire body heaved with each
breath. She stank of sweat and fear and fury. Every pore
oozed pure hatred. Blood ran down her face and dripped on
the floor. She had no idea where she'd been cut.

"Kenna," Patrick rasped.

As she hurried over to him, a scuffle behind her made her
spin, knees bent, rifle ready. "Reload," she called.

Ready for the creature to rise up again, she remained utterly
still, waiting, watching, hearing nothing but echoes in her head
and Patrick's labored gasps next to her.

The creature moved.

"Damn you," she said under her breath.

It didn't, however, leap up. Didn't resurrect itself like some
hideous monster from a horror flick. The Tate-wolf's image
buzzed—a noise that didn't come from within the creature
but from around it. The werewolf's right claw trembled, then
began to shrink.

Humming, the claw's knifelike nails receded. The wolf's
tail disappeared. Human legs replaced fur-covered ones. The
being slimmed and shortened. In seconds, the creature was gone
and Tate lay before her, nearly naked, with a blue Virtu-Tech
infinity logo tattooed near his shoulder. His blond head reclined
in a bloodied pink mess, his features almost angelic in repose.

Except for the bullet holes punched everywhere, he looked like he could have been sleeping. Kenna's index finger eased from the safe position to caress the trigger. She almost wished the bastard was still alive so she could kill him again.

"Kenna..."

Blood chugged out from Patrick's right side. He blinked with effort.

"Oh my god, Patrick," Kenna said, kneeling next to him.

He tilted his head toward Trutenko, who lay motionless on the floor. "Save him. Save my brother."

"I'm saving *you*," Kenna said. She grabbed Patrick's chin. "Look at me," she said.

He clenched his eyes, grimacing. He blinked several times and tried to meet her gaze.

"Look at me," she demanded. Tightening her grip on his chin, she adjusted herself to see his eyes. Red rings circled his irises. "None of this is real," she said.

He coughed. Blood spurted from his side. "Feels pretty real."

"Patrick." Her voice rose in panic. "You're perfectly safe."

He pulled in his lips, held himself in check for a moment before his words burst out in a gasp. "Too much. Too long. Can't...handle it."

The rim around his iris widened, and the red grew more intense. The pressure behind his eyes had to be unbearable.

"We've got to get you out of here."

He wore no signal medallion. Tugging hers from her neck, she started to put it over Patrick's head, but he pulled away. "No," he said, nodding toward the floor again. "Get him out of here."

Trutenko had regained consciousness enough to lever himself into a sitting position. "Oh dear God," he said, grasping his midsection. "I had no idea it could be like this." A second later, he faced his brother. "Take her medallion."

With effort, Patrick shook his head. "I'm tethered at headquarters, Celia is there. Tate is there. Armed security is there. How long do you think I'll last? Go now. Before they come back."

"Where are you exactly?" Kenna asked Patrick. "What floor? I'll send help."

"It's too late."

"Where. Are. You?" she asked again.

"Third floor. Capsule number two." Patrick coughed. "Liberty, Kenna, liberty. Everything is at stake. You must stop them. Find Maya. She knows what to do."

"Maya got me in here," she said. "I won't leave you now."

"You have to," he said. "Or liberty is lost."

FIFTY-NINE

Kenna threw her headgear to the floor. ""Where are Maya and Aaron?"

"They left as soon as you were in." Stewart pointed. "Doing whatever they can to get into Virtu-Tech headquarters."

"Get one of them on the phone," she told Stewart as she raced from her capsule. "Trutenko's here?"

Stewart nodded.

"Where?"

Stewart indicated the next room. "What do I tell them?"

She stopped at the doorway long enough to answer, "I'll talk. Just get them on the line." A second later, she turned back. "How's Jason?"

"Alive when the paramedics took him," Stewart said. "What happened?"

Ignoring the question, she made her way into the chamber Trutenko occupied. "Are you all right?" she asked when the older man emerged from his capsule.

"I think so," he said.

His face ashen, his gait unsteady, he didn't seem very well at all. But right now, Patrick was her immediate concern. "How can I get inside Virtu-Tech's headquarters?" she asked.

"Without a valid badge?" he asked. "Impossible."

"Unacceptable," she said. "We need to get your brother out of there. Do you have your security pass with you?"

"Of course, but security has probably canceled my authorizations by now. If we attempt to use it, we'll bring all of Virtu-Tech down on our heads."

Stewart ran in, phone in hand. "Kenna."

She grabbed it. "Patrick's fighting absorption," she said. "I don't know if he's going to make it. He's at the Chicago headquarters, third floor, chamber two. Can you do anything?"

"On it," Aaron answered. "Meet us there."

"How will I get in?"

"Improvise," he said.

When Kenna hung up, she snatched her jacket and slid it on. Trutenko grabbed her arm. "I'll come with you."

The man was still reeling from his VR encounter; he could only slow her down. "No, you and Stewart stay here."

"I can't sit back and do nothing."

"Fine. Give me your pass."

"But it won't—"

"Just give it."

When he complied, she tucked it into her jacket pocket. "Where might Celia be if she's not with Patrick?"

"Her office is on the fifth floor," Trutenko said.

"Got it." Kenna made eye contact with Stewart and then Trutenko. "Now, you both need to do exactly as I say."

✦

When Kenna stepped out the front door of AdventureSome, she was shocked to see hundreds of people milling around outside the nearby Virtu-Tech offices, despite the morning's chill. Her heart skipped a beat. *Is this about Patrick?*

"What happened?" she asked two women standing along the curb. Both wore company badges on lanyards around their necks.

"Fire evacuation," the younger one answered. "They say it isn't a drill, but I don't believe it. These things are always false alarms."

Kenna took off again, pushing her way through the scattered groups that made up the chattering crowd. She kept her head down as she raced around to the rear of the building, where a number of employees were taking a smoke break and fire department access doors stood wide-open. With so many bystanders, there was no way for her to sneak in unnoticed.

Walking past the smokers as though she had every reason to be there, Kenna pulled her jacket tighter. She made her way to the far end of the building, then ducked behind garbage dumpsters next to a door labeled "Keep Out." Banking on it automatically unlocking in response to the fire alarm, she tried the door's handle. Luck was with her. It opened easily and quietly.

Holding her breath, she stole inside to find herself in a tall industrial room that smelled of metal and wet concrete. A black iron spiral staircase led to a catwalk where maintenance workers could more closely inspect the fat pipes that ran along the walls and ceilings and be able to access their giant valves.

The area was empty, save for the thrum of machinery and the hiss of compressed air. She bolted for the staircase and hurried up to the catwalk. Running now, she sped toward the exit door at its far end.

"Hey!"

Kenna spun.

A firefighter on the floor below gestured. "Get back down here," he said. "You can't be inside until we issue an all clear."

She pulled Trutenko's pass out of her jacket pocket, keeping her fingers over the photo of his face.

"Ah…It's an emergency," she said thinking fast. "My medication. I left it upstairs." Without giving him a chance to respond, she grabbed the door's handle. "Thanks for letting me get it," she shouted over her shoulder, even though he clearly had no intention of doing so. "You're a lifesaver."

Thinking of Patrick, she hoped that proved true.

The shabby two-toned beige corridor ahead let Kenna know that she was still in the back rooms of the structure. Although she'd only been inside Virtu-Tech's local headquarters once before, she remembered its open floor plan. This was not it.

She sighed with relief at the sight of the stairway/exit sign at the far end of the hallway. Running full speed now to outpace that firefighter, if he'd opted to come after her, she made it to the doorway in three heartbeats. Stopping, she gently eased open the door and peered in. The stairway was clear.

Breathing through her mouth, she took the steps two at a time, treading as lightly as she could. The less noise she created, the better her chances of making it to Patrick unseen.

At the third-floor landing, she cracked the door open wide enough to get a view of the corridor. This was the Virtu-Tech she remembered. Gray-blue carpet, sky-blue walls, and the kind of indirect lighting that gave everyone's head a golden glow. Best of all, no one nearby.

Quietly, she stole into the corridor, dropping to her hands and knees. The building's center atrium made for a bright and sunlit working space, but the risk of being seen from firemen on other floors was too great for her to remain upright.

Taking in her surroundings, she managed to get her bearings. Trutenko had told her that VR chamber number two was on the building's north side. She was on the east.

"I'm coming, Patrick," she whispered. "Hang on."

How long could his body hold out against what his brain believed? Was it longer than Charlie had fought before he'd succumbed? She didn't know. And what about Tate? Although his werewolf avatar had been killed, had the man survived?

She crept along the wall, hyperaware of sound and movement. On the floor below her, firefighters called out to one another as they made their way from room to room.

"Over here," came a loud shout from the floor below. "Found another one of the tripped alarms."

"That's two down," a colleague responded. "One to go."

A third voice chimed in. "So, what is this anyway? Some kind of prank?"

"Probably an angry employee looking to cause trouble," the first voice said.

"Whoever it is should get his ass fired."

"Better than shooting up the place," the third guy said.

All three men made noises of amenable disgust.

Still on her hands and knees, Kenna crawled along the wall until she made it to the north end of the building and spotted the door to VR chamber number two. Enormous from the looks of it. Kenna tried to guess how many capsules it held. She rose to a crouch and hurried until she was directly outside.

She'd prepared as best she could. This was real life, not VR, she reminded herself. No calling up weapons or changing parameters. Whatever lay beyond this door, she had to face with instinct, strength, and whatever she carried on her person. She drew out one of the two items she'd armed herself with—a heavy pair of shears—and gripped them high in her right hand *Psycho*-style, prepared to attack. She fervently hoped she wasn't bringing scissors to a gunfight.

She wrapped her fingers around the door's handle. Locked.

Unsurprised, she dug out Trutenko's badge and checked her surroundings one more time. If using it did set off an alarm, what better time to do it than when sirens were ringing all over the building already?

She got to her feet and swiped the badge. Rather than a security alert, she heard the satisfying *click* of the door unlocking itself. She turned the handle and pushed.

SIXTY

Frantic activity inside the chamber stopped Kenna short. Startled by her appearance, Aaron and Maya leaped away from the tech stations they'd been manning to take up defensive positions. Both held semiautomatic handguns, pointed directly at Kenna and her silver shears.

A tense heartbeat later, all three took a breath and lowered their weapons.

Kenna started to ask about Patrick when she noticed someone else in the room. "How did you—?"

Maya gestured. "Hurry up. Make sure the door's locked behind you."

Aaron returned to his keyboard.

"Where did you get the guns?" Kenna asked. "When you broke into my apartment you said you were unarmed."

"Would you have let us in if we'd told you the truth?" Aaron asked.

Starkly illuminated, the chamber was even bigger than Kenna had expected, outfitted in blinding white with four opaque VR capsules lining the far wall. The only color came from the computer monitors and the people in the room.

Seated on the floor with her back against one of the capsules, Celia's legs were splayed, her arms limp, and her head tilted down to one side. Dark hair covered much of her face.

"Is she dead?" Kenna asked.

"Unfortunately not," Aaron answered. "Maya worked her magic, but she's only temporarily subdued. Long enough to—"

"Patrick," Kenna interrupted. "Where is he?"

"Still hooked into the system. Over here." Aaron opened the second capsule from the door.

"He's alive?" Kenna asked as she pulled out her phone and began to dial.

Aaron's expression was grim. "His vitals have stabilized, but he's still in bad shape. Maya's afraid we may need to do a cold shutdown."

"Don't!" Kenna spun as though to run back to the control panels. "Patrick's mind is in no condition to handle that kind of shock."

Aaron grabbed her arm. "Hang on. We know that," he said. "Maya isn't pulling Patrick out. Not yet. She's working on something more important."

Kenna was about to ask what that was, but Stewart picked up her call.

"I'm here. It's a go," Kenna said into the phone. When he acknowledged, she hung up. "What's Maya doing?" she asked Aaron. "What do you mean by 'she worked her magic'?"

"When we got here, Celia was running tech where Maya is now," he said as they hurried toward Patrick's capsule. "That woman was plenty disoriented but apparently alert enough to send a replacement in. We assume it was whoever had been running her tech."

Kenna hoped to God that Stewart and Trutenko had followed her instructions to the letter. As she reached Patrick's capsule, one of the wall monitors sounded a new alert.

"No way," Aaron exclaimed as he sprinted for the display. "Patrick's coming out? No way is that possible."

"Yes!" Kenna fisted both hands in triumph. Before she'd left AdventureSome, she'd outlined a plan to send Trutenko back into the sterile-room scenario. Stewart was to remain at the controls but assist Trutenko in arming himself. Most important of all, Trutenko would be sent in carrying in a signal medallion for his brother. The men would wait for Kenna's all clear to send Patrick out.

It was the best she could come up with given the circumstances.

Kenna threw open the capsule, breathing a prayer of thanks that her hastily cobbled-together plan worked. The signal medallion had begun to bring Patrick's mind back to his convulsing body. Patrick lay on his side on the floor, shivering. Though not stripped to his underwear as he had been in the scenario, his shredded shirt offered little cover. He must have put up quite a fight. She peeled off her jacket and placed it across his bare chest.

He took a shuddering breath.

"He's out," she said.

Kenna gently removed Patrick's headgear the moment he was fully disengaged. "Patrick," she said. The man's eyes fluttered. "Wake up. You're safe. You're okay."

"Another subject coming out." Aaron's fingers flew at the controls. He focused on the monitor but called over his shoulder. "Maya?"

"On it," she answered. "Have to reload the program."

"Shut the system down cold," Kenna said. "He won't know what hit him."

"Too late," Maya said.

A moment later, the door of another capsule opened and a young, muscular guy emerged. Dark-haired, formidable, and wearing an expression of biting fury, he grasped his left bicep with his right hand. "What the hell?" he asked. "Nobody told me I'd be getting shot at in there." A moment later, he seemed to comprehend that those surrounding him were not the people he'd expected to see.

Kenna jumped to her feet, pulling her scissors out again. Why didn't Maya and Aaron draw their guns?

"Almost there," Maya said.

With a growl of fury, the young guy lunged. Kenna skipped out of his reach but not far enough. He snagged her by the arm, throwing her to the floor.

"Hurry," Aaron shouted.

"One more second." Maya's voice was confident, though strained. "Now." She twisted to watch.

When the guy lunged again, he stopped mid-motion like a windup toy at its final *click*. Mouth open, he grunted as he took a lurching step to regain his balance. His eyes rolled white. He attempted one more step, but his knees bent and he collapsed to the floor as Kenna tried to get up. He landed hard on Kenna's twisted right leg. She stifled a scream as she heard something pop.

"You okay?" Maya asked.

"Ah, ah." Kenna extricated her leg from beneath the man. Her knee began to swell almost instantly.

"Anything broken?"

Kenna didn't think so. She worked the joint. Excruciating but not immobile. She shook her head, in too much pain to speak.

"Good. Take your time." Aaron blew out a breath. "That's what I meant by Maya's magic," he said. "She wrote a program that temporarily disables a person's implant—and the brain it's attached to. They'll come around in about a half hour. By then we should be gone." He pointed. "That's Nick Rejar, by the way. Celia's right-hand man. Her golden boy."

Kenna nodded acknowledgment as she worked to beat back the searing pain in her knee. She could get through this. She'd been through worse. "What about…the firefighters?" she asked, finding her voice. "How are we going to get past them? How did *you* get past them?"

"That's Aaron's superpower," Maya answered from her perch at the monitor. "They haven't invented a security system he can't breach."

"Usually I need more time to study it," he said with a shake of his head, though he seemed pleased by the compliment. "We were supposed to have another month. I had to circumvent this system with almost no warning and nothing but instinct to guide me." He waved away Kenna's other question. "By manipulating the sensors in the operations office, we managed to convince the fire department that a team had already cleared this floor. We're good." He tilted his head. "You sure you're okay?"

"I will be," Kenna said. The sharp pain had begun to subside but the swelling continued to grow. "We should call paramedics for Patrick."

Aaron made a noise of disapproval. "Sure, and then we get kicked out before the job is done."

Wincing, Kenna lowered herself to the floor next to Patrick again. "Patrick." She laid a hand against his cheek. "It's okay. You're going to be all right."

"Tell him I need help," Maya called from across the room.

"With what?"

Aaron had moved to the last VR capsule—the only one they hadn't examined. They opened it to find Tate lying on his back. When Kenna had left him, he'd been on his side.

"That one." Kenna pointed. "Is he still alive?"

"Barely."

"He killed Charlie. Fry his brain so hard we hear the sizzle."

Aaron sucked in a hard breath. "Ah, Kenna," he said. "No."

Kenna struggled to get to her feet. "I'll do it myself then."

"Don't." Aaron moved to intercept her. "You don't want to do this."

"You don't know what I want."

Aaron placed a hand on Kenna's forearm. "But you don't want to *be* one of them, do you?"

Kenna worked her jaw. Frustrated and furious, she tugged out of Aaron's hold and hobbled back to Patrick's side.

"Come on, buddy," she coaxed. "Wake up."

Patrick's eyes fluttered again but didn't open. Instead, they clenched shut. His mouth flatlined white. Still shivering, he shook his head. Moments later, his lips began to move. "'Everything,'" he whispered, slurring, "'is perfectly safe.'"

From his position at the monitor, Maya swore. "We're not going to get anywhere with him. He's too far gone."

"Patrick," Kenna tried again, "we don't have much time. Please come back to us." When he didn't respond, Kenna looked over to Maya. "What did you need?" she asked. "Maybe I can help?"

"Only if you can escalate my privileges from here." Her fingers never stopped moving. Her focus never shifted from the monitor. "I need to execute the payload Patrick installed, but we're screwed because I was supposed to have access to the security engineer's workstation. It's offline. I've been trying other stations but none of them have high enough clearance. Patrick would know the best attack vector, but unless he regains consciousness soon, my capacity to corrupt will be limited."

"How much damage can you cause?"

"Enough so that they'll have to scramble to recover. But that's not good enough. I'm blowing stuff up as I go, creating chaos," she said. "Patrick dropped the program into the system weeks ago. It's been copying itself across the network waiting for the command to execute the payload." At this, she turned to Kenna. "If I could do that," she said with a frustrated nod toward Patrick, "we could take down Virtu-Tech permanently."

SIXTY-ONE

Kenna held Patrick's hand, hoping that physical contact would help restore his mind-body connection. "You're out. Your family is safe. You made it." She and Aaron exchanged an anxious glance. "Maya is here, too. She needs you. We need you."

"'Nothing,'" Patrick said, slurring again, "'is real.'"

"Maya needs escalated privileges," Kenna went on. "She can't get there without you."

Aaron took up a position next to Maya's. "What can I do?"

"Scan as much as you can. See if anything pops. Looks familiar," she said. "Knowing Patrick, he would have dropped the program in more than one location—" She stopped at the unmistakable sounds of employees returning to work. "Damn," she said quietly. "Door's locked, right?"

"It is," Kenna said. "But what's to stop an authorized person from coming in?"

"Not a darned thing," Maya said as she scanned the data before her.

"Wait," Kenna said, clumsily clambering to her feet. She ran over to Celia's lifeless form and reached around the back of the woman's neck. "Would logging in from Celia's machine help?"

"If I could find hers, yeah," Maya said without turning. "But from here I don't have visibility."

"Celia's office is on the fifth floor." Kenna turned around with a flourish. She held the woman's security badge aloft. "And *this* will get us in."

✦

Minutes later, Maya and Kenna stole out of chamber number two with Celia's badge around Kenna's neck and Nick's around Maya's. Aaron stayed back to keep watch over Patrick and ensure their Virtu-Tech captives didn't cause trouble. Kenna's scissors and wire had finally come in handy. When Celia, Nick, and Tate regained consciousness, they'd find themselves bound and unable to move.

"And if Celia's machine is password-protected?" Maya asked under her breath as the two made their way along the corridor. "Then what?"

"Then we're no worse off than we were before." Kenna tried hard not to limp. "Aaron is doing his best to continue 'blowing stuff up' as you put it. We have to hope that Celia is so supremely confident in the strength of this pass"—Kenna grabbed it by a corner—"that she doesn't log out every time she steps away."

"That's a whole lot of hope you got there," she said.

"Yeah, well, what else have we got?"

On their way to and up the stairwell, they passed a handful of employees returning to work after the impromptu evacuation. Not one of them paid Kenna or Maya any attention.

As they stepped out onto the fifth floor, Kenna headed to the right, striding with purpose, ignoring the pain in her leg, and scanning the area for clues. Maya followed. "This is the way to her office?"

"I have no idea," she whispered. "But if we look lost it'll be obvious we don't belong here."

"We got lucky," Maya said. "It doesn't seem as though anyone has gotten back up here yet."

She was right. The entire level appeared deserted.

Across the atrium, Kenna spotted a set of ornate double doors with an unoccupied desk set outside of them. She gestured with her chin. "There."

"Yes. That's got to be it," Maya said. Picking up their pace even though every step made Kenna flinch, they made their way around the balcony. Gold raised letters spelled out Celia's name and title on the dark carved door. The empty desk, with papers strewn across the blotter and a half-empty water bottle next to the computer monitor, made it look as though its occupant—nameplate: Drew—had been unexpectedly called away.

Kenna pulled her badge up.

From their left came the distinctive sound of an ascending elevator.

"Hurry," Maya whispered.

Like she didn't know that.

As the elevator slid into place, dinging with its arrival, Kenna swiped.

With a *click* and push, they were in.

Shutting the door quickly, Maya started for the giant desk across the room. Her pace slowed slightly as she made her way around. "This is crazy," she said. "How much room does one person need?"

This was the first time Kenna had ever been in Celia's office, too. "I don't know, but talk about intimidating." She stared up at the portraits on the wall. Vefa Noonan and Simon Huntington watched them from above. The two geniuses who had brought VR to the masses. They'd envisioned a better, stronger society. A happier world. Not at all what Virtu-Tech had planned. And if she and Maya were successful, everything the two men had ever worked for would be destroyed.

"I'm sorry," she whispered to them. "But there's no alternative."

Maya settled herself in Celia's chair.

Kenna made her way across the room to stand next to her. She held her breath.

A moment later, the desk phone's intercom sounded. "Celia, I'm back." The voice was youthful, masculine. This must be Drew from the messy desk outside. "Is there anything you need?"

Maya and Kenna turned to each other shrugging helplessly. Kenna leaned forward, pressed the button, then grunted a negative, "Nnnn-nnn."

She disconnected. "Hurry."

"Celia wasn't logged in," Maya said. "Give me her badge."

Kenna complied.

Maya examined it and smiled as she set to work. "Let me in, pretty baby. Let me in. Let me in." She whispered it like a mantra. A moment later, she smiled in victory. "A lot of people record their passwords on their ID badges. *Tsk, tsk*. Very unsafe."

"You're in?" Kenna asked.

"Yup," Maya answered, feverishly tapping keys. "Should be a simple matter of double-clicking." Scanning the display, she said, "Yassssss," then double-clicked.

Instead of executing, a box opened, presenting more choices. Reminding Kenna of a zip file, it expanded to offer a host of options. There had to be two hundred of them.

The intercom sounded again. "Glen is on his way over," the young man at the outer desk said. "He said he's having trouble accessing the inventory files."

"No surprise there." Maya said to Kenna. "One of the things I blew up."

Kenna pressed the button again. "Mmm-hmm," she said. She hoped that would be enough to keep the kid happy. With any luck they'd be long gone before this Glen guy showed up.

Maya ran a finger along the row of files. "I know what Patrick did here. He played it safe by installing it on as many privileged machines as he could."

"No one noticed it?"

"Not if he hid it in a slew of innocuous-looking files. Hiding it in plain sight so that an IT manager wouldn't notice it. So that Celia wouldn't notice it."

"But he didn't tell you the name?"

"He never got the chance. We had to accelerate our timeline, remember? Patrick was convinced Celia suspected Trutenko. He thought he was safe. None of us could have anticipated what she had in mind for Patrick down there."

"What can we do?" Kenna asked with a glance at the door.

"Try them one by one," Maya said. "What else can we do?" She clicked.

Nothing.

"Scroll down," Kenna said.

"Why?"

"Like you said to Aaron downstairs. Something may pop."

"Could be a waste of time."

"Could save time." Kenna pounded the heel of her hand against the desk. "Scroll."

The icons slid by alphabetically: Adams, Autonomy, Bartlett, Democracy, Franklin, Freedom, Gwinnett, Jefferson...Names and words having to do with the founding fathers, the Revolutionary War, the heroes...

"That's it!"

"What?" Maya asked.

"Liberty." She pointed. "Right there. Patrick's nickname. And he said it to me before I came out. He said it."

"Got it," Maya said as she double-clicked. "Patrick has a nickname?"

"Yeah, Liberty. Because of Patrick Henry. Remember from grammar school? 'Give me liberty—'"

With an exultant shout, Maya thrust two fists in the air. "Oh yeah! Payload!"

The intercom voice came back. "Are you all right, Celia?"

Kenna clicked the machine again. "Mmm-hmm."

Maya studied the program's progression, her smile growing wider by the second. "Oh yeah. That's what we want to see. Right here."

"You designed this virus?" Kenna asked.

"Team effort," she said. "Simon's the one who gave us the idea. He saw where things were going and decided to come up with a fail-safe. Charlie knew we were working on it. A couple of the others—Aaron, Sabra, Edgar—helped brainstorm, too. I brought the final version home. And Patrick dropped it where it needed to be."

Kenna blew out a breath of relief. Her shoulders relaxed. Even her leg felt better. She stood next to Maya and the monitor with a sense of serenity she hadn't expected.

Patrick was still in danger. Jason, too. But they'd at least accomplished what Charlie had originally set out to do.

"We need to get medical help for Patrick," she said.

Maya nodded. "I'll call Aaron."

As she did, Kenna phoned Stewart to give him an update and get help. "We're stuck in Celia's office right now. Aaron is on the third floor with Patrick. There's no way any of us are getting out of here without being noticed."

"Got it," he said. "I'll see what I can do."

The intercom again: "Glen is here. Should I send him in?"

Kenna pressed the button. "No," she said in her best impression of Celia. After disconnecting, she turned to Maya. "We can't stay here. What now?"

"Back door," she said pointing.

"Excellent," Kenna said. "But what if they shut Celia's computer down?"

"There's no stopping the program now," she said, grinning. "Boom! All their data, all their technological research, all their ability to control VR globally is about to disappear forever."

"How long will it take?"

"Hard to say," she said. "Give me a couple of seconds to delete our footprints here, and we'll sneak out the back way."

"What are you doing?"

Two men stood in the doorway. The younger one wore an expression of pure panic. "I didn't let them in," he said to his companion. "I swear."

Kenna recognized the voice from the intercom. Drew. The other one must be Glen.

He strode forward, Drew in his wake. "Who are you?"

"Security," Maya said, waving Nick's badge. "We heard there was trouble up here with the alarms."

Drew stepped closer. "Where's Celia? Does she know you're here?"

"Of course," Kenna said as she eased around the desk, pretending she felt no pain. "She's tied up with a delicate matter on the third floor, so she sent us up here to check."

"Let me see that ID again," Glen said. He turned to Drew. "Call security, I want them up here just in case."

Without a thought of her injuries, Kenna sprinted at the two men. Grunting with effort, she swung at Drew's back, knocking him face-first into the ground, hard. Breath shot out of him with a *whoosh*. "Sorry, kid," she said as she hobbled around to face the other guy.

"Glen, I assume?" she asked through shallow breaths. Older than Drew, he was taller, too, with shiny dark hair and a soft paunch.

"Who are you?" he asked. Pointing at Maya, he said, "Get away from the computer. Now."

Kenna stood between Glen and the door. She might not be at full strength, but she wasn't about to back down from this guy. "Why should she?" Kenna asked, spinning the man to face her. "Because you're afraid you won't sell enough Flaxibars or soap to keep investors happy?"

A muscle twitched near Glen's eye. He bared big teeth. "I'll have you both arrested," he said.

"Actually," Kenna said. "I think it may be the other way around."

"Fine. Stay as long as you like. See what happens," Glen said. Setting his jaw, he made to push past Kenna. "I'm getting out of here."

She stepped sideways to block his path.

"Get out of my way."

"Nope." She pointed over his shoulder. "Not until my friend gives the okay."

Glen spun.

With her gun barrel aimed at Glen, Maya widened her grin. "Listen to the lady. She makes a lot of sense."

Glen's hands went up. "Whoa, whoa," he said. "Let's not get crazy here. What do you want? I'm sure Celia can arrange to help you out with whatever money you need or—"

"Don't you remember? I told you Celia is tied up," Kenna said. "I meant that literally."

Glen blanched.

On the floor next to her, Drew rolled onto his back. Heaving, he grabbed at his neck as though trying to pull breath out with both hands. Kenna studied him a moment. "You okay down there?" she asked.

He glared up at her.

"Yeah. You'll be fine," she said.

Glen turned again. "What's really going on here? What is it you want?"

"How about a signed confession?" Kenna said.

"Of what?"

"Don't play coy, Glen," Kenna said. "Time has come to fess up about plans for Celia and Nick to win the primary and then the general election. In landslides, no less. Landslides so huge they'd be mind-blowing." She waited a beat. "I meant *that* literally, too."

"I don't know what you—"

"Sub Rosa is dead," Maya said.

"We killed it," Kenna said.

"All of it." Maya pantomimed an explosion, complete with sound effects. "Bwooosh!"

Glen glanced between them again, the twitch in his eye becoming more pronounced. "I don't know what you're talking about."

"Of course you don't," Kenna said. "But don't worry. Plenty of other people do."

SIXTY-TWO

Kenna made her way across the parking lot, favoring her braced right leg just a bit. It would be a long time before she'd heal completely. Until then, she'd follow the physical therapy regimen her doctor recommended and she'd do it in a real hospital environment like this one, not in a VR chamber.

Up ahead, she watched people enter and exit the revolving front door, some with flowers in hand. A few wheelchair patients sat outside in the sunshine, afghans tucked around their laps, friends and family hovering, keeping close watch.

As Kenna crossed the small street that separated the parking lot from the hospital itself, she heard laughter over the unmistakable grinding of a garbage truck. Two giant trucks pointed opposite directions sat blocking the entire width. The drivers leaned out their respective windows in animated discussion, elbows braced on their doorframes.

Two other men busied themselves with picking up trash piled on the ground next to the overloaded dumpsters. Kenna stopped in her tracks.

One of the guys noticed her. About thirty years old, he was trim and handsome beneath the smudges and sweat. He swung an overstuffed bag into the back end of one truck and waved hello. "Hey," he said, showing white teeth that gleamed super bright against his dirty face. He tossed a careless look over his shoulder. "You like watching men work, do ya?"

"To be honest," she said, "I'm just looking at all those Flaxibars." Chuckling, she laid a hand against her purse. "I don't think I've ever seen so many in one place."

"Yeah." The guy set his hands on his hips and surveyed the stacks of unopened snacks. "What did the idiots buy the things for if they didn't like 'em?" The corner of his mouth pulled up on one side, "But I guess I'm no better. Last week I picked up a case of Flaxibars myself. Couldn't get enough. Today"—he made a face and pointed to moldy vegetables spilling from a ripped bag—"I'd rather eat that."

His buddy yelled, "You planning to do any work today, Tommy-boy?"

Tom's smile widened and he shouted back. "Can't you see I got better things to do here?"

"I should be going," Kenna said.

"So soon?" Tom said. "I get off at three. Give me an extra hour to shower and shave—I clean up pretty good."

"I'm sure you do," she said with a smile, gesturing toward the hospital. "But I'm here to visit a friend."

He winked. "Well, you know where to find me," he said with a wry grin. "'Bout this same time, every week." He waved and went back to work amid his buddy's good-natured complaints about slacking off.

The sight of all those discarded Flaxibars made Kenna's pain feel like a badge of honor. With a sigh of contentment, she continued her trek to the front door.

Inside, the hospital's antiseptic tingle and chilly air enveloped her as she headed for the elevators. She pressed the button for eight.

But when she got to the floor, room 812 was empty. The bed pristine, unslept in.

Kenna spun, panic kicking her forward, charging toward the nurses' station. As she passed a small visitors' parlor, she caught sight of a lone figure seated in a wheelchair. She skidded to a stop.

"Jason!"

He looked up and smiled. His dark eyes crinkled at the corners—coaxing Kenna to grin in return.

"You're up!" she said.

"Where else would I be? Can't wait to get out of this place."

Kenna sat in a blue vinyl chair next to him, serious now. "How are you?"

"They're holding me for observation. Worried I'll start hallucinating or something." His expression tightened. "What about Patrick? How's he doing?"

"He's in the psych ward at Saint Constantine's across town. Mallory's with him."

"So in the scenario…they weren't…?"

"They were both virtuals. Just like we figured. Thank God, they weren't real. But Patrick's got a long, tough trek before he's back. It's a good thing his family's there for him."

They were silent a long moment.

Kenna suddenly remembered. She opened her purse. "Say, I brought you something."

When Jason leaned over to peek, she moved to shield her bag. Digging her hand inside, she grabbed the plastic-wrapped item and brought it out like a magician producing a bouquet of fake flowers. "Ta-da," she said.

When he saw the Flaxibar, his eyes lit up. "How did you know?" he asked, tearing it open. He took three fast bites, filling his mouth with the crunchy snack, making Kenna cringe.

"How can you stand those things?"

Cheeks full, he smiled. Then winced. "My brain thinks it should still hurt to swallow," he said. "Don't know how to convince it otherwise."

"Time," she said. "It'll take time."

He took another, smaller bite. "Thanks," he said around the mouthful.

"If you want more, believe me, I can get them for you cheap," Kenna said. "People are dumping them by the caseload. In fact"—she grinned at him—"if I hurry, maybe I can snag a few cases before the garbage guys finish back there."

"Ha, ha." He took another bite. "I'm starving." His eyes met Kenna's, and he seemed suddenly hesitant. Swallowing, he licked a crumb off his lip. "What about the queen bitch?"

"Celia survived. She's in custody, along with a few other Virtu-Tech executives," Kenna said, watching him. "I didn't kill her, but God knows I wish I had." Her hands fisted, and she worked hard to loosen them before continuing. "Regardless, she's out of commission. Her former minions are proving eager to turn on her in exchange for leniency."

"Trutenko?"

"He's providing all the information he has. Completely turned on her." Kenna explained how Trutenko had helped the dissidents save Patrick and the mission. "Tate's dead but I didn't kill him, either." She shrugged thinking about how close she'd come. "When he came in to fight us, he was wearing an envoy implant."

"Where did he get one of those?"

"Black market, and probably defective." Kenna shrugged again. "Definitely not calibrated properly."

"Geez," Jason said, finishing off the last bite, grimacing with each swallow. "Didn't he know how dangerous that was?"

"Maybe. Either way, he's gone and I'm glad. I just wish we could have nailed him before he killed Vanessa."

"You know that for sure?"

"Yeah," she said. "He wasn't particularly careful when it came to killing people." Kenna pulled out a second Flaxibar.

"You're a good partner," Jason said, reaching for it.

"You're not so bad yourself."

"What about Stewart?" Jason asked. "I got the impression he invested everything in his AdventureSome franchise. What will he do now?"

Kenna made a so-so motion. "Stewart's taking it well, all things considered. The losses of Charlie and Vanessa are still too fresh in his mind for him to worry about himself at all. He's a smart guy; he's convinced this is a sign for him to develop new technology himself but this time make it incorruptible."

"Like such a thing exists," Jason said. He tilted his bare head in a thoughtful way. "I'm kind of disappointed, actually."

"Why?"

"Well," he said, "with all that the dissidents accomplished—with everything we did to help them—it looks like we put ourselves out of a job. I was just starting to get used to you."

"Going forward, we won't have the same jobs we had, that's for sure. Maya managed to erase all the technology that supported Virtu-Tech's proprietary information. The quality of VR that's left is like what we had when we were kids." She chuckled softly. "The news is filled with people complaining. They're furious and disappointed to have lost their favorite toy. Little do they know how close they came to losing a lot more than that."

"So I shouldn't whine then, should I?" he asked.

She wrinkled her nose. "No, you shouldn't. We're young. We're healthy and talented. We'll find our way." Staring out the window, she thought of Charlie. Her throat caught. "We've all made sacrifices to protect our freedom," she said. "And I wouldn't trade that for anything."

✦

FOR IMMEDIATE RELEASE

In a surprise announcement, media giant Virtu-Tech, once virtual reality's most popular entertainment provider, has confirmed that the company is going out of business effective immediately.

Worldwide, VR fans are reacting to the news with shock, disappointment, and anger. Already, other firms—small players whose technology could never match that of Virtu-Tech's—are stepping up with vows to their customers to re-create all that was lost with the giant company's dissolution.

Claims by Virtu-Tech executives in their Washington, DC, offices that last week's fire in Chicago caused permanent damage to the corporation's systems have been met with skepticism by experts in the field of virtual entertainment.

More likely, as someone close to the situation who spoke on condition of anonymity reported, Virtu-Tech's top executives are likely to be charged with assault on a grand scale. Employing heretofore undisclosed technology, our source alleges that these executives knowingly inflicted beta testing on unwitting consumers despite the fact that several of Virtu-Tech's early subjects died or were rendered permanently brain damaged as a result of exposure. The scope of damage done may never be completely known.

Investigations are ongoing.

ACKNOWLEDGMENTS

This novel would never have made it into your hands without enormous assistance from many supremely talented and generous individuals. Thank you, Jamie Freveletti. A dear friend ever since our serendipitous meet-up all those years ago, Jamie invited me to contribute a manuscript to her Calexia Press. I didn't need to be asked twice. If there's one thing to know about Jamie, she gets things done. I'm thrilled to have delivered *Virtual Sabotage* into Calexia's capable hands.

Many thanks to the Mystery Buffs of Lombard Area AAUW for their help in vetting titles. They were kind enough to offer opinions on all the options on the list we'd provided, but—better yet—they came back us, suggesting *Virtual Sabotage* completely on their own. I loved the title. My publisher loved it. Everyone I tested it on loved it. Thank you, Mystery Buffs, so very much!

Although I've undergone a bit of firearms training, I knew that my limited knowledge wouldn't be enough to realistically portray this novel's gun scenes, so I turned to my awesome cousin Mickey Schuch. Mickey listened carefully to my requests and provided a selection of weapons to choose from. Thank you, cuz! If there remain any errors in gun usage or terminology, the fault is entirely mine.

A huge thank you to systems guru and all-around cool guy Rich Quaid for reading my convoluted descriptions and then—unbelievably—understanding what I was trying to achieve in key scenes. Rich provided guidance (and the oh-so-important proper jargon) to help my characters navigate the story's technology. Here again, any mistakes are mine.

Thank you to my friends and family, all unfailingly supportive and enthusiastic. They cheer me on over daughter discussions, Rook games, wine adventures, and pizza from Home Run Inn. As always, heartfelt thanks to my husband and awesome kids. Love you guys!

ABOUT THE AUTHOR

Julie Hyzy is the *New York Times* bestselling author of the Alex St. James Mysteries, the White House Chef Mysteries, and the Manor House Mysteries, along with several stand-alone novels and numerous short stories. Her work has won the Anthony, Barry, Derringer, and Lovey Awards.

More information about Julie and her work can be found on her website: www.juliehyzy.com.

✦

SHORT STORIES

"White Rabbit" in *Manhattan Mayhem: New Crime Stories from the Mystery Writers of America*

"Strictly Business" in *These Guns for Hire*

"Five Sorrowful Mysteries" in *At the Scene of the Crime: Forensic Mysteries from Today's Best Writers*

"Destiny" in *The Future We Wish We Had*

"These Boots Were Made for Murder" in
Crime: A Fiction River Special Edition

"Dissident" in *All the Rage this Year:
The Phobos Science Fiction Anthology 3*

"Efflorescence" in *Star Trek: Strange New Worlds V*

"Savior" in *Star Trek: Strange New Worlds VI*

"Life's Work" in *Star Trek: Strange New Worlds VII*

In addition, the following nine of her short stories
are available in an e-book collection, *Made for Murder: A
Collection of Suspense*:

"These Boots Were Made for Murder," "Strictly
Business," "Evenings for Vylette," "Travelogue,"
"Sanctimony," "Criminal Intent," "Panic," "What's Real,"
and "Dissident."

ALSO FROM CALEXIA PRESS

Blood Run

Jamie Freveletti

978-0-9835067-1-3

The smallpox virus was eradicated over forty years ago. Or was it? Six newly discovered vials found their way to a village in the Sahara. Biochemist Emma Caldridge, there on a humanitarian mission to deliver vaccines to remote villages, must run to stop the plague from being unleashed again. Surrounded by insurgents, she has no choice but to head through the desert, finding and freeing hostages as she does. Caldridge must lead her ragtag team to freedom...if the Sahara doesn't kill them first.

✦

calexiapress.com